THE LOST SOULS' REUNION

On a hill overlooking the grey sea, in a house filled with the past, a woman gathers her ghosts for one night to hear their story retold. This is Sive Moriarty's tale, beginning with her grandmother's ill-fated marriage. It is a strange and beautiful tale of love between mothers and daughters, between men and women, and between individuals and the land they live on. From the grotesque bustle of sixties London to the magical landscapes of coastal Ireland, it is a story that paints, most beautifully of all, the landscape of the human heart.

Born in 1968, Suzanne Power has been an athlete, journalist, broadcaster, traveller, teacher, care assistant and skivvy. She is a columnist, reviewer and profile writer. She lives with her partner in Dublin and London, and is the mother of twin boys. *The Lost Souls' Reunion* is her first novel.

SUZANNE POWER

◆

THE LOST
SOULS' REUNION

Complete and Unabridged

CHARNWOOD
Leicester

First published in Great Britain in 2002 by
Picador
London

First Charnwood Edition
published 2003
by arrangement with
Macmillan Publishers Limited
London

British Library CIP Data

Power, Suzanne
   The lost souls' reunion.—Large print ed.—
Charnwood library series
   1. Mothers and daughters—Ireland—Fiction
   2. Ireland—Social life and customs—
20th century—Fiction 3. Large type books
   I. Title
   823.9′2 [F]

ISBN 1–8439–5020–0

Published by
F. A. Thorpe (Publishing)
Anstey, Leicestershire
Set by Words & Graphics Ltd.
Anstey, Leicestershire
Printed and bound in Great Britain by
T. J. International Ltd., Padstow, Cornwall

For Chubb

Prologue

The Leave-Taking

The cards are old, frail friends. Spidery outlines and shadows. They come alive in the right hands.

Most of the Scarna townland has come looking for the fortune-teller. They do not come again because I tell truth as I see it, not fortune. They choose to make me the mad woman of the town and I am content with their choice. It means the three miles between them and me is rarely crossed. I am left to my madness, they to theirs.

The cards. All of me contained and lost in them. We have shared much past, and the future is an honest place in their company.

They called to me from a dark corner of the house where they rest in the quiet of their wooden box. They had advised me on Simon's leave-taking before now, told me we would have one more year.

So before I spread the truth in front of me I knew what it was. The card of the Leave Takers fell between the Fruits of the Earth and the Wanderer. The Leave Takers shows a man and woman on opposite sides of a valley, their arms outstretched to each other.

It is more often than not related to death or the loss of a loved one. The last time I saw it

1

Simon's chosen father was dying. But the presence of the fruits, encased in the womb of earth, told of a parting between mother and child.

It has happened.

I closed the door on Simon's departure this morning and found a hole in my life. The shape of his leave-taking all around, too good a man and son not to be missed.

My mothering days are at an end. These are the days now of goodbye and alone.

He was conceived in the worst moment of my life and he protected me from that moment. He sustained me by inviting me into his resting place in the womb, giving me the peace of the unborn for a while. When I put him to my breast for the first time I knew no lover's lips would bring that kind of joy.

My bold, strong boy grew into the gentlest of men. We are not alike; you would not look at us and see a mother and son. Simon has always been my opposite. I am dark to his fair. I have always been old, to his all-young soul. He was my teacher and I was his. We fought only because my love was all around him and above everything he prizes free breath.

When he was five, he went to school wearing one of my skirts with a gold belt. I could not persuade him to take it off with words and I have never laid a harmful hand on him. I waited for him outside the school gate and soon he appeared, his face red, laughter following him, ringing through the gaps in the old, worn windows.

Today leaves me with the same feeling that I had then. Put him now where he has always been — put the long bulk of him in the too-small bed and the feet too big for most shoes on either side of the bed rails. Put him in the barn and have him lift bales as if they were feathers. Put him on the shoreline with the white horses racing in to meet him with his wild blond hair, laughing back at the playful and delighted waves. Put him with the animals that are sick and lost and watch the bucket-sized hands move fine and deft and restoring. Put him with the people of the town and his big head reaches down from the air of giants to the smaller ones who want words with him.

We all want Simon. Anyone near him is alive. I gave him life and he brought it back to me. What is there for me now? My fate is the only one the cards will not shed light on. There is no self-prophecy. Everyone needs mystery, or we would lie down and die. The cards tell me only of Simon's journey.

The Wanderer's appearance, wind and purpose snapping at his heels, impatient for the long stretch of road and discovery ahead, showed me the route for my son will be into the heart of things.

Simon is passionately involved with the world. He has a place at its centre. I find fear for myself in that. I am here, where the edges meet the past and remain forgotten. All my life I have taken care of people, now I have only people to remember.

* * *

The animals have fallen strangely quiet since Simon left this morning. His old tired mongrels trail closely, pine with me, sniffing the sense of loss and lack of purpose in the air. We cannot find comfort.

My eyes are drawn to the open fire. The smoky heat stings them, the orange glare forces them to close and the first tears begin to fall. I cry until I sleep.

When I wake the fire has gone out, my body is frozen and curled. The cards call, with my red eyes I ask: 'What am I supposed to do?'

The card of the Storyteller makes itself known — a mouth at the centre of a circle. The card of tales told and tales to come, on lips that have spoken and lips that do not speak.

I run a bath and step into the hot swirl. The water opens my skin and runs through to the empty places, brought about by loss and separation from all those dear to me.

In the long glass I see a woman of forty-two years — all present. My skin shows the blood of many races runs through my veins. I press my hot body against the steamed-up glass, gasp at the coolness and leave my imprint: the curves of my breasts, hips and abdomen, the points of my nose, chin and forehead.

I rub oil into my skin. In the glass I watch my eyes. I leave the look behind and put on my dress, green velvet, worn smooth as eels in cool waters. It has no shape but my own for I made it with these hands, empty now of purpose. The

4

shape of my life these past twenty years it has. I could wear no other dress on this night. Like my mother I do not wear shoes.

I leave the bathroom with a steam cloud that follows me down the long corridor. I open doors to rooms that have been shut off for many years. Behind each one friends wait. Together we walk down the staircase to join others who have assembled by the fire.

I am aware of Simon's absence, he is the only other living being who belongs with these people. But then I see the crib beside my chair and he is here, as he was in the first year of his life, smiling in his sleep. I sit by the fire. The cards have been left out on the side table.

The new moon is watching us through the open window — her eye narrowed to a cautious slit. Summer is almost gone, the world is changing. I have to think about where to start and, from the company assembled, I find it to be at a beginning before mine. A long way back. We will be here until morning.

The room is small so most of my friends have to stand, but in the chair on the other side of the hearth, Simon's chosen father, my Beloved, sits. He is as I remember him and love him. Myrna and my mother Carmel together on the old, threadbare couch. Myrna's black eyes watch. Carmel sits with her knees curled up under her chin. She is wearing her blue dress. She has found something I never knew her to have.

It is as if they never left.

I turn the first of the cards and, still, the Storyteller. In the Storyteller the weave of past history and present intent is to be found, in the Storyteller the threads of the future are to be found and gathered together.

The story is told in and from the place it began. In the old house which knew such despair and came to know what joy meant. Solas is the name of the house, the place where the lost souls found refuge and it will always be so. It is protected by the long arms of time.

Sive is the name on me. I am the Storyteller. I am the last of the Lost Souls — reunited for an evening.

1

Hoar Rock

The tide of storytelling, which ebbs and flows between past and present, brings us to the shoreline that Solas overlooks. The waves wash around the bare feet of a young woman, whose soles are so hard she has run across the stones like they were bog cotton. The wind whips hair across her face; her skirt twists around her swollen belly.

The sun sets on her.

She raises her arms above her head, slides into the dancing water, wincing as it creeps around her hips. She waits for the big wave, starts to count them:

'One . . . two . . . ' The sand shifts and she can no longer stand.

'Three . . . four . . . ' The air is warm, but the sea still has a cold bite and from the waist down she is numb. 'Five . . . six . . . '

She breathes out. Her ribs reach for her lungs.

The jaws of the seventh wave open wide and swallow her, she curls up, sinks like a stone. A body now more water than flesh. She does not fight the change.

'Take me down. Take me away.'

The sea tosses and turns like a restless sleeper and the woman, thrown now on to her back, can

7

see the dark liquid clouds of evening closing in the light. A heron skims across the wave tops, as if searching for silver gleams of mackerel. But it wants the woman with the red-gold hair. The heron dives and meets with no resistance, catching her by locks that are the same colour as this drowning sun. Heron and woman break the waves fast claiming all that is left of the day.

The thunderous roar of air drives the limpness out of her; she thrashes against the bird's grip. Whole hanks of hair are torn from her head, but the heron holds fast and the beat of its wings is steady over the short distance to the shore.

Once the woman reaches firm footing the heron can no longer hold the weight and retreats to a rock. It rests with all the stillness and all the grace the drenched, spewing woman stumbling on to the shore lacks. The heron curves its long neck into its breast. The light of owls is thickening.

★ ★ ★

When the woman wakes it is to find the heron gone, and that the waves have once more turned to melting copper under a sun now rising. She wonders if she tried to drown again this morning whether death might be warmer.

But there is the dull ache of defeat in her bones and the knowledge that the heron would return. She is a child of the sun and it has risen, asking her to live another day.

Up the long laneway from the beach to the house, Carmel Moriarty walks with a worn look about her. The wild desire for freedom has gone and her shoulders slope with the weight of what is ahead of her.

She wraps her hands around her belly, whispers to it — 'God protect both of us.'

Her father is waiting, a strap pressed against his thigh. As she squeezes past him in the doorway her body folds in on itself. He stares down the road she has just walked up and closes the door.

★ ★ ★

Carmel Moriarty grew up in Solas. Then it was known as Hoar Rock — a cold place. Once home to a large family, the line had dwindled to the nothing Joseph Moriarty knew he was.

The land did not co-operate with farming, running along the shoreline as it did. It turned Joseph Moriarty into a demon. He put care into the stony soil and it spat rocks back at him. That taught him only to hate the earth. His crops were miserable, their growth stunted by the harsh, salt-laden winds.

He took his frustration out in public bars, where he never stood a round of drinks. No woman would go near him until Noreen.

Noreen Byrne, then, had the reputation for being fast and loose in times when the fast and loose were good to roll around with in woods and fields but bad to settle down with.

The image of Noreen stands before me now.

You were a fine, strong woman, Noreen, with a ready laugh! But you enjoyed life too much,

9

that's what they said. You reached twenty-eight and realized no man wanted to share your years with you and even if they did their mothers wouldn't let them. So you cast your eye around and found the truth in a short man with granite features and no real smile, only the cruel kind.

Sit, Noreen, while I tell them.

The truth was Joseph Moriarty was the only one if she did not want to die alone. The others slid off to safer territory with tighter women and paid the price of being bored all their lives.

In time you wished to be alone, you learned. But at twenty-eight you had different wants. You had no proper home. Your parents were in a tied cottage, which would be lost when they died. You cleaned and gutted fish. Who would want to do that for the rest of their natural born days?

So you asked him to dance. He would not. So you sat down beside him and asked him to talk to you. He would not. You followed him around like a puppy dog for five solid months, swallowing everything like pride, before you got him.

He never bought you an engagement ring, or a present, or even a drink.

You never kissed while you were courting. You never kissed after you were wed.

A woman with Noreen Byrne's bones and laugh, a terrible shame that no one should have kissed or made love to her in married life! All of us assembled agree on that one.

I can feel the cold-to-the-bone presence of the man I never met. Where are you, Joseph Moriarty? Show your face.

His eyes are before me now, telling me he would plant me like one of his crops into the stony soil with half a chance. He is here because he is part of us by blood and incident.

The spirit of Joseph Moriarty is welcome to stay in a room full of friends, but only until his part is played and I promise that the truth will not be changed in his favour. It will be put in front of him.

2

The Road of Swords

The truth is put in front of Joseph Moriarty as it was in front of Noreen when she crossed this threshold for the first time on her wedding day, to find nothing but broken bits of furniture and dirt. The house had been fine, two storeys, with an oak staircase and many rooms.

People prosperous enough to appreciate fine sea views, in days when most sheltered from them for the sake of warmth, had built the Hoar Rock farmhouse. But the Moriarty name now came down to one man and that one man had closed off all but a few rooms to light and to habitation, not just because of cold. There was dark in him, a weight put on him from the first breath of his life.

The father and mother of Joseph Moriarty had put all their hopes on to the one child they could have, along with the burden of their ill health and dwindling prospects. He was left to work at what he did not want to be, a farmer who did not have a farmer's instinct, not the first one of the Moriartys to be born that way. The best fields had been sold over four generations, leaving him with the ones that brought more in the way of work than reward. His only means of income, unless he would walk into the world with nothing, was to work them. They could not be sold. He turned his back on anything like hope for a future. He turned his back on the reputation for romantic notions the Moriartys were once famous for and it did not make his farming any better.

A wife had never fitted into Joseph Moriarty's plans. There had been no one willing to take on the sourness and the lack of prospects. Until Noreen who, like Joseph, was afraid to leave the town for uncertainty. Though brave within it, she had spent little of her life beyond it. What could not be seen, well, it was glorious until you came to live it, so those who had been to beyond and come back had said.

Noreen had wanted to go beyond, but only with company. None had offered to take her. So Noreen stood in front of Joseph Moriarty long enough for him to notice what there was in her he needed. Some said that she had already got reason to need to be wed. If she had, she had lost it by the time Joseph looked back at her. She fooled herself at the prospect of the big house and the fields with the fine views of sea and harbour. She had romantic notions about helping Joseph in them and turning his bad temper around. Noreen was a fish gutter, not a farmer's daughter. Any farmer's daughter would have told her fields with fine views of sea and mountains are bad fields. No farmer wants the soil such scenery offers.

They had been married after ten o'clock Mass, with only her family in attendance. His were all dead and other relatives wanted nothing to do

13

with him. Noreen paid for tea and scones for the women in the Harbour View Hotel. The men bought their own pints. Joseph sat among them but did not speak. She had thought they might go somewhere for the day afterwards. But he was keen to be home.

'There's a bed in the back room for you,' Joseph said, sitting down at the kitchen table, not offering to carry her small suitcase.

A cloud of dust rose from the sheet when she lifted it on to the mattress. Fine echoes of laughter and loving times rose along with it. This bed had not been used in a long time. There was to be no pretence of love. Joseph Moriarty had married Noreen for the work in her. In that same night she would beat out the dust of lives gone and her own hope of times to come.

'Where will I find a wardrobe?' she called out to him.

'Your family might give us one as a wedding present,' he laughed without joy. 'Haven't I given the roof?'

Noreen née Byrne, now Moriarty, put an apron over her new dress to make a start. She had expected nothing and got worse than that.

'Have you any kind of soap?' she asked him, standing over the sink, staring at her reflection in the clear water. It seemed it had changed since morning.

'Have you not brought any soap?' he enquired. 'Do you not wash yourself?'

'Household soap, Joseph, for the kitchen.'

14

He pointed to a press.

She wished now she had gone off with one of the casual labourers who came into the town, or one of the actors in the fit-up theatres who spoke so well.

'Well,' she thought, six hours after marrying him. 'There's always the hope that he might die before me.'

And he did, but it took many years and by that time she had already lost herself.

'I suppose I do have a present for you.'

Noreen spilt some of the hot tea she had made for them, having scrubbed the kitchen around his seated form. It smelt of carbolic, the windows opened wide to let in the betraying sunshine, which gave it all the appearance of a happy place.

'There's a plot out the back you might do something useful with.'

He also gave her six hens to look after. From that day on he took the surplus and left her the six. When one died he cursed Noreen as if she had wrung its neck herself. What she got from him on that first day was all she got.

She was left alone at night in the back room. Occasionally he would push open the door. He was not the first for Noreen but he was the roughest and he did not like her to make a sound.

★   ★   ★

The child, Carmel, came into the world quickly — as if not to cause trouble. She did not cry

15

until they tried to put shoes on her.

An only child, her companions came out of her imagination. Her dreams were filled with kind people who could only love her since she had created them and she had not a spiteful bone.

'Get wise to the world, girl, or it'll walk all over you!' Noreen tried to teach her when they were not under Joseph's eye.

Once they had left him. Noreen's family had sent her back, warning her they would tell Joseph the next time. They reminded her how lucky she was to have married a farmer.

After that day Carmel did not meet or know her grandparents who lived three miles away in another world. Joseph did not like his wife and child to go into town unless it was absolutely necessary. He did not like to pay for shoes or clothes.

Noreen's last pair of tights laddered just before her daughter was born. She made dresses for her girl out of her own clothes and was left with little to wear for herself. She did not go into town if she could help it.

When Joseph had drink on his breath or a look in his eye the child had been taught to go to the barn until she was called. Sometimes Noreen was not well enough to come out for her, so she slipped into the night and learned the ways of a cat, prowling until the first light.

That was how Eddie Burns came to know her, a streak of flame through Gamble's wood, hiding and watching him with her green eyes, from a safe distance. They did not say hello to each

16

other over the years that they turned into man and woman. What was between them needed no words.

Welcome, Eddie. There's a place beside Carmel for him, as there has always been.

★   ★   ★

Eddie left school at thirteen to take over his uncle's window-cleaning round. He could cycle over thirty miles a day, which did not worry him as he liked his own company and his work did not take him out on wet and windy days. On those days he liked to walk through the wood and feel her watching him. In bad weather, woodland gives the best shelter, without a soul to disturb it.

Carmel was rarely to be seen in Scarna. People would have forgotten her mother only they caught an occasional glimpse of her in early morning or late evening, shopping for a few bits. Their hearts went out to the big woman reduced to a bag of bones. Joseph was seen more often in the town and avoided. The word on their girl was that she was simple.

Noreen tried to put manners on Carmel, but there was no reason for her to keep them. They were far enough away from the town for her to grow up without a friend. On the days Noreen got her to school, by dragging her, the teachers sent her home by lunchtime. They could not keep her at a desk and she took off her shoes continually.

When they asked her a question she would not

answer them. She did not write well and could barely read.

She would only be seen near the town when the fit-ups came. The travelling theatres brought life and colour and dreams into the grey hours that made Scarna days. The town would see Carmel and Noreen then, slipping into the back row when the performances had started. Dreaming with the town and aching with the town for the stories that happened on makeshift stages — Noreen and Carmel were seen and not noticed. The town had its mind and heart on the stories too.

Carmel watched one woman one year, a woman called Sive who played the leads in plays best forgotten in a way she could never be. Carmel watched her on stage and in the town from a discreet distance.

The woman called Sive had seemed more fine and free than any woman. She had sauntered through the town with men all following with reasons to talk to her, with women all watching their men. She had caught Carmel watching once, out walking on the Shore Road. Her male company was not pleased when she had called Carmel over and touched her hair and said, 'Like fire.'

From that day, Carmel was allowed to follow her. Until the day when Carmel went to the theatre tent and found it gone.

This was one week in a life which went on in a manner where little changes, until Eddie's eighteenth birthday. His father took him for his first pint to the Slip Inn on the harbour front at

Scarna — where fishermen and farmers met in a back bar where no stranger stayed for more than one drink. Too many eyes on them; even enemies in the town of Scarna united against the unknown who entered. The men were talking of Joseph Moriarty, who had just been asked to leave.

If the drinking men did not bait him, and they tried not to, he would rise to imagined insults. That night's had been a concern about the state of Joseph's crop in Stone's Throw Field, which ran right along the shoreline. The only thing that could grow in it was cabbage. The rubbery leaves fought the salt winds well, but the first, tender shoots were not able for the fight in the same way.

The farmer whose family had acquired good Moriarty fields in other years and done well from them, put it to him, 'No way a cabbage will raise its head now, Joseph. Not after the fourth week of salt winds. This is no summer.'

'Is that right?' Joseph had spoken back, with a calm they all knew to come before a blow-up.

A good foot or two of space round him cleared, the enquirer drew back also. From behind him, someone who knew his face could not be seen, said, 'Mark you, everyone loves a bit of salt on their cabbage.'

The laughter lasted for as long as it took for Joseph to rise and belt the initial enquirer. Belt the smugness his fat and happy fields gave him.

It was done quickly — four lifted him and four put him outside and bolted the door as Eddie and his father came through it.

'Why do you keep him as a customer?' one asked the barman. The barman did not have to answer that Joseph was in most nights and worth the trouble for that reason.

The usual insults were thrown at Joseph's back once he was safely gone. Then the conversation turned to his family and they talked of the daughter, who roamed at will, as they would one of the beasts they farmed.

'A fine thing, well stacked at the front.'

'You'd have to hobble her to keep her still.'

'Don't go getting ideas about Carmel, lads. She has the colouring of a fox and she scrawms like one too!' Poker O'Toole cackled. He was forty if a day.

'And how would you know?' Eddie asked.

'Well I tried to get acquainted with the mite once. I went home the beach way and came across her, in her nip, having a wash in the sea. In the dead of night! Took off like that when she saw me,' he clicked his fingers sharply. 'When I caught up on her she took the arm off me, bit into it she did.'

Eddie was not outspoken on any occasion and did not utter a sound as he smacked his fist home, nor did he say a word, but left with the stunned silence still about them all.

His father looked long and hard at the door his son had just walked out of. The men took no offence and Poker was out cold so could take none either. They all put it down to Eddie being unused to the drink.

★　★　★

20

On this night Carmel was sixteen years old, sitting over a dinner which she had not eaten. Her father at his full height was two inches shorter than her and took great exception to this. She had been ordered to get him some more meat. As she stood up, he said into his meal, 'I can't see how she could be mine.'

'She's yours,' Noreen answered. 'My side are all tall. She takes after me.'

'That she does, which is why she has not worked a day in her life. No child with my blood would miss a day's work if they could help it.'

Noreen finished his sentence off in her mind. 'I've tried to get her work. They don't want to take on a slow one.'

'No child with my blood would be slow.'

It ended with him telling Noreen he would give her money to feed only two people in future. And starve some sense and inclination to work into the lazy trollop. Carmel faded from the room. Her mother still told her to leave, always. Carmel had not the sense to realize it was beatings meant for her that Noreen was taking. She had the sense to know the more she stayed away the better it seemed for them all.

★   ★   ★

When Eddie found Carmel she was asleep, curled up into the trunk of a great oak. He got the sense if he moved nearer it would crush him to protect her. She was more part of this world than his own. And he would have left her if she had not stirred then. Once her eyes opened she

21

held her arms out to him. Her milky white flesh shone in the moonlight on this soft night full of kind stars. He knew it would be better to wait but the salt of her skin drove him to a thirst. He drank more than his first pint that night.

Her legs were strong and she wrapped them around his waist, locking him into her hot darkness and not a word out of her but groans and moans. Not soft whispers but wild, feverish gasps that brought the night sky in around them so that neither could breathe. They could be free with themselves since there was no one around to hear but the woodland creatures.

His head fell between her breasts and he put his hand on a rose pink nipple reaching towards the stars. She grew cold beneath him and shifted, and he looked into her eyes, afraid that he would find a bitter fear in them, but he saw she had been filled in the same way he had been.

Still, when he gathered her, shivering, into him he felt hot tears on his cheek and found they were his own. What he had done with her was what other men wanted and she was not wise enough to the world to stop them.

'There are other men who want this from you, Carmel,' he said into her soft hair. 'It's my job to keep them away.'

Carmel did not hear. She had fallen asleep to the drum of his heart.

3

Roaming Done

Am I right to tell them, Carmel? You, loved for the first time in dark-night moments that turned golden.

You gave birth to me and I never knew the inner workings of your heart.

Eddie was the only person for you.

My mother. Her hair is red, her skin as pale as the white-gold rays of the sun. Her eyes glimmer in the dark. Green, with flecks of gold, reminding us that the sun is in her.

Her feet walked her own way from the earliest day; she was not one to be pointed away from her fate. Her toes so broad and flat she had to wear brogues from the men's section of the shoe shop. These big feet looked like they were not part of Carmel, who was tall and thin like a willow.

Once Eddie and Carmel began their loving no power in the world could stop it.

'Keep away from the woods, Carmel,' he told her. 'Unless I am with you, don't go near the beach. Don't go anywhere you shouldn't.'

And to please him she stopped her day roaming and waited for night before joining him.

★   ★   ★

23

There was some part of Eddie that did not belong with Carmel, but with the narrow town. He would not be seen with the slow Moriarty girl and her big feet in men's shoes. He had been taught that decent girls did not behave in such a way. But he had not been taught that one true to her feelings did. And he felt that true love and it found a way into his bones. It frightened him that his bones were now not his own but called out for her.

Carmel, under Eddie's instruction, stayed close to home. Carmel stayed under the constant eye of her father now. Since no one would employ her she was put to work in his fields.

The glimmering girl was replaced by a deep, mournful shadow that bore sorrow as a friend. A lost, hollow woman with a worn mouth. The only vibrant thing left was her hair. My mother could set fire to the world around her with that.

★ ★ ★

'Who would marry this one, the whore from Hoar Rock?' Joseph cut through the heart of the mother and the daughter with these regular words and rants. 'Who would take on a lazy, idle, useless good-for-nothing trollop, just like her mother before her? It was a sad day the day I got saddled with you pair,' this spat at them with fine, dry pellets of spit that had no moisture or feeling in them above contempt.

The whore of Hoar Rock, the baby in her belly. Her father now adding blows to the words.

'You should burn for what you have done,' he

24

told Carmel, who the heron had saved for this fate. They were in the kitchen. Carmel's hair full of the cooked food she had not eaten the night before.

The night before Joseph had gone from the table into the pub. The night before Noreen asked her daughter if there was something she should tell her mother. It could not be hidden on such a thin frame. Carmel did not know, so Noreen had to tell her. The pair might then have held each other tight against the near future and what it held, but with Joseph near and between them, they had not held each other in a long time.

Noreen now only felt despair that the daughter had allowed another man to take the only thing she had been able to make sure Carmel kept. She thought of the nights when she had stood between Joseph and his daughter's door. For one moment she wanted Carmel to have suffered as she had suffered, to learn that to give willingly is to give foolishly. For willing women of that time were led to places where only the foolish go.

Then she cried out and she did not wish it any more, she did not wish for her flesh and blood to know all that she had known and she knew she would once more put herself in the way of the punishment.

When Joseph came home, she told Carmel she would tell him and Carmel lit out the back door.

'Whose is the dinner?' he wanted to know when he came in.

'Carmel's. She was not hungry.'

'Then let it sit there and she can have it for

25

breakfast. I don't put good food on the table for it not to be eaten.'

Noreen, knowing that every moment they waited was a moment in which he might realize for himself, told him why he had more reason to be angry than a dinner.

She bowed her head and waited. He said nothing, took the belt off his trousers and went to sit, in this spot that I am sitting in now, by the fire. By morning he had not let the belt out of his hand. Noreen was out looking all night for her daughter, to tell her not to come home. But she was not used to the night and was afraid of it and could not go into its darkest places where Carmel found most comfort and Noreen felt most fear.

Noreen had returned, grey faced, at dawn, only minutes before her daughter. Joseph saw her at the end of the lane and roared.

'Come up to the house and get clear of me.'

She had gone to wait in the good room she kept up only for the visitors who had never come. The door to the house had been left open, so Carmel could be seen by Joseph coming up the long lane.

Not by her mother who could not help her now. Her mother was in the good room, with the radio turned up loud to drown out the squeals. She rocked back and forth, crying slow tears. Joseph was roaring between thrashes, 'Who's the bastard's father? Who did you spread your legs for, you little whore? Was it Poker O'Toole? I have heard the way he talks about you. Or young Nolan with the motorbike, or McGuinness, the little weed with his big talk? Or ... was ... it ... all ... of ... them?'

The blows becoming heavier now, taking the breath out of him.

Noreen could not see, but she could feel the spittle rain from the corners of his mouth, the chewed lower lip and the bulging eyes, the veins on the back of his neck hard and prominent.

Carmel did not tell.

Afterwards, Noreen dressed her daughter's welt-covered back and bruised face with ointment and combed the fibres of food from her matted hair. She listened to the dry, soft sobs and felt the thin trembling bone and flesh.

'I have money, Carmel,' she whispered as she smeared the cool ointment over the roaring, opened skin. 'I've been saving out of what he gives me. Needless to say it isn't much. But it would be enough to get you away from this house, child. If you stay, the baby or yourself will be injured.'

They could not afford to wait until the bruises had healed. He would come back worse from where he had gone. Before that happened, Noreen Moriarty packed a few things in a small cardboard suitcase that she had kept hidden in the barn and she walked her limping daughter to the bus stop.

★ ★ ★

Noreen pulled the black hat down over Carmel's face, casting a shadow over the swollen features. She asked again who the father of the child was,

27

but her daughter made no answer and in some ways Noreen was glad not to know. She had enough men in her life to blame. The conductor urged them to get on, or miss the bus.

The mother and daughter held each other then and the holding could not make up for all the times they had not held each other before and would not hold each other in the future.

As the bus disappeared over the brow of the hill, Noreen could not stop herself thinking that it was her who should have been on it, resenting her only daughter's escape. Then she thought of what the price had been.

★　★　★

Carmel caught a bus, a boat and a train. The voices of what had gone before came with her. She did not speak, they did not give her time to, so insistent and incessant was their chatter.

So, it was as well that by the time she stood on a station platform, dominated by a large clock, she had been found by Constance Trapwell, who had met her on the boat. Constance had informed her, 'All roads lead to London for those who can't afford to go to America.'

'Do they speak a different language in England?' Carmel asked Constance now, looking at the clock, not recognizing the Roman numerals.

'No,' Constance replied. 'We speak theirs. But not well enough for their liking. We don't pronounce properly, the English say about us.'

It was a bright, sunny afternoon and a part of

Constance wanted rid of this girl who she had spoken to only out of curiosity to know where the bruises came from. But she was still curious. Carmel seemed frail and rigid in the fastness around her. Constance knew it was only a matter of time before it swallowed her. She remembered her own first days of knowing no one in this city and would not wish it on her worst enemy. But the thought of sharing her narrow single bed was not pleasurable. Carmel would have to make do with a blanket and the floor.

'We'll have to hurry if we want to miss rush hour.' Constance did not even ask if anyone was coming to meet Carmel. 'But you haven't much luggage anyway.'

A small cardboard suitcase, which had less weight in it than the belly with the life inside it, that is what Carmel amounted to.

The London Underground air stung the throat and nostrils as if it had been laced with vinegar. To make conversation Constance talked of the place that had been her home for five years, as one would talk of a lover who has never met expectations.

'London is close enough to home to make sure you never forget it, but far enough away to make sure home forgets you.'

Carmel did not answer and Constance felt annoyed that she had not yet expressed gratitude. It was as if Carmel assumed she would be looked after and if it was not Constance's job it would fall to someone else.

'I'm kept busy here in case you're wondering what I do.'

29

Carmel had not wondered.

'I sang at Mass and at weddings at home,' Constance went on. 'I'm up the West End all the time looking for an audition but they won't let me in the door without an agent. I can do all the numbers from every musical. I can do any number you care to mention. But my accent gets in the way of me. It keeps breaking through in my singing.'

A bare pause for breath from Constance and no visible breath from Carmel.

'Never mind — I have the man to fix that. Mr Lawton says I'll be a mouthful of plums in no time,' Constance laughed in a hard way. 'I don't care for plums myself but I'd eat a tree of them for a spot in one of them Park Avenue clubs.

'It was Mr Lawton's idea I should change my name. My real name's Bridie. The Trapwell part came from the Trapwell Institute for Finishing, or is it Finishing Institute? I went to it when I first came over to put manners on me. Manners cost in London I can tell you. I expect you're wondering where I got the Constance from?'

Carmel was not wondering.

'Well, Daddy used to call me Lady Constance because I went around with my nose in the air. And what would he know about it? Someone who never looked up from the paper but to ask for something? I don't know why I go home for holidays now Mam's gone. All him and the others want is the contents of my suitcase. This time they even took the suitcase. That's the last time I go home.'

Constance had the high talk of one who had

gone a long time without a friend. Carmel could be made, a part of Constance realized, into whatever Constance needed her to be.

She was pleasing to Constance Trapwell in all but her silence. No thanks given. Constance stared openly at the girl with the clasped hands. She could be pretty underneath the bruises and the hat. What kind of figure she had Constance could not tell, for she was wearing a big lumpy coat. It was Noreen's coat and Noreen had worn it into the house called Hoar Rock on her wedding day over eighteen years before. She had given it to Carmel as the only coat she had. So she looked like one of the simple unfortunate country girls to Constance. But her face was not broad and strong and expectant. It was thin and hidden and afraid. She had a sickly look and the sickly look, Constance knew, was a look only real ladies had, ones that did not swallow big spuds and lumps of bacon from a pot. Those heifer women made their way over here to skivvy and fall in love with exactly the same kind of man they would have married at home. But home had no jobs for the men, so the women followed.

Constance ate like a bird and she watched her figure like a vulture. This girl was a breed apart, as Constance felt she was herself.

She would not like to see another girl stuck as she had been. Time enough for her to learn the more people are around you the lonelier you are.

The girl had not freshened up once in all the time they had been travelling. A girl's got to freshen up, look her best, feel her best, Constance thought. Dull hair spells a dull mind,

31

but this one was a natural red. It would go down well in some of the more select clubs around town. Cut the right way she would look like a Maureen O'Hara.

Constance touched her own bleached and rolled locks. She hoped she did not look too like Betty Grable, an old-hat star, a forties fling-back.

'I had this done while I was at home,' she said to no one at all.

Carmel was further away from talk than she had ever been. She looked beyond her reflection, examining the black closeness. She had imagined under the ground to be comforting, what could be more comforting than the earth? But this Underground was a hollow place filled with a despair and unreality she could smell.

She could smell the sweet, stinging lacquer on Constance's hair and it reminded her of her mother, Noreen, one Christmas when Carmel had been a child. Getting ready to go out the door to Mass and Joseph had said it was not Mass she was going to but the whore shop and she had not gone. Later, when Joseph was downstairs listening to the radio her mother had called her and Carmel had gone to her in the bedroom and had been given her stocking. When she reached to kiss her mother she saw her lips brimming with blood, which poured, now that Carmel had touched them, from her mouth and on to the pillowcase.

The scent of set hair lacquer and fresh blood filled Carmel's nostrils and hot salt tears slid down her cheeks and into her own mouth through swollen lips that ached when she moved them. So she did not speak. Her mother had been in bed a long while that time and her face had gone as white as the sheets she lay in. But she came back to Carmel.

'I should have waited till I got back and gone to someone decent.' Constance continued on with her hairstyle and the intricacies surrounding it. 'I couldn't find a magazine under three years old in the shop. I want to look a fifties woman. Modern. With the times. I'm a great one for the times. You'll learn that, Carmel.'

Carmel saw Eddie in their place, Eddie alone and wondering where she had got to. She saw her long stretch of rocky shoreline and she felt the soreness of her beating and the tightness in her head where the heron had pulled her ashore.

'I expect you want to know where we're going,' Constance broke in. 'Hammersmith, Piccadilly line. That's the decent line you know, Carmel. The Irish are all off the Northern. Slums full of the dregs. That's what they are. You're lucky you fell in with me, Carmel. I'll keep you out of there.'

The carriage was crowded. Few spoke. This place robbed them of their voices. Without warning the train left the tunnel and the grey evening cast shadows, lights came on to drown them.

In those shadows Carmel saw Joseph Moriarty raise his curled fist and bring it down upon her.

'Burn. Hell.'

And a woman called Sive, touching her hair.

'Like fire.'

When the doors opened at Hammersmith she felt the autumn chill bite at her and could not see the sky for all the buildings peering down on her.

4

Shod

Carmel slipped off her shoes before climbing the grey, uncovered stairs. Constance had told her to do this, because she slept like a sparrow.

'I never heard feet like yours. A herd of elephants rampaging through Hammersmith.'

Constance slept through until afternoon most days. Her new job at the nightclub had her up until all hours. She got up as the sun began to set and she put her feet into a tin bucket and Carmel poured hot water on them. They soaked until they withered. Constance towelled them dry and massaged cream into them and pared corns and pricked blisters.

When all this was done she would slip them into comfortable slippers and begin to wind her hair with rollers. Carmel watched her do all of this and then would go into the kitchen and make tea for them both which Constance would sip and sigh, 'My feet might be blistered, but I'm making the right connections. I'll be swapping my uniform for an evening dress and a microphone, you see if I don't.'

Sometimes Constance brought a friend home and would wake Carmel, putting her out of the bedroom they shared now an extra bed had been bought, on to the cold linoleum floor of the kitchenette. On these nights Carmel would open the curtains and look for the stars she had lost.

The noises from the bedroom put her in mind of Eddie and what she had shared with him. But that put her in mind of the empty part of her that would never be filled and the tears came.

The hollow in her stomach had grown worse with time and the voices in her head more insistent. In the six months they had been living together Carmel answered Constance Trapwell's beck and call like a laboured donkey. It was not that Constance gave nothing. That much had been proven in the weeks when Carmel had first climbed the grey, uncovered stairs to their small piece of London and pulled off her coat. 'So that's the way is it?' Constance spoke to the rounded belly. 'Well, I had the same trouble myself when I first arrived. It's dealt with if you have the money.'

But Carmel did not want it dealt with. While the rest of her had grown cold there was a heat from her unborn that kept her warm. Constance let her rest a day or two 'to get your bearings', but Carmel did not even leave the rooms, just sat at the kitchen table staring at the patch of grey sky.

Constance felt she would need to grow more patience in dealing with this one but could not stop herself pointing out, with a harshness she later regretted: 'If you've money, you'll pay rent. But your money won't last long if you don't get a job, and you won't get a job when you're having a child.'

'I can't part with it.'

'You'll have no choice when it's born.'

'I won't part with it.'

'That's what they all say. I wasn't mug enough myself. I had prospects. Mind you it nearly killed me. They had me in bed three weeks, tipped up to stop me haemorrhaging. I knew if I got through that . . . '

Constance was lost in her own thoughts, of a back lane and an old woman who smelt of damp sweat, of a wall with peeling, mud-brown paint. She had drunk the vile-smelling liquid, scalding hot. It took away the insides of her mouth and she had wanted to cry out with that pain until another, far worse, came.

'Most girls arriving here on their own have the trouble,' Constance said softly to the remembered mud-brown wall. 'The trouble has to be sorted or it will sort you, Carmel.'

Carmel slipped out. She walked to the small park near their home and around she went as a prisoner paces an exercise yard. The lone trees and tortured flowers in angled beds made her want to cry out. When she grew calm she slipped out of her shoes and felt her toes spread out in relief.

Rain began to fall on her and she felt clean. The brainfire put out. The coolness was a balm and she lay on the clipped grass, pressing her lips against it. A man walking his dog on a lead watched her and looked away, a woman parked on a bench with her pram and responsibility beside her, felt obliged to call to her, 'You'll catch your death, missy.'

Carmel sat up, shamefaced, like a dog caught

rolling in a scent. She put on her shoes and left the park but her feet would not turn to home, they walked the streets until she felt near dropping.

Then up the grey, uncovered stairs in her bare, tired feet. Into the room she slipped like the shadow she had become to find Constance Trapwell, waitress with notions of stardom and splendour, naked and bent over with a peacock's feather between her buttocks and a pair of high shoes that made her wobble like an unsteady building. Constance's clothes were folded neatly on the end of the horsehair sofa. Constance treated clothes reverentially.

A man had stayed well-dressed but for his dropped trousers. A pair of glasses balanced on the end of his nose. Constance turned a face that wished the whole thing was over with in Carmel's direction. And saw her watching eyes and high colour to her cheeks.

'Show's over, Johnny.'

Jonathan Lawton, voice coach to stars and feather producer to would-be's without the money to pay for his services, was busy pulling on his clothes, leaving the premises in seconds, not forgetting his feathers.

'I'm sorry, Constance,' Carmel said.

'No need. He'll be back and I'll have to start charging him. But you should have bloody well knocked and saved us all a red face.'

'You told me not to.'

'I know what I told you. I didn't tell you to sneak up on me. Who pays for the lion's share of this palace? Who?'

Constance did not finish. Carmel had slid into a pile as neat as that of Constance's clothes.

★   ★   ★

The fire in her belly was what woke her. She let out a scream that brought Constance into the bedroom.

'I have work you know, Carmel, I'm late as it is.'

Carmel folded up and clutched at the cramping pain.

'I'm burning!' she screamed. 'I'm burning inside!'

Constance pulled back the bedclothes to find what she expected — the sheets bloodstained.

'Look at the cut of you! Well at least you didn't have to pay for it.'

Hours later a slither of deadness was delivered without a doctor into Constance Trapwell's hands. It had been a boy. Constance blessed it with water from the kitchen tap.

'God forgive a heathen like me doing this,' said Constance, and flushed it into the London sewer.

When the doctor finally came he advised bed rest for a fortnight. Once he had left, Constance set the terms, 'If you're not up in a fortnight you're out. I've nowhere else to bring them as yet, but here.'

Carmel got up four days later. Constance helped her to find work cleaning, in the early hours of each day while the world still slept. She knelt and with each circle of the wire brush rubbed out the face of the dead child staring at her. She begged those inside her not to talk so loudly in case others overheard talk of her badness. Those that did encountered only a strange woman on her knees, a stream of talking and scrubbing.

During the day she cleaned whatever mess Constance and her men had made.

When Constance learned Carmel could barely read or write she said, 'You ought to write home. I'll write a letter for you and you tell me what to say.'

Carmel sent a letter to Noreen Moriarty, care of the post office, requesting it not be delivered to the house.

> Mammy.
> All's well here. I am in London and settled. Here is my address. The baby is gone.
> Carmel.

She did not write one to Eddie. How could she when she had lost their child through her badness?

40

5

Meeting with the End

Constance Trapwell had advanced in the world, though not in her chosen profession.

Carmel, hidden now entirely under the beat of Constance's wing, had moved with Constance to a small but tastefully appointed place of residence in Shepherd Market, W1, a stone's throw and a far cry from Soho. It was a place where the more select women paid court to the more select gentlemen.

'It's an honour to be here,' Constance reminded Carmel. 'Two girls from the bog, one posh accent between them. Strap me up.'

Constance would write letters for Carmel, which went unanswered. Still Carmel would ask her to write and she would watch as her words were put on to the page, as if a miracle was happening.

Once or twice the mistress had to take Carmel to task for answering the door to the men barefoot.

'Giving them the wrong impression altogether, Carmel, with those big feet of yours. Keep your shoes on and your mouth shut and we'll all be happy.'

The stairs were no longer grey and uncovered — they were carpeted with a plush pile that cushioned the well-heeled from the world and made their coming and going noiseless.

Carmel did everything but wash Constance and feed her. Since neither could cook they were often seen in Soho cafés, Carmel lighting Constance's cigarettes, playing with the pearl lighter, passing her hand through the hot and single flame until Constance grew impatient and snatched it from her. Then nothing to do but listen to Constance's endless talk of the same things.

'I'm earning more than I would in any show, Carmel. Most showgirls do what I do for nothing but a dinner and a bottle. By the time I start withering I'll have enough put by not to worry.'

'I'd like to go home then,' Carmel whispered.

'What's home got for us? A priest to tell us where we went wrong and a town to talk about us? If they don't pity you they'll hate you, Carmel. No, we're done with that and that's done with us.'

Constance and Carmel had spent many nights like this. Now one was thirty and the other nineteen. It still rankled with Constance that Carmel had never once thanked her.

Carmel was younger than her mistress, but not as well decked out. She dressed in Constance cast-offs as before she had dressed in Noreen's. A dress of her own was a world and a dream away.

That was not what she was thinking when she felt a pair of eyes on her, brown eyes with long fringed lashes. Eyes of the man who might have been my father.

Gomez was at another table, drinking strong black coffee, waiting for his shift at the restaurant to begin. He was a dishwasher who insisted on being a paying customer before he put his apron on. That was his pride. A pride I inherited, if it is his blood in me.

Carmel was thinking about putting her hand over Constance's endlessly moving mouth. But this time Carmel felt the eyes and the eyes said: 'Look at me.'

When she did she was lost, for she recognized the look and felt she had returned home in it. It was only later, when things were different, that she realized. The eyes that Gomez had cast on her had been those of Joseph Moriarty, an expression in them that stood for a hatred of the world and all those in it who had stood against him.

Gomez came across to their table and introduced himself. Carmel's face came alive and something in Constance's heart said they had met with the end.

*　*　*

Carmel, now, could have all that she had not had before. She stood in the dress shop, afraid to touch anything.

'You have to look, to try on, otherwise no point,' Gomez said impatiently.

She had always accompanied Constance into dress shops, had never been the one to choose. Now colours and fabrics and styles surrounded her. The clothes called out, 'Choose me!'

And since she thought she would never have another chance to choose she chewed her lip and could not decide.

'OK, I help.' Gomez walked through the rails and took up five dresses, held them against her milky skin and sighed.

'Such a woman. My woman will be beautiful in these.'

He ran his hands over her to judge a size he already knew. It was a Monday morning and the shop was deserted. A bored assistant came across to them to see if they wanted anything.

'No help,' Gomez dismissed her with a look that was long.

The assistant put the counter between them and did not appear bored any more. She looked at the door, hoping and waiting for other customers to come in.

'Carmen, change now into these.' Gomez had taken to calling her Carmen.

He held up three, all blue, and he gave them to her and she had not chosen any of them.

In the empty changing room Carmel looked in the mirror and saw nothing but the midnight blue satin she was covered in.

'It's like wearing the sky!' she whispered.

'Ready?'

Gomez parted the curtains and saw a slight woman with full breasts whose beauty had been hidden under hand-me-downs. Exposed now. A beauty he wanted in front of those mirrors. He walked up to the assistant and gave her a pound note to keep everyone out. She put the pound in her purse and the closed sign on the door.

Gomez went in to Carmel and closed the curtains behind him. Carmel was not looking at him, but at the sky around her. He lifted the starched skirt, his hands on creamy thighs and buttocks.

'My Carmen.'

She was cold to the touch and this was what he liked about her. Being inside her was like swimming in a night sea. With the hot ones you learned everything quickly — with the cold ones you would never be satisfied. A secretive woman.

'Mine,' he said, pulling the neckline of sky away to expose a breast.

Carmel looked in the mirror. She did not feel any of his touch until he placed his fingers on each breast and twisted the nipples hard so that she whimpered and then he emptied into her and took his tissue from his pocket and wiped her and himself before zipping up.

'We don't take this one,' Gomez said.

Carmel did not smile and took it off and stood naked in front of the mirrors without the sky around her.

'We take another,' Gomez said. 'This one is used.'

He picked a turquoise blue.

'You got to wear underwear now,' Gomez reminded her, for she often didn't. 'You in London now.'

He paid the assistant and the assistant thanked them both for their custom and snapped shut the till before going back to a magazine which told her all about the violet eyes of Elizabeth Taylor, and how to get them with new eye drops. She avoided the green eyes of Carmel and the brown eyes of Gomez.

* * *

Carmen. Gomez gave her things, new bright things that she had never had. Her hair was cut in the latest style, her nails were polished and her feet were dressed in pointed shoes that cut them to ribbons. She did not know if she needed or wanted them but everyone else who had these things seemed happy.

All she had to do was give little and Gomez knew how to do things well. But he could not reach beyond her skin. When he was inside her, her eyes looked for Eddie's.

* * *

Constance Trapwell's successful business was going downhill. It was nothing to do with her technique going stale. But her clients were always somehow dissatisfied.

She could look no further than Carmel. It didn't do to have a better-looking maid. Nothing personal, lovie, but you'll have to move on to where you're going quicker. Remember what I said. He's trouble. Bye now. Call anytime.

And once more Carmel was on the street with a suitcase. Gomez was waiting.

46

6

Professional Love

No loving was in store for Carmel Moriarty, though it had begun well enough. When she had turned up on his doorstep Gomez had moved Carmel into his attic flat in Brewer Street without a word.

Was she comfortable enough? Did she need any more clothes? Shoes?

Over the days they bought more new bright things and then they went straight back home. No more dinners or going to the pictures.

A bed and a wardrobe in one room; a bathroom in another; a stove, table and two chairs in the kitchen; blood-red linoleum and pale green painted walls with the marks of all the lives that had lived here. This was home.

Carmel looked at the sky through a sealed skylight window, a sky so close to her now but no longer familiar. They were strangers to one another.

Gomez brought a friend, a much brighter woman than Carmel, to help her with make-up. The friend used to work in theatre. She knew how to put a bit of slap on still, she told Carmel who did not utter a sound, who watched as a brush whispered against her skin. Her paleness was painted in and her lips smeared with a rich gloss that spoke loudly.

When the friend departed Gomez spread some receipts out on the table.

'It is so expensive to keep a woman. See. You cost me twenty-three pounds and six shillings, for new dresses, for shoes, for make-up. You wear underwear now. I pay for that. I pay for everything. I take extra hours at the restaurant. I don't mind because you are a beautiful lady. You are mine.'

Carmel sat looking in the cracked mirror, which Gomez used to shave in. The results of the bright woman's painting were plain to see — she had coloured in the memories, brought fresh blue bruises to the eyes, made the blood pour from Carmel's lips as before. The sky was closed out and Joseph's hands were raised over her. Burn Carmel. Burn in Hell.

'Carmen,' Gomez was standing over her. 'What you do for me, now?'

She did not answer and he punched her neatly in the abdomen, not touching the face that was the picture of Carmel's memories, brought to life once more with paint and with powder.

She lay on the floor gasping like a fish on dry land, seeing the sky she had lost so clearly now. The clouds parted to reveal the blue that was not hers any longer. The colour in her skin drained, leave the paintwork set against white. She pulled in breath because that is what a body does.

Gomez bent down and whispered quietly in her ear, 'You do what I say, Carmen, and I say I don't wash dishes no more.'

He had the first man on top of her three hours later. He was old and he worked long hours at a factory and would die of lung failure in a short time and he was lonely without his wife and needed company. He was kind to Carmel and he sobbed as he pushed into her and he wheezed loudly and the mucus in his chest rattled as he called another woman's name over and over. And Carmel, now Carmen, put her arms around his neck when he had done and he said, thank you, pet. He would come again and again to her, spending his overtime and his savings, which should have been passed on to children, but he'd had none. He would come again and again because of the way she would pull him against her at the end. He did not realize that she held him on her breast so she could see the lost sky.

★   ★   ★

Three years later, Carmen was no longer special. She was one of many. Most found her cold, too cold. Long after they had left her bed they felt they would never be warm.

Three years later in the dead of night she woke and saw Gomez beside her. He did not call so often now as he had other girls. When he felt a bad wanting he would come to her, because she was still cold to him. The other women moaned but Carmen did not utter a sound.

'Carmen. My best girl. You give professional love.'

He would give her a lot to drink. She liked a

49

lot to drink. Every day. But it did not change anything except her eyes, which lost their stare and swam in a listless sea.

She could not feel the child growing inside the same way she could not feel the men who entered her. Nothing made her warm in life. But dreams protected her as her belly swelled. In them, she held me through her skin and spoke softly to me of the crib that Eddie was building. She saw him planning it. Telling her the walnut and rosewood was worth the price: 'Nothing but the best for our baby.'

He told her how he had searched for the right nails, copper, because he was not a real carpenter and could not make dowels, join or turn wood. But he was a neat worker and he would make this like it had just unfolded, for their child.

'Like a fairy cot, Carmel, it will be. The child will sleep sound in it,' Eddie promised.

She did not admonish him for the time spent on it, only she wished he would look at her, as he had always looked, as if he could not get enough of her and would be happy to die trying. She was happy just to have him near when she was cold. The cold even caught her in sleep. Him being close by, though preoccupied, drove the cold away.

'Don't worry about the cold now, Carmel. The baby is growing too fast for you to keep up with it. You sleep and let nature take away your weariness,' Eddie spoke gently but all his attention was turned on the work.

'Sometimes, Eddie,' Carmel put her hands on

50

his shoulders, bent over the task, 'I wish we could live in a place always sunny.'

'When the baby is born it will be always sunny,' Eddie promised.

And Carmel smiled at that.

* * *

It had been too late when Gomez realized, and it had gone badly for her when he did.

'You make them wear a johnny,' he shouted, 'or they don't do it.'

Carmen did not know who was with her or what they were wearing most times.

Now she was seven months pregnant and Gomez had told her she would work until the end because they would not take her now down the back lanes, as she was so far gone.

'Some men like this. They pay more.'

Nothing had been said about what would happen after the child's birth. But it would not be Carmel's decision.

She did not know if the child was Gomez's and he would not have claimed it anyway.

Hundreds of men had put into her. One had a disease and Gomez found her a good doctor to put her right. He also found the man and put him in hospital.

'My girls are not dirty.'

He looked after them all. They had things to wear and places to go. But no money of their own. Gomez was with them when they shopped and when they went to parties to meet new men. Gomez was always there.

She lay beside him now, listening to the night sounds of women doing their job with men on floors below her. She watched the lost sky and counted the stars that were framed by her window. Carmen was a woman who did not deserve the stars now. Eddie was a long memory away. But she went to the place where they had once been and she knew that once there had been heat in her and fire and she wished for it now, for she was frozen.

The small of her back ached from the shape of the bed and the weight of the men. She wanted to get up; she had not been up all day and all night. It was coming up to Christmas. It was busy.

She tried for sleep because Eddie always arrived with the crib soon after it. But the day's work had taken up too much of the night for that. She got up but she could not get away. Gomez's breathing was deep but if she made to leave this room he would be awake and asking her to wait for him. She never left the place alone. She never received visitors. The letters to her mother had stopped, with no one to write them.

His cigarettes and matches were beside the bed. She took them and went to light one for herself, curling up against the cold on an armchair. The bottle of spirits was almost empty. She drank what was left.

Even in sleep he did not appear vulnerable. His mouth was hard set and his jaw clenched. What he had asked her to do that night she did in order to end things quickly.

'This way does not harm the baby. This is my place.'

She was in pain, bleeding. The cold light of morning near. The child in her rested quietly, but even when it moved she did not feel it. By day it was the child of Gomez. There was no joy in its growth, only a reminder of another child lost.

The voices grew. Burn Carmen Moriarty. Burn the badness out. Fire to keep warm by.

She looked out at the sky and at that precise moment it opened and released a powerful shower of rain, which rattled loudly and came through the leaking places in her roof. Gomez stirred and did not wake, but fell into a heavier sleep, brought on by the drum of the night rain. The baby kicked hard and sharp against her left side. She put out her cigarette.

She took the clothes, which had been bought for her, from the wardrobe and placed them in a pile at the foot of the bed. The room was small, its function did not require much space and space was much in demand in the Soho of my mother's day. The match light was crisp and clean. She held it until it burned her fingers, could not feel anything. Another.

Then the whole box. She rested it on the clothes and knelt. The flames took hold quickly and licked through the colour and form of her soft chains.

She spread her hands and smiled at the sudden warmth. It grew now and it was as if the fire had pierced her veins and ran through them. Carmel had known it would, had known this was the way to come alive again. The voices in her formed song and chorus as the flames journeyed.

If Gomez had felt a hand on him or heard a noise he would have woken. But the flame is soft and silent and does not announce its presence. The fire crept like a great cat and pounced on prey aware of nothing until it roared victory in Gomez's ears and took what it wanted. He screamed but the rain fell louder and it could not enter the sealed window. The sky he had sealed out claimed victory.

Carmel watched the figure thrash and cry. She did not answer it but stared open mouthed as the fire claimed the small, sad space. She stood waiting for the flames to notice her, their mother, and come to her. The door burst open and hands pulled her out.

Standing on the street with the other women in their tired collection of silks, lace and nylon and simple cotton, she watched the flames shooting from the roof of the building. The men who had been with the women had disappeared in various states of undress back to their lives and their explanations.

Carmen Moriarty had a dressing gown to keep out the cold. Even that was not hers. One of the other girls had thrown it over her in the street. She had less in the world now than she had on her first day in London.

★ ★ ★

When the police delivered her to the former address of Constance Trapwell, an irate woman opened the door. Constance Trapwell had left a year before with a small bald man in his sixties. She had moved to the south of France with him.

They took Carmen to a cell for a night while they made enquiries.

7

The Daughter of Life

She walked the grounds of the home by day, and by night they learned to lock Carmel in. That did not matter — the dreams could grow in the daytime now there was no Gomez to prevent them. No men to lie with.

Only Eddie to watch. It's coming on grand, Eddie.

'It will be ready, Carmel, or I will not be the man I think I am.'

She was in a place that was my mother's harbour, and mine for a while. She wandered the gardens barefoot and was not prevented.

'Remember to stay close to yourself,' she whispered to me. 'Remember what your mother forgot. When the crib is ready, we will see your father. Won't we, Eddie? You're too busy now.'

The old sister in charge was kind to Carmel, in a way she was not with any of the other women. The police had made it known the kind of life she had led, the kind of place where she had almost been burned alive.

And while she gathered strength I grew inside her, but I could not be held. She let me go early and I was a small and shrivelled excuse for new life. I was afraid before I was born; it travelled from my mother's heart into mine.

I clutched to her insides, turning this way and that. When they dragged me out with forceps they dragged most of her life with me. I was cold from the long fight out of the comforting darkness and into the harsh light.

Being born too soon I shrank from the sunlight. My mother's womb had been a dark waiting place. I would not have formed if it had not been for the dreams that led us to the places where my mother had walked freely, away from what she had become.

She lost everything in my birth. The dreams left her blood and the harsh voices remained. The colour of my skin said Eddie would not be coming for us. I would not be laid in the crib that had been finished only the previous evening.

'One more plane, one coat of wood oil. No varnish for the child. Let the child feel the wood proper, wood is good stuff to be felt. We know that.' Eddie was more in a hurry now than before. His desire for neatness overtaken by the desire to be done in time.

'Don't worry, Eddie,' Carmel tried to rub his shoulders but they were knotted now with intent. 'The baby can sleep with us in the big bed for a few days.'

'That's no place for a baby — a big bed. The child will be lost in the bigness of it. The child needs its own place, to start off in the world knowing where and what it is.'

Carmel had watched, without words, until the pains began.

They did not expect either Carmel or me to live. But my cry grew stronger and I was calling for Carmel. My mother did not hear it. She had slid down the long passageway up which I had just travelled. How and why she came back into her body is a mystery. Perhaps the heron still held her.

When she recovered I was already two months old, had been held by her only a handful of times. The voices had returned to her and my mother fought with them this time, for the sake of the child that I was.

The voices wore habits and said, 'Do what is best for the child.'

Carmel could write her name, but she would not sign the papers that would have given me away. When my mother had me in her arms she knew she would not let this child of dark skin and unknown parentage go.

'This child will be a liability to your life,' the old sister in charge said gently, 'but a blessing to others. Leave her with us and find a life of your own.'

My mother called me Sive. It came to her from a time in Scarna when a theatre company had come to the town and brought with them a woman more fine and free than any other woman had seemed.

Sive was not the name on my certificates. The nuns who ran the home we had been placed in chose that name. They changed my name just as they changed the young woman's name from Carmen to Carmel when she first came to them.

The certificates that made me known to the world said, Mary Moriarty. Father unknown. Mother: Carmel Moriarty. Place of Birth: St

Margaret's Home, Ealing.

She was asked to leave. The nuns bid us both farewell with a heavy heart, but their conscience intact, for they could not offer her anything while she remained a woman with a child and no wedding ring.

Where else was there for us to go?

8

Back to the Streets

Back to the streets Carmel went, back to Carmen.

Carmen's madness protected her. The ponces did not want the woman who it was said had started a fire in Brewer Street in which one man lost his life. They did not want a woman with a child, who walked the streets now talking to herself.

'Will you write a letter for me?' she would ask the world.

Only the poorest and most desperate would pay for her now and since she had no place they would have her in back alleys.

We lived in a basement room, far away from the sky, with leaking pipes and a view of feet moving in the world above, unaware that eyes watched below. There was no bathroom. There was a sink from which no water ran. There was a two ring stove with one ring working. The walls were salted with damp and Carmel would stop me from putting my tongue against them. To touch anything was to be part of rot and damp — even when you did not touch, the smell came to you until you became one with it.

I was fed when Carmen remembered. Dreams came when Carmen left me tied to the cot at night and dreams untied me. In them a long thin woman, tall as life, with grey hair and black eyes watched over me as if I was her own.

In all, I should have died, but life wanted me as it had once wanted my mother. I was kept in a room below the world for the first two years of my life, except for the times when Carmen would strap me to her and walk, sometimes for miles. We sat in Soho Square and she would watch me as I played with green blades of grass that were my fascination. We picked flowers when no one looked and brought them home to our flowerless world.

As I grew, the dream lost its hold and the woman with it and I stepped into my mother's place one day on sturdy legs that took me out of the door and up the stone steps worn down by feet before ours, into Soho. I followed my mother's wasted legs in torn tights and shining red shoes that disappeared into the grey-black of the thickening crowd.

I cried and wandered until my cry was heard and a woman picked me up in her arms. She carried me into the café close by where her friends sat. Carmen also sat, alone.

Carmen looked up from her copper-stewed tea and took me.

'She's a grubby one, could do with a wash, and what is she doing on the streets?'

The woman who had carried me put spit on her thumb and leaned down to wipe my mouth.

'I didn't even know you had a baby, Irish.' She smelled of the lavender sweets she sucked perpetually.

'How would you?' another said. 'We don't even know Irish's name.'

'You'll have to take her home.'

Carmen shook her head and whispered, 'Work.'

Carmen put a sugar into her cup and did not stir it. She held the cup to my lips.

'Don't!' the woman who had carried me screeched. 'It's too hot! Sergio, get the little girl some milk, there's a good lad. I'll go and get a towel and wipe some of the muck off the mite's face. Keep a child clean they'll grow clean — no one ever tell you that, Irish?'

''Course not,' another new face said. 'Them Irish is savages — they have about ten kids apiece.'

'That's rich coming from you, Lulu, your mother had twelve.'

Lavender woman came back from the bathroom with a steaming towel. She scrubbed hard. The wail I sent up shook my own bones and lavender woman's dusted cleavage was suddenly a prison as she pushed my face into it to get at the back of my neck with a practised hand.

'Why is it kids the world over hate being bathed?'

'I don't go with that. Every one of us growing up was cleaner than this one.'

Lulu took out a compact and bothered already perfect hair rolled in a chignon. I watched her apply blood-red lipstick and smear kohl on the upper corners of her eyes. She stood up smartly and grabbed a patent leather handbag and powder-blue coat — both as new as Carmen's were worn.

'There she goes, Lulu — as French a fuck as anyone from Leeds called Nancy.'

Lavender woman blew smoke at Lulu. Lulu was on her way out the door when she stopped and stuck her head back in again.

'That's rich coming from a prostitute called Fanny.'

Sergio, a large man with hands that had no business cooking, put a baby's bottle of milk and an almond pastry in front of me.

'I'd best be off too,' Fanny smiled at Carmen who did not smile, but rose herself and walked after Fanny.

'Look, Irish, you can't just leave the child here. Sergio has a living to make too. I've got to get on. We all have our own worries.'

Carmen did not move. Fanny gave her an impatient shove towards me.

'Go on, girl, look after your own. I have four waiting at home.'

Sergio was shaking his head and the other customers were waiting on the outcome. I was eating my pastry and drinking milk.

The door opened. In came a woman tall as life, and wearing a blue-grey dress. Her hair was silver white and her eyes a glittering black, her face unlined though there were years on her. Her step was a silent one and her presence spoke loudly. I went to her as one I had known all my life and she welcomed me with the practised kindness of one who had seen me each day. Sergio went to a table in the far corner nearest the counter and began clearing it.

'Here, Myrna,' Fanny popped a lavender sweet in her mouth. 'You about for a while?'

'Yes,' she spoke in a voice that was not loud and everyone heard.

Myrna took my hand and the world was in hers. Her skin had something past warmth and beyond cold. She led me to the table Sergio had cleared and I spent all day, and many after that watching her.

That was how I came to be known to all the women of Sergio's Café. There were women who worked behind closed doors, there were street women and show women and then there was Carmen, who worked where no one worked. I went with her to the café each day and one or other of the women took care of me. Mostly Myrna.

The women of Soho, our increasingly bright Soho, no longer secretive but with its uses and skills displayed on garish signs that spoke of now and not tomorrow, all knew of Myrna.

Where Myrna came from no one knew. They once tried to deport her and could not, because she had no home place, no placeable accent, no relatives. She had shed all dutiful ties and links with the past. Her choices were always her choices and she could see no other way of living.

Some of the oldest colleagues and acquaintances of hers — women who had worked in the gentlemen's clubs of the twenties and some even before that, said she had always been there and had always been alone.

What she did to survive was what they did.

She went with the men. But they got nothing of her. She went with them in such a way as would make a man continue to want her for the rest of his days. They would spend a night with her and in the morning it was as if they had never been there. It made them come again, a wanting in them.

The old women of Soho remembered Myrna young. She arrived with nothing but a grey dress and shoes that were held together with two rounds of string and a small miracle. She wore nothing but grey all her life.

By the time Constance Trapwell and Carmel Moriarty had found their way to that world, Myrna's working days were long over. But she continued to live among her own. Sergio's was where she spent her afternoons and nights. In Sergio's Café I watched her and I learned from her and I never knew all of her, even, in times to come, when she told me all she knew of herself. She could never tell me all she was. The details of her life do not explain the mystery. By her ways Myrna told me all she did not say was all she did not know.

Sergio's was where the women of Soho came to discuss the business of their days and nights and to do so without fear. Sergio was that rare thing — a silent Italian who could not cook. He made up for it with warmth, comfort and plenty of tea, coffee, sandwiches and pastries. They were my food for six years.

From Sergio I learned the value of silence. When I learned to talk I also learned to stop talking, because I heard the world better then. I did not look at people, but I watched their every move.

★   ★   ★

When I close my eyes now I can see the café. I smell the cheap scent and cigarettes of the working women. I see them check themselves in the mirror over the counter as they leave and come in, a mirror that had lost its silvering over the years as the women lost their brightness, rubbed out by hard-edged lives. I hear the high chatter and low confidences. I see the dark-wood tables scraped with names and longing and the chairs with tatty cushions in bright brocade curtain material, sewn by Sergio's long-gone wife. She had been the one to cook and make the place into a proper restaurant. He had been lost when she had left.

Sergio threw out what threatened, but he would never throw out anything his wife had made in case she came back through the door, which tinkled as it opened and shut.

I see Sergio, always with a cloth in his hand, cleaning in the way that men do — without seeing the dirt. He cleaned slowly and with thought in his eyes. He would wipe away the condensation from the half-curtained window on cold days when the women's breath had filled the room with welcome warmth and clouded the view.

I see his balding head and large belly under a grey-white apron and the heavy arms folded when the window is wiped clear and his eyes on the street outside.

Myrna would come and stand beside him and whisper, 'Make some more coffee.'

The café held the combined sadness of the women who worked and the man who served them. But it held their laughter and hopes too, their speculations on silver linings and sunshine around corners that, for most, never came. The women and Sergio were the first evidence I had that lost souls make good together with what they have.

When you have nothing you always have conversation. Women with little to lose, sharing what was left.

It was a kind of home.

★   ★   ★

Carmen became afraid to stay in any one place. We moved around the narrow streets, leaving no marks behind for her sake. I was eight when I put out Carmen's first fire. She had torn the pages from a phone book.

'The way home is here, Sive, but I can't find it because I haven't the right eyes.'

She put a match to her efforts. I quenched the flames quickly enough with a pan of water. It had begun.

I found food for us, washed us and dressed us from the cast-offs the other women gave me. Once more Carmen was in things not her own. I took her by the hand to the kind doctor with the soft voice and thick glasses who came once a month to clean the women up as best he could.

My mother was beyond cleaning.

Fanny and Lulu prided themselves on not having need of that kind of doctor. Fanny because she only took 'respectables', Lulu because she only did kinky.

'There's no use having money for trimmings and no teeth, now, Lulu,' Fanny warned. 'You're best with those who want little of it.'

'Why is it you never mention the word sex?' Lulu barked. 'You've been working as long as I've known you and you never mention sex.'

'Well, it's not as if I enjoy it. You ever tried to feed four and clothe four kids on coupons? Well that's how I got started. What's your excuse?'

'I'm just a tart,' Lulu said in a hard way that hid the softness of her story.

'Well, there's no one to dispute that. When I got going I had a bed settee and five of us to sleep in it. I had two pairs of shoes for four pairs of feet and me own. Now I got a nice flat and keep it nice. I got lino, curtains, dressing table . . . '

'You got clap, too.'

'I never. All mine wear French letters or they don't get near me.'

I watched them all from Myrna's table. Myrna was given respect because she did not ask for it. The women all knew her to be one of their own and yet apart from them. In a place where many shared their stories Myrna did not share hers. But she told many of theirs. Myrna read cards and told fortunes by palms. The women would ask for this and more often than not Myrna would say no. Why not? the women would ask.

It's worth a few bob to you.

'I tell the truth, you don't want to hear the truth.'

Myrna would say nothing more, but look at Sergio. He would put a hand on the woman's shoulder.

Myrna drank coffee black as her eyes. I tasted it once and found it bitter.

'You are too young for such sourness,' Myrna smiled a rare smile.

★ ★ ★

I did not have proper schooling, but one or two of the women would give me lessons. At eight I wrote and read but not well. I wrote letters for my mother, to a place she knew from memory. I wrote as much as I could of what she asked me to say to Noreen. I wrote my name, over and over, while she told me to write all I could not. When I had done writing, my mother would come close to sleep and give into it, peaceful only in those times. I would take the words and paper and hide them where she could not find them. I put my head on her lap and went to my dreams of places other than Soho. No one begins like my mother, I learned in those dreams. All are innocent.

9

Welsh Lucy's Request

I was sitting with Myrna when the young girl with the white face came in and walked straight up to Myrna.

'Are you the one reads fortunes?'

Myrna looked at her a moment and said yes for the first time in many days. She spoke nothing for a while. The girl looked ready to run out the door, there were sweat pearls on her forehead — she rubbed her hands together, palms flat and kept looking at Sergio.

'He safe?'

Myrna nodded.

'I'm Lucy. Welsh Lucy the girls in my building calls me, as distinct from the French girl. I come here because they told me you could help me with my work. I'm not doing it the right way.'

Welsh Lucy's whole body was shaking. I stared at her.

'Tell the child to stop looking at me.'

Myrna looked at Lucy and said, 'I can tell you what to do with the men and it won't do you any good. You're not cut from the cloth that's suited, Lucy. Go off somewhere.'

'What sort are you anyway? I need to have some lessons to do what I do better. That's all. Will you tell me what to do?' Welsh Lucy urged.

'Or do I have to go on myself trying?'

'Take the child to another table, Sergio.'

Sergio moved me and Myrna spoke in a long, low voice to Welsh Lucy. They talked for a while and when Lucy left she was not shaking. But I saw the shadow with Lucy and I ran to Myrna and pointed to it.

'You see it?' Myrna asked. I nodded.

'Then you have the eyes.'

Myrna drank more coffee that day than any other and spoke no more words. I played with the sugar grains, pouring them down my sleeve and piling them back into the sugar bowl. I reached for Myrna's sleeve to do the same and she caught at me and I would have shrieked but I was silent on that day, as I was on all days.

'You remember the eyes of Welsh Lucy, Sive. Eyes full of shadow. You remember,' she hissed. 'When you see eyes in *your* head like that then remember this: it is best to walk away from all you have known, with nothing to remain or remind. Get ready to leave, Sive, leaving is upon you.'

★ ★ ★

Two months later Welsh Lucy's body, a knife through her young heart not yet hardened, was found in the kind of laneway that had seen it all before, opposite Sergio's Café. The police had been crawling around all day and reporters were slipping women a few quid for stories about Welsh Lucy that may or may not have been true.

When there was a murder, in those days there was a stir. The women gathered in Sergio's and talked rapidly and smoked as much, sucking life and calm from cigarettes, and put off going to work.

'What we have to do!' Fanny broke her lavender sweet hard against her back teeth and pulled on the cigarette harder. 'Take my last punter. There's him sweating like a pig and me panting and the business finally done. When it's over he says, 'I hate people like you.' Don't know why, but I burst into tears. The old bastard got to me!'

'They all hate us,' Lulu rooted in her handbag. 'He's only saying what they all think. They hate us because they need us. That's why you get them to pay before — once the need is gone so is the will to pay for it. And they're strange buggers. I've no respect for any man has to pay for it with me.'

'What about your fishy fella, Lulu?' Fanny urged as Lulu struck a match like she was striking out all the ones who'd had her and would have her again.

'Well,' Lulu lit her cigarette and poked it into a pearlescent holder. 'He brings up a big salmon in an ice box and gets me to whack him with it on the arse. It's frozen solid at the start and by the end the smell of it would put you off all fish, even caviar.'

'I had caviar once,' Fanny laughed. 'Tasted like snot.'

'What we need is for rich men with bad eyesight to love us out of all this,' Fanny spoke as

72

if no one was there at all. 'We need some of Myrna's stuff.'

'You need to find the man first before Myrna can do anything,' Lulu reminded. 'Personally speaking, I wouldn't be bothered loving a man who paid me. But I'd marry a rich one all right. Loving and marrying — two different things.'

I had seen Myrna take the hopes of more than one woman seriously and turn them into reality. I had heard a woman tell Myrna of a man who had been brought to her, a shy man, too old for his first time, but his first it was. Could Myrna read her cards and tell her if he would come back?

Myrna had taken the cards from the wooden box and unwrapped them from the piece of cloth. I watch her hands shuffle, long fine rivers of fingers flowing through the pack. No rings on them, no marks of anyone or thing but herself.

The woman picked some on Myrna's request. Myrna spread them and read, looked up from them and smiled.

'You'll have him. When he comes back to you it will be for you. Give him some of this,' she reached into her bag and pulled out a small bag of powder, 'in a glass of whatever he is drinking.'

The woman thanked her all the way out and was not seen again on the streets.

Carmen came to the café door and called for me. I went out the door, pushing past Lulu who patted me on the head and tried to plant a kiss on it, but I shrugged it away.

73

'She's getting stranger,' Lulu said, miffed at being snubbed in front of everyone.

'She doesn't look eight, with those big green eyes looking back at you.'

Myrna said, 'Not much longer for her now.'

10

All Small beside Him

The café had the quiet of Welsh Lucy's death about it when the man who had to stoop to come through its front door entered. Sergio was small beside him, all were small beside him.

The man put hands on Sergio's counter.

Words were spoken. Sergio looked at him a long while and finally pointed to one of the stools and poured him a coffee. The women sniggered at him sitting on the stool — an ostrich on a canary perch — then again at his wincing on the roughness of the coffee.

Black, he took it, no sugar. After one mouthful he spooned a heap in and stirred. He continued to murmur to Sergio — long, slow and deep — like thunder in the far off distance.

I watched the man, as near to a mountain as I had seen. His hair was brown with strands of silver grey and his long neck ran out of it and down into shoulder blades that stood sharp against the cream shirt he wore.

He turned away from Sergio only once, to glance at the surroundings in a way that left the women out of them. I needed only one moment to catch the eyes — their blue not like anything I have seen before or since. Almost black this blue was, the colour of dark sapphires.

'Photographs,' he said the word to Sergio.

Sergio shook his head. The place had been full of photographers since the death of Lucy. But this man was different; otherwise Sergio would have shown him out the way he had shown all others.

The women sniffed money and asked for it.

The giant said no. He did not pay. He was here for a story on Welsh Lucy and the women she worked with. Myrna came in and Sergio beckoned to her. I went up to the giant man behind her.

'Perhaps,' she was saying, 'you could tell us your name?'

'Thomas Cave.'

'The women work, Thomas. It would be good to give them something in return.'

Thomas Cave shook his head.

'If I pay then you do what I want, rather than what you want yourselves.'

He pushed away the coffee cup, emptied at great pains to himself and thought, slowly, as if the world would end in moving quickly. His skin was a light tan. He would be fair on most days of the year away from sun.

'I could,' he offered, 'buy you all lunch.'

The sunlight came at the same moment and fell on the giant who had come to make my world so small. His voice was calm in his dealings, but I watched the backs of his hands placed on the counter, the skin raised on them, light fighting through the white hairs, standing on end. If he had lifted those hands they would have been shaking. He did not lift them.

76

'Lunch,' Myrna said, 'would be delightful.'

The women she turned to did not reply. Sergio's lunches were not famous for being eaten. More women left than stayed and the giant seemed content with that. He had once had chestnut-brown hair and it had lightened to grey. I wanted to touch it to know what made the rivers of colour run their way.

The giant Thomas Cave was not for touching or talking. He ate with us at Myrna's table, before photographs. I watched him and he asked, 'Who is the child?'

'She is Sive.'

He did not do the small talk adults insist on using with children.

'Where did you get your green eyes?'

I looked away from him.

'From the same place as her mother. The same place you come from,' Myrna spoke.

Thomas Cave's turn to look away. He did not discuss himself. Where, he asked, after a while, did Myrna come from?

'Here,' she said as if there were nowhere else.

The giant Thomas Cave held his knife and fork awkwardly; they were too small instruments for such hands. After lunch he got his camera and behind it he was a different man. The giant's awkward presence smoothed into invisibility. The women forgot he was there; he was patient in letting them forget him. They talked among themselves, did their coming and their going.

I did not forget — I watched all he was as he worked. And Myrna watched me. The hands that held knife and fork so clumsily were deft with

77

this black box, small as a toy in his hands, but part of them.

He passed it to me once, when he felt my eyes on him.

'Look.'

I saw all I needed to know about my world. Carmen came and he put her beside me and we shared our green eyes with him, we were the only two he asked to look directly at the camera. Myrna turned black eyes on him, but not on his lens, and said it was the first time she had allowed her image to be taken away from her. He said that he was privileged. The reluctant subjects eased into the work he did with them. Sergio put his arms on the counter and leaned into a smile.

Thomas Cave took all we offered. Then he was gone. With his camera he could make an almost unseen exit so unlike his cumbersome entrance. Only Myrna and myself watched his departure and took his thanks. Myrna put her hands on my shoulders, said, 'Watch, Sive, for when he comes through your door again.'

★ ★ ★

Six weeks later photographs arrived of all of us, bar Myrna. A note from Thomas Cave said her image could not be taken from her as it had refused to develop. The days came and went the same way, Welsh Lucy and Thomas Cave forgotten but for the photographs pinned to the mirror behind Sergio's counter.

11

Noreen, by Way of Dreams

A woman I did not know came to us by way of dreams. Before they and she came to me, Fanny Martin and I were sitting in Sergio's Café. The rain coming down too hard for the punters to be about, Fanny's talk was as full as the rain. I pointed to the place where Myrna always sat and Fanny said, 'Well, we all want to know more about her. What I learned about Myrna from her own mouth I could write on a postcard. But I know her. There's two kinds of women, Sive, women that do this work out of need, that's me and most of the girls in here. Then there's the women who do it out of choice. Myrna belongs with them. She's no tart, but she's too fond of freedom for the times she was born in.

'She couldn't settle and in our days, not yours, women who didn't settle had no life. She could have married any man she pleased and it didn't please her. I know she was born with nothing, because she's left with it now. I know she lived with gypsies for a time because of her potion-making. I know she learned that from them, because one called to Sergio's once, begging, and Myrna spoke to her in the gypsy tongue. Mind you, she speaks more than gypsy, she speaks — ' Fanny broke off, suddenly

79

unwilling to continue before adding, 'There are girls round here who turned into old ladies and into gravestones and Myrna's still alive. There are some who think, and I'm one of them, that Myrna's lived forever.'

The door tinkled and Fanny sensed it was Myrna, even though her back was to it.

'Well,' Fanny said. 'Wet enough for you?'

'Have you been boring the child?' Myrna asked Fanny.

'No, Sive likes to hear the old stories.'

'Do you think, Sive,' Myrna asked quietly, 'that you would like to come for a walk with me?'

I took Myrna's hand and we walked out into waiting Soho.

'I take this walk most days before I come to the café. It's a walk you will like, Sive, a walk into the past. All places are somewhere different before they become what they are. They move on to become somewhere different. Just like people, Sive. Like you and I. You and I will be very different in the years to come,' she said, as we walked down Berwick Street. The doorways to Soho were doorways to worlds of many choices and the same end.

'What happens here,' Myrna said as we walked along, 'is the same as happens anywhere else. All you have to do is look to see the same stories told time after time. Mine is just the same as yours, Sive. It's started somewhere else and has ended up here. This place has more than its fair share of past.'

She stopped at a fruit stall and picked two

bright red apples, bloody with ripeness. She bit firmly into hers.

'Soho has sold everything from the apple to Eve herself. Life is for sale here, Sive, and death in some places. This is life, Sive, this is how you must learn to treat it. Be fierce with it and it will not beat you, be tender with it and it will not harm you. At each moment you will be told what is the right way to take hold of life. Listen well and do only what your heart tells you. Do only as you please. There is no other way of living unless you prefer death as life.'

She put her hands on my shoulders.

'You are a great find, Sive. Don't be afraid of ghosts, they only appear to the living they find worthwhile. The ghosts will come to you, Sive, because your eyes invite them. One day, when I am long gone, you will remember that.'

Myrna and I walked on. I was given in those hours and that talk a sense of all that could be done with a future. I wanted to rise up and out.

Myrna saw the stir in me and she smiled at it. We walked back to the familiar café.

'You can walk between two worlds, Sive, but you're best off picking one. If ever you need me I'll come to you in dreams,' were Myrna's last words to me before we went through Sergio's door.

★ ★ ★

My first memory of my grandmother Noreen was that she filled the room early one morning in a big green hat with a yellow band. She came by

81

way of dreams — with hope of mending what had been long broken.

★ ★ ★

Carmen and I had found our way from the room under the earth to a room near the sky. But it was my sky now. I sat at the open window and stared at it and was a part of it. My mother Carmen did not look at it.

The woman who lived in the flat below had been growing a sunflower in a window box. I had watched it reaching up for our window and each day I strained to touch it, but the wind snapped its life in two before that.

'Did you take the sunflower?' I thought, when I opened the door to Noreen.

'I am glad you like my hat.' Noreen said, in answer to my stare. 'Can I come in?'

I let her enter the room, not like me, who ran from strangers in the same way my mother went towards them.

Carmen had not been home that night. Noreen sat in my watchful silence.

'Where is she then?' she asked.

She did not expect an answer. She looked down at her feet, which were swollen in the new shoes. Her ankles had no shape, they were straight lines pinched into the cutting edges of leather. She was a big woman again, but she perched on our chair as if she was small.

'Are you hungry, child?' she asked after a long while. 'I know I am.'

The key finally turned in the door. Carmen

did not recognize Noreen under her hat.

'Mammy,' she said, after long minutes at the door with the cold wind of the day travelling up the stairs behind her. Noreen removed her sunflower hat to reveal a sweat-drenched scalp covered with hair that had grown grey and thinned and in places come away altogether. It was the only part of her that had given way to Joseph Moriarty and lost.

'Mammy,' Carmen cried softly.

'Carmel.'

Noreen watched her and said the name and did not draw close. She knew London had been no kinder to her than the homeplace had been. 'I would have written to say I was coming, but you didn't give me an address.' Noreen began the talk with the distance between them.

'How did you find us?'

'An old woman in a café told me the place. I would have cooked a breakfast for the child, but she wasn't keen. The child needs a wash, as do you.'

'How did you find us, Mammy?'

'By asking. I found the letters last month, one of them was Hammersmith and the other few were postmarked Shepherd Market. I went to Shepherd Market and found out what they do there. Then I was told to come here. I asked until I was told.' Noreen spoke with a softness that did not hide the shake in her voice. 'The child won't tell me her name.'

Noreen almost could not face what she had come to face. That is why she had bought the summer hat. Even though it was autumn it was brightness she needed.

'That's Sive — go for bread, Sive,' Carmen told me.

I did not want to leave. I hovered by the door while Carmen fished about in her purse. A crumple of well-worn notes, each with their separate story, fell to the floor. Noreen put her head in her hands.

'Sive, take the pound note and count the change like I told you. Go to the Italian baker. You can't trust the Italians, Mammy; they'd rob the eyes out of your head. You can't trust anyone round here.'

Carmen's voice and her eyes were moving rapidly around the room, her breath was short. I went to her side.

'Go on, love!'

My spindly limbs were pushed out the door. But I waited in the hall for a while. I heard the big woman's voice.

'She's very small for eleven.'

'She's eight. The other baby's gone.'

'Gone where? You said in the letter 'gone', too. Gone where?'

'Dead.'

Noreen sighed.

'I didn't get the letters until last month. Your father had hidden them. She's not going to burn in the sun like her mother, is she?'

By the time I returned with hot steaming bread wrapped in newspaper, both their faces had changed. They sat close together. My grandmother stood to make tea, but I was there before her. There was no kettle, the pan had to be boiled on the gas ring. I kept the matches in my skirt, away from Carmen. I wanted to shout at the old lady with the half-bald head, 'She is having a good day today. On a bad one she won't speak to you and she might even try to set fire to you.'

'Eddie called to the house many times to look for you,' Noreen talked as if I had spoken. 'I told him you'd gone to London. He came here.'

'Eddie?' Carmen asked. 'Is he still in London?'

'No, he's back home. Not long back.'

He had heard my mother's voice, crying for him in the night. He had not heard it well enough.

Carmen went into the bedroom to change. When she came back she had washed herself clean of all that her mother had seen at first. She was Carmel — loudness wiped away.

She would not have done this for me, even when I poured the water and pointed to the flannel. Noreen saw her daughter's broad feet, scarred and tortured from the pointed shoes.

We ate the hot bread with smeared butter and we drank sweet tea, even though the summer was with us again for a time in autumn, and it was too hot for food. Our window was wide open but it did nothing to relieve the closeness of the air. Pearls of sweat appeared on Noreen's cheeks, growing fat then running a river into the damp neck of her blouse.

'I bought this on the way here,' she said, showing us her hat. 'I always fancied myself in a hat and when I saw this in the window I knew it had my name on it.'

Carmel laughed a high laugh, not sure of where it would lead her. I went for the pill bottle and gave her one. She took it.

The talk began to pour on the second cup of tea. They forgot about me. I was afraid of this talk, of the peace it brought with it.

'Where is he?' Carmel asked finally.

'Gone,' Noreen said.

★ ★ ★

As the bus disappeared over the brow of the hill Noreen could not stop herself thinking that it was she who should have been on it, resenting her only daughter's escape. Then she thought of what the price had been.

Late that night, Joseph returned, full to the gills, ready to wreck the house on the back of a crooked look.

He opened the door of the house and slammed it against the wall so that the damp plaster cracked, split, fell away. He liked the noise, it sounded good in his head. He went to his gun rest and found his gun gone. Up the stairs, slowly, the spots of anger in front of his eyes and the drink making his feet unsteady.

He opened the door to his daughter's room and he turned, expecting the mother to rush out pleading for her like a bleating sheep. The mother did not come. Again he pushed the bedroom door against the wall with a force that drove a picture off the wall. The glass shattered into thousands of fragments so tiny that they could be felt underfoot for a long time afterwards.

Joseph shielded his eyes from the light of the hallway, for the room was in darkness, and he found his wife sitting bolt upright in his daughter's bed, pointing his own shotgun at him.

'You wouldn't dare,' he snarled.

'I would and I will, and what's more I know I wouldn't need a second bullet.'

Joseph stopped at her voice, which had all but disappeared into a soft whisper over the years, now grown again. Even on this first night Noreen seemed bigger, filling out the large bones and flesh that had grown limp on them.

'I am ready to kill you,' the grown voice said.

'Why don't you?'

'Because killing would be too good for you. I am spending no time in no prison for your carcass, unless you make me. The girl's gone. You will beat me no more because I have no reason to let you any longer.'

The trigger was cocked; the click rang in his ears. His wife's face had a new expression.

He left, treading on the shattered picture frame. It was a forced Christmas picture of the three of them. Carmel had wanted it put in a frame and on the wall. Noreen Moriarty lived under the same roof as Joseph for many more years. He never raised a hand to her. Now and again he tried the handle of the door to Carmel's room. Each time it was locked. Once he put a shoulder to it. The click of the shotgun put a stop to him doing that again.

His revenge was simple; he never gave Noreen

another penny. The town remarked on how the big woman must have turned simple, to let her husband do all the shopping, pay the bills, even buy her few bits and clothes right down to her underwear. It was decided Joseph had turned over a new leaf. The reason for his chronic temper was the wife he had at home who would not lift a finger for herself or him. Time can distort as well as heal. The distortion left Noreen without a person in the world to enquire after her.

She ate because Joseph could not cook and he had to bring her the food to do it for him. She spat in his dinner each night.

The letters that came from London never reached her, since she no longer went into the town. The postmistress had delivered them into the hands of Joseph.

★   ★   ★

Eddie called to the house seven days after Carmel had left when he was sure Joseph was away in the fields. Noreen said nothing to him for a long time — a man who would wait seven days before enquiring about a woman he was supposed to love was no man at all.

'I came after Carmel, where is she?' Eddie said outright, after a silence in which a tea had grown cold. The kitchen was clean and bare. It made him want to cry to think of the thin girl he loved growing in this place.

'Gone,' Noreen said into a sink that showed her a reflection that had changed as much as she had expected it to and more since the first time she had looked at it.

'Gone where?'

'London.'

Noreen told him the truth, that Carmel had gone away with a child in her belly. From the look in his eyes she could tell it was his, as if she did not know already. She did not sleep nights, thinking she had two wandering souls on her hands now, not just one.

It took Eddie a month to follow. He had never wanted a big city in a different country. The windows of Scarna were his and he had wanted no others. He thought she would fade from him but in the fourth week the pain in his chest was worse. A woman and child of his, elsewhere.

Eddie left. On the night he arrived in London, Carmel was walking up the grey stairs and in on Constance Trapwell, complete with peacock feathers. On the night of Carmel losing their child, Eddie lay on a bed with no sheets and reached into his sorrow, pulling out the tears he had not cried.

When he was not working he walked the city looking for her. But she only came to him at night, in a dream. It was the same dream always — her eyes on him, with the naked flesh of another man between them. He reached out to pull the man off her, but his hands were tied.

Then the dream changed. In it, he saw her waiting, with a full belly, on him to do something for her and the child between them.

'What can I do?' he asked. 'I can't grow the child. What can I do for the child?'

On the way home from the factory where he did work he did not care for, one of many jobs, he saw the crib in the window of a shop. The finest of wood and hours of making gone into it. He could not prevent what happened then, went in and asked how much it was, as if he was an expectant father with all that to look forward to. The sales assistant had smiled at his shyness and said she was not afraid to serve a man, though she had not served one before. Maternity business was the business of women.

She gave him the price and he nodded and went to his wallet and found it would be more than one month's work to pay for it. He made excuses and left, promising to return since she had agreed to keep it on hold.

He never walked that way home again for fear he would see her and feel the shame of not calling. He would have gone back, with the saved money, but he had the dream of Carmel again. It was for him to make, no stranger.

'Why, Carmel? Our child will have outgrown this.'

'Because we will have another. That's why.'

And he could not prevent himself from buying the finest of woods — walnut and rosewood. He could not stop spending all his half-day Saturday searching for copper nails. For he was no carpenter and could not make dowels or turn or join wood. He worked at it and each night he continued the work in dreams and felt Carmel at the back of him.

'I don't appreciate you standing over me,' he growled, but by it he meant he wished that he could have the reward of her face and the look on it as she saw what he was producing. Even he was proud of it. He lay in bed each night and watched it take shape and took time in shaping it, for something in him said this was something that should be made to last.

The men who shared the digs with him, with rooms of their own, peeked in and wondered about the fine work and who it was for.

'A nephew.'

They could get no more out of him. He looked for Carmel each day that was his. In all the places where the Irish gathered. He could not look where he could not bear to find her so he had no hope of seeing her.

* * *

Then he stopped looking and let the dreams take over. In them he had her company, although unseen.

'I want to see you,' he would say.

'Not until it's done, Eddie. Keep at the work.'

'It will be perfect, Carmel. Like a fairy cot, Carmel, it will be. The child will sleep sound in it,' he promised. As the work grew nearer to finishing he could feel her hands on his shoulders, her breath on him, the swell of her belly against his back. Into his spine the delight passed and he thought he would never be rid of it.

'One more plane, one coat of wood oil. No varnish for the child. Let the child feel the wood proper, wood is good stuff to be felt. We know that,' he said.

Then he had finished and watched the crib and its gleam told him the love would pay off. He would see her.

That night he did not dream. The following night the dream where she was under another man returned.

Once, years into living alone in London and knowing few people and wanting to know less, when he could bear the dream no longer, Eddie went to the place where women work with men and took comfort with a woman he called Carmel all through the night. He left her room with his rent money on her dressing table and felt he had come to an end of something.

Across the street he saw a dark-skinned child leading by the hand a woman who had hair the colour of Carmel's. But it was not Carmel; this woman had no fire in her and limped awkwardly in high shoes Carmel would never have worn. She was thin, broken and slow.

In that moment he decided he had cried and looked enough. He left London with nothing but the crib he had made. He came home to settle down to a life alone and was lucky enough he had not sold his ladder, for he began to window clean again. The windows of Scarna had waited.

He put the crib in his room, where there was little else. It was the last thing he saw on sleep and the first thing on waking. Then he heard that Joseph Moriarty had died and Noreen had left the town. He walked out to the coast road and got into the Hoar Rock as anyone in the country did at that time, through an unlocked door. He set the crib by the fireplace, where it is this night, and knew that it was in the place where it should always have been.

Eddie Burns went home to a lonelier life that night, alone but for his guilt and thoughts of the child who might have kept him company.

★   ★   ★

Joseph Moriarty died, at the age of fifty-seven. His heart gave way under all the hate. Noreen watched him fight for breath, globs of unswallowed morning porridge spilling out of his mouth, one hand clutching his breast, the other fastened to the table edge. She smiled as he fell and his eyes rolled until they showed only white. He took a long time to go. She did not bless herself or him; she did not put a sheet over him, left him to survey the bareness of the kitchen. She pulled on his great coat and left the house quickly.

Late that night she came back to it and his open eyes. She pulled the place apart looking for money — and found Carmel's letters of so many years before.

Following Joseph's funeral, attended only by the curious and lonely of the town with little better to do, Noreen caught the mail boat to London and began her walking. Her steps had more purpose than Eddie's. She knew where to look because she knew what was in her daughter was also in her and she could go where he could not.

The working women did not surprise or shock her. She would most likely have become one of them if her way had not been different. In Sergio's Café they told her that her daughter would come.

'Thank God someone turned up,' a woman with rust brown hair and a cockney accent said. 'It's a mother those two need.'

'It's two of them, is it?' Noreen asked Fanny, who had not introduced herself. None of the women had. The man behind the counter had watched her with slow eyes and purposeful movements. She would be made to leave if he felt there was reason, or one of the women called for it.

'She has a girl, a little girl grown bigger each day. They're in here most days.'

Noreen stood up; she did not want to meet Carmel in a café after all the time that had been passed between them.

'Could you tell me where she lives?'

Fanny was just about to when the woman with a French bob, dyed black to hide grey and dressed in clothes as new as her haircut, broke in. Her manner was not as elegant as her looks.

'We would not. You know she comes here, you can wait for her. We don't go giving strangers addresses.'

Noreen sat down again and ordered a tea. The man behind the counter served it with the speed of a snail in no hurry. Noreen felt the eyes on her big body at the small table and felt the pricks of embarrassment at the cut of her clothes. She wore Joseph Moriarty's coat since she had given Carmel her own. Her shape inside the coat was lumpen — looks had been lost to Noreen a long time before.

'You could butter yer bread with her accent,' she heard Fanny whisper.

'Where'd she get the hat?' the other one asked. 'A gardener's wet dream that is.'

'Lulu!' Fanny hissed.

Noreen drank the tea eventually set in front of her and almost spat it out. The tiredness came over her. Three days tramping around and no signs of what she prayed she would not find — a daughter who looked older than her. She felt her dreams slide away and the hard watchful eyes of the women told her Carmel was one of them, or worse, because what Noreen knew of her daughter was that she had no ability to harden.

Then the door had opened and the tall old woman came through it and stared at Noreen.

'You've come a long way.'

The old woman's eyes were almost black. She hadn't a line on her face, Noreen envied that and tried to hide her red, chapped hands, but the old woman had already extended a pale, fine one to shake with.

'You won't want to wait until she comes in, I expect?'

'Myrna!' Lulu said.

'A mother doesn't want to meet her daughter

with a circus crowd watching, does she?'

'I wouldn't mind being a fly on their wall, all the same,' Lulu said, when the big woman in the misshapen coat and ridiculous hat had left, after checking herself shyly in the mirror, as if she had no right to.

12

The Quiet Leaving of Noreen Moriarty

Seven years we had. Seven years when we lived a life that was as good as anyone else's.

Noreen understood the way it was with her daughter; understood things could not be undone. But for as long as she lived she would not allow another hand to harm her.

Carmel could not go home. Too much and not enough had happened to make the return journey. So Noreen came to us. In fact she never left us from that moment on, so afraid was she that we might disappear on her.

'We don't want Sive falling into the same life and hands we've had. We must get her away from this.'

She wrote to the solicitors in Ireland, closed up Hoar Rock, sold a few of its fields, but did not sell it.

'What would it fetch? Pennies. Our nest egg that house is, our just-in-case.'

When a small amount of money from Joseph's life insurance arrived in the post she set us up in a rented two-bedroom flat away from places that served to remind.

★　★　★

97

Our goodbyes to Sergio and the café were brief. I let the women who wanted to hug me do so and I let Sergio pick me up and give me an almond pastry with tears in his eyes. I let him tug at my hair and touch my nose with his. When he set me down I went to Myrna and I put my hands on her seated shoulders and looked into her eyes as she had looked into mine. I did not believe for one moment that I would not be back the next day. I was still a child in that way.

Carmel said quiet thank yous and Noreen had one of her own for Myrna.

'For all you've done.'

'All I did was tell you where to find them, you did the looking.'

★ ★ ★

In the new place Carmel and I were not to share a room.

'Sive needs time away from you,' Noreen decided. 'Time to be a child.'

When different hands soothed my mother, my dreams overtook me. Greenness opened up to me, I walked in places I could not find during the hours of waking in the hard northern part of a hard city. The place was filled with people who spoke like my mother and grandmother.

'Our own,' Noreen would call them.

But they were not mine. They had white-blue skin and eyes full of judgement.

I dreamed. Carmel rested. Noreen found work in a shop. It was that work that fed us and kept us. Noreen would dress us in clothes bought by

98

her, which were not splendid, but they were our own.

Noreen tried to get me into school. I proved as keen on that school idea as my mother had before me. I did not take to the rows of faces and the big face looking over them, the lined copybooks and measured learning.

'All right, Sive,' Noreen conceded, after a fight that left her scratched and panting. 'You are your mother's child and if the truth be known I was the same about school. You'll learn what I know and that's not much. But you'll never have to set foot in the school again if you give me one thing.'

I looked at her.

'Your voice, child. You'll have to speak some time.'

I had always known how to speak, and I began by saying, 'I want to go to the sea.'

We took the train to Brighton the following Saturday. Noreen wore her hat and Carmel had a blue scarf tied around her white face. I had a lemon dress, which made me feel like part of the sun that shone through it. People looked at us.

The walk from the station was long and when we got to the sea it was not just ours, it belonged to the hoards of others swarming on the pebbles with their boxes of food and patches of blanket that squared off the greatness until it was much diminished.

This was not the sea of my dreams, but another sea. Still I went towards it, holding my mother's hand and it welcomed us as an old friend.

We slid into it; I looked at my mother and the

shadow of a bird passed over her face.

She smiled a smile that made me so warm I dived into the cool of the waves. I kicked and turned and saw the whites of my mother's legs beside me. I held on to them and they were firm to the touch as if they had taken root in the place where they ought to have been all along. The water made us clear to each other.

'Let go of me anytime you like, Sive,' she said when I came up for air. 'You'll swim like a fish.'

And I did. Just like my mother, said Noreen, minder of our belongings and our cares, when I came out of the water, but only after my skin had turned blue and I looked like I had been born in it.

★   ★   ★

There had been no noise from their bedroom all morning, so I had slept on. I dreamed of Myrna's dark eyes on me, after seven years. It was a long sleep and she had plenty of time to come to me, to stroke my brow and learn the shape of my face and body with her hands. It had filled out from a straight to curved form only in the past few months.

The child was passing and the woman time was coming. This was what I was proud to tell the run of her hands. You have grown into yourself, they told me in return.

She had not come to me in all the times that we had Noreen to protect us. I remembered words that had come to me from her without being spoken, when I had put my hands on her

100

shoulders: 'You have a grandmother now. A good thing to have. Grandmothers do the job I do, only better, because you share blood.'

Still I did not trust the woman in the sunflower hat, she did not mind her own business, as Myrna did. Myrna, reading me, had tilted my head up so I could see the full blackness: 'You don't want to leave me now and before you grow another inch you won't remember me.'

Now that Myrna was with me in dreams, I felt none of the guilt at having forgotten her. I felt the child's gladness. An old friend had returned and it was as if she had never left. The air was filled with lemon scent, so I had no wish to wake.

She sat over me and we shared a silence that drove the angry hum of the city, not only from my ears, but also from my heart. I wanted to reach out and touch her skin, to find what made it so pale and fine, but the dark eyes held me. We watched and waited, this old woman and this girl-woman that I now was, until the screaming of my mother carried.

I moved in its direction, still half asleep, the dream-giver fading away. Then, in front of my opened eyes, I saw Carmel, kneeling beside her mother who was already cold to the touch. Seven years she had been with us and provided for us. My mother had grown quieter and I had grown lighter in her care.

'Who will mind us now, Sive?' my mother wept. 'Who will mind us now?'

I did not know. But I cried my first open tears.

101

We put Noreen in a soft grave that promised to care for her as she had cared for us. The man in black watched my mother with a curious concern as she watched the box being lowered into blackness.

'We should be putting her into her own ground,' she whispered over to herself.

I took her by the arm.

'Who will mind us now?' she asked of people, who had come to know Noreen enough through her shop work to pay their respects at her last resting place. They looked away. London was where they had learned to look after themselves.

I asked my mother to be quiet, my stomach turning at her beggaring us.

★ ★ ★

At home, Carmel went to the wardrobe to look for the shoes and satin Noreen had long since thrown away. She talked all the while, to herself, until her lips moved without forming words in that way that tiredness brings.

When we were on our own in the dark kitchen, sitting over food that had grown cold, I made the promise to mind us, if only she would go to bed.

She went, and I sat up with the long dark night and waited for morning.

★ ★ ★

At the corner shop the owner said with great reluctance he could not have me to fill Noreen's place. He had two more family members coming from India and, besides, at fifteen I was too young.

I knew where to go and what to do.

★　★　★

It was not the same. Sergio was not there. Myrna was not there. Harder, older versions of Fanny and Lulu were at the same table they always sat at. I walked up to them and they told me to push off and mind me own.

Then Lulu looked at my eyes and said, 'It's young Sive. You're not quite filled yet, are you?' Lulu looked sidelong at me. 'Still a bit of work to do there, girl.'

I sat down and a young man came to ask me what I wanted. His eyes were cold and I did not hold them. Coffee, strong and black please. For the first time.

'Myrna's drink,' Lulu remembered.

I tasted it, winced and had to put two sugars in it.

'Where's Sergio?' I asked, when the man had gone, though his ears stayed with the table.

'His own food got him,' Lulu said simply. 'Heart attack.'

'And the fella behind his counter is his nephew. Got the place and came over from Italy and didn't even go to Serg's funeral. We went,' Lulu reminded herself and Fanny. 'Antonio lets in anybody. No peace in here these days.'

'We still come in though, nowhere else to go,' Fanny looked at me as if I might have another suggestion.

'Where's Myrna?' I asked.

The two looked at each other. Lulu bit at one of her nails and tucked her latest hairstyle behind her ears. It was too soft and too long for her face and neck, which were hard and taut, fighting slacking skin. There were two small scars above her lip and one bigger one at her hairline. Veins like red stitches poking through too much make-up.

Fanny finally spoke. 'Gone, Sive. We're the old girls now!'

'I'm off.' Lulu got up abruptly and went out the door, stopping to check in the tarnished mirror that was no longer there. She did not seem to notice.

'Poor old Lou,' Fanny sighed. 'She's on the sauce big time. Can't tell her. Still looks well though, don't she? I got four girls, as you know.'

Sergio's nephew, I could see out of the corner of my eye, was watching me. Fanny noticed and interrupted herself with a whisper.

'He's a git. Pay no mind to him.'

Fanny was working as a maid now.

'I gave up that business when my first two left home. I haven't heard from them since. I'm gone down, Sive, and I know it.' Fanny touched the hair more rust than brown now. 'But Lulu keeps herself nice. So she's not gone as far down.'

'And Myrna?'

'Myrna got as old-looking as she never was. She was here the day Sergio died. He lay in her

104

arms and he called for his mother so they tell me. A big man like that. After that we never saw Myrna again. We heard she was in hospital — that's the height of it.'

I felt the empty spaces in the café and the people who should have occupied them. The photos were no longer stuck to the mirror behind the counter. It was as if we had never been. I sat a long while with Fanny until it suddenly occurred to her to ask why I was here.

'Work.'

'Right,' she stood up and brushed off a worn coat. She saw me look at it. 'Maids don't earn as much. Come on, we'll get you sorted.'

* * *

I took my clothes off carefully the first time, as if my body would disintegrate without them. He had asked to take some photos, the man at the bottom of the stairs in the dark room. The photos were to be put in the glass box so men could decide what they would come to see.

The man agreed with Fanny that this was the best way for a young girl to work, and the cleanest. When Fanny left he said to me I could get extra money doing extra work, but that was up to me.

Our new Soho room was not clean, but I had learned from Noreen to make it so. Carmel had grown wild again and had to be tied to the bed while I went out, as I once had been. But, unlike me, she had no dreams to stop the fear and the fire that had begun to burn in her again.

105

Myrna did not return to my dreams. I put my head on a pillow each night and listened to my mother's ragged breath. I turned my back on the fresh green dreams, they brought too much feeling into the grey days I knew lay ahead.

Some nights I would cry for Noreen and some nights for Myrna and often for both.

Days wore on and led to endless nights. The shape of a full woman formed under my skin and I shrank from it as I had from the sunlight on the day of my birth.

I knew the time was coming when I would give more, because I needed more. I remembered Lulu telling me once: 'It's like this. It never seems so bad after you've done it.'

Carmel took more and more caring for and I was left with less time to make the money we needed. She ate only what I put in her mouth. She burned us out twice and landlords came to know us. The women would keep her in the café while I went to see places and I brought Carmel up at night to the newly rented place when no one could see her. She never left them until she found a way to burn. Then we would both have to leave.

★ ★ ★

One night Antonio asked to talk to me.

I gave Fanny a look that made her wait for me.

'I give you thirty pounds if you let me,' Antonio offered, annoyed that Fanny had not gone away. 'Me and my friend, together.'

106

'Well, love,' she said after he had gone. 'Mine was given away for nothing to a wanker who left me with wet knickers. It's good money. By the looks of him, by the swagger, I'd say he won't last more than five minutes.'

The long Road

13

The Way Home

I put the thirty pounds in my pocket walking up the stairs. The sulphur smell snaked under the unopened door.

I felt the hard walls close in around me, I moved quickly, expecting to find Carmel passing her fingers over flame or pressing it against her flesh and watching it blacken. I had doubled the knots I tied her with and still she found a way out of them, tearing at them with her teeth until her gums bled, lying in the foulness she could not contain.

I thought my eyes deceived me. Carmel sitting at the table, drawn to a flame held by an old woman. This could not be Myrna. The woman tall as life was bent over and the fine bones turned to gaunt longings for lost flesh and muscle.

The aged shadow of Myrna talked soft and soothing to Carmel, she talked like a river and the flame flowed like a river and my mother was quiet with watching. My mother's eyes closed and her head rested on her arms. The red marks of bondage on her wrists angry, not a stitch of clothing on her stretched tired body.

I found my voice, 'She dirties herself — easier to keep clean. I dress her in the day — don't

109

leave her like this all the time. It's only me looking after her.'

Myrna held her arms out to me and I knelt and put my head against a jutting collarbone, no soft remained. Myrna spoke and softened the cold grey light of morning.

'I went in my dream to the place where you were sleeping. Then Noreen came for me every night and shook me awake, wearing that hat. She showed me a place where we can go. A place by the sea and away from people. These bones want to go nowhere quickly. They talk to one another as I walk. They say: 'Stop, Myrna, stop walking.' I told them, Sive, I said, 'One last time.''

* * *

In Sergio's Café Lulu just nodded when we made our final goodbyes. Fanny stood on ceremony more, asking for our address and putting it in a special compartment of her purse.

The bus to the station took us up the long stretch of road, past theatres, offices, flats and homes all within walking distance of my life but I had never entered this world. Past the people who lived in this other world we were carried, who did not know the contents of mine, or those like me. I was nineteen and it was as if my whole life had been lived.

So I felt no regret or loss when our train pulled out of the station and heaved its way out of the grey vastness into greener times.

Nor did my mother who had her eyes trained

on home. The way home cost thirty pounds. I paid for it.

★   ★   ★

The ship's blast took my throat. We marched up the gangway with hundreds of excited voices, ours silent among them. Myrna and I sat Carmel by a window and not once did she move from it, not once did she take her eyes off the harbour or the rolling sea which followed.

The movement of the ship took my stomach by surprise and I felt it would not settle unless I went above to the deck.

'On you go, Sive, I'll mind her,' Myrna said.

So I left my mother, I had to have the wind on my face.

The day was cold and bright and the wind sharp with it. I had no jumper and was all goosebumped flesh. My heart stayed warm. I saw the first island off the new shore and I was filled with the sense of knowing it. Voices raised, the ship's blast said: 'I am bringing them all home!'

Shouts and cries as people on deck recognized waiting faces on the pier, a rushed clearing of the deck that left me standing alone and waiting for someone I would recognize.

There was no one, but the town spires and the faraway hills said, 'We welcome you back.'

The seagulls added their cries of homecoming.

Below, I found a different mother with the same old woman. Carmel's face had come alive and flushed. She was in her place and knew it.

Myrna smiled at us both and our feverish talk

of what way we could make for home.

'The train to town, Sive,' Carmel was saying. 'Then the bus. Then home.'

★ ★ ★

We arrive in the town of Scarna at dead of night, with nothing but emptiness to greet us. The old tired woman and the young lost one look to the one between them, the middle one knows the way.

Carmel left Scarna from the same spot to which she has now returned. She comes off the bus on to ghost footprints, which are her own. Her steps are strong and sure. We leave the town quickly, out into the blackness, and I am afraid. All is familiar about this night to only one of us. All is the same as it was before the path broke up around her. The night greets her like a purring cat, wrapping itself around her.

Carmel bends to unstrap the shoes that have bound her. Her feet released, they carry us over ground known to them. Myrna cannot keep up and I am afraid to be led. Afraid of choking silence and the stray pairs of eyes belonging to the night creatures and spirits who line the way, belonging to the hedgerows and high trees which line the way. All the eyes have come to mark the return.

Myrna and I trail further behind, hold hands and strain to retain sight of the pale legs slicing through the night way. And for us the walk is a forever walk, to us it will not be kind, because we are strangers to the place and the pitch black of the unlit night. We have the smell of city and its disregard on us, we are not open to the ways of the country. Not like Carmel. This is her own. None can take it away. Her pale legs ahead disappear from view and we have to follow up an overgrown laneway with brambles which screech and throw misshapes into the sky and scrape at bare skin. I am afraid of these and Myrna sighs and takes my arm. 'They will know you, too.'

Where is the way leading?

Upwards and upwards and the shape of a stone house appears when the full moon changes mood, casts off her cloud shrouds and chooses finally to shine and her white light bathes the path and the prospect for us.

Myrna reaches for my hand and says, 'The house that Noreen brought me to. This is the shape of coming things.'

Where is the way leading?

Up to that stone house surrounded by ghostly trees.

There is an open door and Carmel is there, before it, breathing fast and remembering the last time she walked through it and she says, 'I cannot go in. I cannot go in.'

And her sweat-glistened face is cased silver in the moon-light and out of the shadows the ghost of Noreen appears and beckons her. She follows then and we follow Carmel and that is how we find the place called home.

A place with no lock on the door, but our presence is marked as an intrusion by the creatures that have made it theirs in our absence. They do not flee when Myrna whispers, 'Stay.'

The ghost of Noreen leaves us.

Carmel knows the way things are to be done. Myrna and I sit while my mother makes light in the darkness with that which she has always sought to make. By the fireplace the crib is waiting. She runs her fingers along it, removing the dust of years with fresh tears.

'Were you kept in it?' I ask. She shakes her head. Myrna tells her it is beautiful and Carmel knows that it is.

A fire of welcome is lit for us.

Home.

★ ★ ★

The new place crept up on us and gave us its heart. Though in the first few days of being there I did not want it.

Noreen had sold all but a few acres. The sold land was farmed still, so curious neighbours did not surround us. The house was whitewashed once and grey patches invited by the salt-laden winds peered through the white. Because the building is on a slight incline, though trees conceal it, the gales laugh at all attempts to shelter the house.

We learned, when a north-easterly blew, to stuff the windows at the front of the house with newspaper and still they rattled and the wind let out shrill whistles of derision. When the weather brought rain to visit the newspaper would soak and drip and the puddles needed mopping up every half hour.

Hoar Rock was once home to a well-made

114

farmer who could afford the view of the harbour at the far end of the grey crescent of rocky shoreline. The house was built at a time when many dwellings huddled away from the elements. Hoar Rock courted them and its first prosperous owners had the means to run fires all year. In the leaner times, when the good land had been sold, Joseph Moriarty was left to farm the rocky fields more sand than earth. The fires were lit only for a few hours on the coldest days and the Hoar Rock house contained a chill that was present even at the height of summer.

This was the house we had come to, and the house, glad to be occupied by the living, whose voices hindered the tormented calls of the dead, asked for the sun to shine on us for the first morning. So when we looked out of our windows we saw the trawlers fishing a glassy sea, a smoothed and polished sea, a rare jewel in the depths of winter. We saw the colourful fronts of the harbour buildings and heard the seagull cries and seal barks carried to us along the shoreline from the harbour three miles away, so still was the air.

'A day for shirtsleeves,' Myrna said, and I could answer the cheer with a smile because the sharp nature of the fresh air had brought life to my city-dulled lungs. We pulled chairs outside and had our mugs of tea watching the new world.

Afterwards I went to the barn at the side of the house to find what was left in the way of furniture. What was left was home to families of mice who did not take kindly to being disturbed.

Two stray cats came from nowhere, like striped shadows. They pounced on the newly exposed nests and carried away the hairless babies. I tried to stop them, but they moved quicker than I will ever learn to. Behind the barn were the remains of Noreen's chicken run and an overgrown track led to a patch of garden, which Noreen had tried to tend to bring some beauty to Hoar Rock on its ugliest days. A few resilient wallflowers had taken over whatever else had been cultivated but now, in winter, these had died back leaving withered evidence of their intentions.

How could anything have grown here?

The sun faded in the mid-morning and I went inside with Myrna. When I saw what had to be done, it was all I could do not to go back to where we had come from. Spots of rain hit the corrugated roof, painted red. The spots told me that when rain fell you would hear little else in the house.

Carmel was nowhere to be found. I thought to look for her, then realized this was her place. She would find me.

There were eyes waiting in the town. The bank was happy to take my English money as most people in the town were going in the direction from which I had come. When I left the bank I had a handful of strange notes between nothing and us.

In the shop the woman put my change on the counter — afraid to touch my skin. On the corner a group of boys-near-men was listening to a transistor, their fingers curled around the last drags of a cigarette or stuffed in their pockets with small change that could take them nowhere.

'Phil Lynott's sister, lads, it is!' one said, and the others shouldered and cawked, eyes on me then, in the manner I knew men to look.

Later, women with shopping bags full of idle speculation would hear from each other, at Mass, that Carmel Moriarty had come home, with an old woman and a dark woman. We were to remain outside.

★ ★ ★

In the soft woodland of before morning a woman walked a path familiar. Her tender feet pinched by branches, her walk not as sure as it had once been.

In the soft woodland of morning a middle-aged man took the stroll that was part of his bachelor's ritual, part of a day that was the same as any other. He had places of pilgrimage.

It was not surprising to him to find the object of prayers under a dark tree, her back to him, hunched over, nursing her ribbon-cut feet. Her wild hair carpeting her back, not vibrant, as it had once been, duller with strands of silver. But the same hair and form.

He was convinced he imagined her. His imaginings were more real now than the day in which he lived, worked, ate and slept.

He sat with her and she did not move, so he knew he had gone a little more mad and sorrowful to have aged her so, even in his fantasies. But she was real — when she turned her face towards him she had the lines and marks of the years that had come between them. Her eyes no longer glistening, her eyes faded. A face familiar, yet strange and weathered as his own was.

He put his arms around her and his Carmel had grown cold, as if she had risen from the bottom of a grave or a sea and he was sure that it must have been one or the other, and he was all at once grateful and afraid.

He was fearful for the story behind the lines and marks and fading, what must it tell and would he be made to hear it?

Her look said he would not. She had no words to put on the time apart.

The weight of years lifted and settled between them as a permanent loss, which nothing could be done about now. She knew him still, and he knew her.

The heat in her rose, but not as it had as a young girl, only enough for him to know she was living. In the new place which was the same as the old but had her in it again.

This time she would not be lost to him.

★   ★   ★

Myrna grappled with the strangeness of the land she viewed through the open window and the dreams that had made it familiar to her. She knew the curve of the beach, the point where it changed from rock to sand. She knew the house, the long laneway, and the trees that surrounded it. All of these Noreen had shown her.

She knew the marks of the land held history in

them. The call of the sea close by spoke reminders of that history.

Myrna would have walked to the sea on this first morning but her bones spoke loudly. She had lived a great many years and had enjoyed her own company and would be sorry to lose it. The goodbyes to herself had begun.

The thought of being light again was pleasant to her. She had been heavy a long while. The green of the place they had come to was a place like that out of her childhood and startled her with familiarity, so long had she lived in the grey city.

She let out a laugh, surprising herself at how deep it went. She felt a shiver down her long spine bone of separate and connected lives and she stepped out of the dark house. The sunlight laughed with her and she found a spot to bask in it. Time to rest before the time to work.

She thought of her own life and the rich tragedy and quiet happiness of it.

She thought of the men she had lain with and the women who had wanted to learn her secret way of loving. No secret did she have but knowledge found in a world that wanted to give it. Now she would give what she knew to Sive and let Sive do with it what she would. Myrna hoped she would grow roots and grow solid. Myrna herself had chosen shadows. Soho had suited her — a place where women come and go. In Soho no one asked you to become real.

There had been a time when she had been as Sive had been — a child alone, a stranger to all in the world. Life had stepped out of the shadows and taken her by the hand. She had grasped that hand and lived to the full, until she realized she had become a prisoner of the freedom she had always courted. The price paid for chains refused.

Once she had been held — not by the arms of man or woman, but by what grew inside her and made her heavy with the need to rest. The child had been born and taken away at a time when dead children were commonplace. Myrna took to wandering on the day the baby had been put in the ground.

In all her years and what they had contained she had only one regret — that she had not mothered. Now life had given her that with the girl-woman Sive and the future Myrna must help her secure before life pulled her down and tied her. Myrna knew Sive's heart was not a wandering one — it was one that needed refuge.

Myrna hoped she was not too tired to give what she had. She longed to release her last breath — but it had to be held. It had to be held.

The ghost of Noreen Moriarty, wearing a sunflower hat and worn smile, watched Myrna from the kitchen window. Myrna looked over her shoulder and shaded her eyes. She waved at Noreen who raised a hand. They both turned back to look at the sea.

14

The Card of Beginnings, of Dreams

It was a quiet evening and it was many days since we had arrived. The beginning was wearing on and it did not offer much in the way of hope for a future where we could pay our way. I had not seen my mother except in the mornings when she left wild-eyed and in the hour before dawn, when she came home wild-eyed.

Myrna caught my anxious eyes and said, 'Your mother has other preoccupations now. She is in her own place. Perhaps you need preoccupations.'

'What we're going to do for money gives me enough to think about. Or do you have an answer for that, too?' I answered her.

'None, except to say I am aware you must regard me as an extra burden. I will not be that to you.'

'I didn't mean that.'

'If I tell you we will be looked after you will think I am leaving you to find the answer.'

'No, but I'm the only one fit enough to work.'

Her laugh was wry and filled with distant kindness.

'Sive, you have feet of stone you are that

121

rooted to practicalities. How will we lift your eyes above them?'

'It is easy for you to say.'

'It is far from easy. None of us knows what will happen from one moment to the next.'

'How will we eat next week? There's no work here,' I asked. 'Unless I do what I did before.'

'There will be no need for that kind of work here. Your grandmother will not allow it.'

'My grandmother is a ghost. She can't work; neither can you and neither can my mother. That leaves me.'

Myrna twisted her back to me and poked the fire.

'We will all find a way soon enough. We are only at the beginning, Sive, learn patience.'

From my silent time I was still the holder of few words, so I had none to answer her and went outside.

★ ★ ★

I sat on the window sill, watching the evening fall softly on the waves, the wing-beat of the heron flying over them in time with their meeting with the shoreline. All the world seemed to have its rhythm but me. The weight of choices made by others long before I was born seemed to gather on my shoulders.

Myrna came and stood beside me. With my mind's voice I asked her: 'Why does life want me to continue?'

I could not speak it out then, to speak would

have been to show too much of what was inside me.

'You have a hard tone, Sive, that does not live in your heart. Life asks a lot of you. Give gladly or not at all,' she answered as if I had spoken aloud.

I felt the deep pull towards her and put my head on her shoulder. She combed her fingers through my hair, tracing the shape of my hairline.

'The way your hair meets your skin, there is ending of smoothness and beginning of wild-ness!' I heard the soft smile in her voice and body. 'Will you remember in this, I will not see you harmed?'

I said I would. Then she was gone from talk a while and I felt the uncertain creep up by degrees. I turned to face Myrna and watched her as I would a stranger.

Her body-flesh hung like straight curtains on wide shoulders and slim hips. Its paleness all the more evident with the black jet of her eyes looking out of it. The silver markings of her hair, the blue-veined fineness, gave her the look of a long-beautiful one who has not mourned the passing of youth and the arrival of soft old age. There was nothing soft in Myrna's form — there was a strength and purpose that ran through her like all the tomorrows were still hers. She held her head high and was proud of her body and the story it told and more proud still of the story it did not tell, but which she held inside her.

'Mine is a body on its way back to the earth and into the sky that clings to it. They claim a

123

little more each day and I claim them,' her old bones and skin and hair sang.

Myrna smiled and her eyes touched me, then she put her hands where her eyes had been. The feel of her skin, the skin of a long life, so transparent I could see through it into her very bones. But she wanted me to disappear into my own, my own skin which opened and let me into its quivering heat and insistence.

'I had your fears,' she spoke soft enough for the dead to hear. 'I wandered, eating nothing, drinking nothing. I was afraid to go into the world that was calling me, so I stayed hidden and grew more afraid until the dark-eyed woman came to me in a dream and said, 'Look in the mirror,' and I did, and I saw that my eyes were now her eyes, blacker than night. She said to me then, 'Leave behind all you are, take nothing but your dreams.' And that is what I did, Sive, the very next day. In dreams you came to me. Your first cry drove straight into my heart and bound me to you. I waited long and patiently for the next cry. It has not come yet.'

It came then. I cried all the waves I had watched and more, as I cried I had the memory of tears unshed for fear of drowning under them. My want was under them all — the want of a warm life, with love and good fortune in it.

'You do not smile at all, Sive,' Myrna said. 'You have forgotten that we met in dreams before we met in person. Even when times are at their most dark and ravaged you have the freedom of dreams. The breath of them fell on you before my eyes did. Let your mother to her

124

wildness and you to yours.'

I understood this even as she spoke it, but she went on.

'Dreams will always be enough, even when they are all we have.'

From her deep pocket she pulled her cards, her companions, and drew one. A blank card, a white space, nothing more.

'The most important card of all, of dreams. It represents beginning. The space for you to fill as you wish. Dreams will bring warmth when there is none to be had. Do not try to live without them. Do not dismiss them as foolish — they are as real as the breath you take. Tonight let your dreams give you the courage to keep going and the patience to wait for what will surely come,' Myrna said, leaving me to the last light and the view of the sea.

★　★　★

With the new dawn, my courage and waking sense returned and I saw us lying in the dusty remains of other lives that had ended.

So I rose and I began to scrub and clear the traces of the despair that clung to the walls. I opened windows and let in the sunshine that Noreen had once let in.

Fresh times had come. Though I had no reason to think that I could feel it. I sang as I worked and Myrna crept into the kitchen so that I found her sitting at the table listening to me without being aware of her arrival.

'You always arrive without noise,' I smiled.

'I leave the same way,' she replied. 'Your grandmother is delighted with what you are doing about the place.'

'Tell her to send work then,' I said, not ready to hear of those dead and gone. 'And none of us will have anything to worry about.'

But even as I said it I was doing more, and happier about it.

'Later I will go down to the beach,' I threatened.

I was losing my fear of straying far from the house, in much the same way as my mother could not be kept in it.

I placed the crib in a waiting place, under the stairs.

★   ★   ★

Carmel came up the laneway with a small, dark man wearing a shy expression and clothes that had no female hand in choosing them. I put down my scrubbing brush and watched. I thought she might have gone back to the old ways. Myrna rested a hand on my shoulder.

The pair of them were joined together by hands that would not be separated until they came into the house. Their eyes would look for each other during the small talk of introduction and tea-making.

'Where is it?' Carmel asked.

'Below the stairs,' Myrna answered. 'Sive put it there, for safe keeping.'

Carmel took Eddie by the hand and showed him. He did not look at it or me. He had thought to pretend the crib was not something he had made, but it had been one of the first things Carmel had told him about, told him she had admired him making it.

He shook his head, there was a lot here to get used to.

'There's not much left in the way of furniture,' Eddie remarked quietly. 'I have a few bits of things my mother left me after she died and no use for them. Could I drop them up to get you started?'

'We'll manage,' Carmel said.

'We'll have them,' I said.

Eddie smiled.

'That's settled so.'

'Would you know where I could find work?' I asked him.

'Not much in the way of work. I'm cleaning windows on half and full empty shops these days. Only people who have money and work would be the religious. The religious have their favourites though, them that have their tongues stuck to the altar rails when they're not licking the arses off them.' He blushed red then. 'Sorry, the only talk I get these days is bar talk.'

Eddie saw our strangeness and knew we would need help in this tight town. He saw my skin. The town had crippled his own life's possibilities. He would do what he could to make sure it would not do the same to us.

So work in the town was out of the question for the dark girl of Carmel's.

In the hours he had spent with Carmel he had reached once for her deepest heart and she had curled up and away from him.

'You can't go there any more,' she told him.

All she had given before was still in her eyes. It would be a question of loving through the help he had denied her before. St Manis's came to him.

St Manis Home was where the old went to live out their last, unaccompanied days. He cleaned its windows and he saw too much of what went on inside to wish to live to a great age. But it was a place where he knew I would find work. The nuns would favour a dark girl for work in order to show her the straight and narrow.

So it was that I found myself tramping the road of Pass If You Can, which wound into the Black Hills behind our house. I found myself before a grey building with an air of silence, which said life stayed away.

Sister Mauritius was expecting me.

15

A Lost Place at the Edge of the World

'Sive. What kind of name is that? Do you have no Christian name? Have you even been baptized?'

Sister Mauritius studied my completed piece of paper.

'I have no other name,' I did not know the nuns before had called me Mary. 'I have been baptized though.'

My mother had told Noreen this when she enquired.

'What age are you?'

Sister Mauritius had poured herself a cup of tea, none was offered to me. She posed the question because it was hard to tell with dark skin, she had come across a lot of it in her London noviciate. A woman of the world was Sister Mauritius.

'I'm nineteen.'

'Have you done this kind of work before?'

'I've cared for my mother when she was ill.'

'Your mother would not be old,' she said warningly. 'These people are old, they need more minding and watching. But it's good enough you have some experience. You're a big girl, you'll be strong enough to lift the men and

129

there's a job going on their ward. You will be expected to clean, serve food, make beds as well as take care of them. Now. I cannot put down Sive here. That is not a Christian name. You will be called Mary here,' surmising that I was needing of work and so would agree to having my name taken from me. 'Sign here.'

I bowed my head and signed with Sive.

'No, that will not do.'

I said I could not sign Mary since I was not Mary.

'Very well then, Mary Sive it will be,'

And she put the Mary in front of the Sive I had written.

'Where is your father?' Sister Mauritius asked.

'I have none, Sister.'

Eddie had warned me not to look her in the eye and to say sister to her.

'No notion of who he is?'

'None, Sister.'

'And your mother?'

'Carmel Moriarty, Sister.'

'That's a quare accent you have.'

'From London, Sister.'

'I was in London myself, London ways are not our ways, you'll pay mind to that here.'

Her eyes came over her nose, they nestled under the large bridge of her forehead and ample eyebrows. So it was that Sister Mauritius always looked down her nose at you.

The money she offered me I could have earned in one night.

She pressed a buzzer and a small, squatty

woman with large feet flapping before her came in. She did not look at Sister Mauritius either.

'Margaret, this is the new worker for St Michael's. Starting tomorrow. She's big, so you might not have anything to fit her in the line of uniforms. Give her one of Magdalene's if so. Call her Mary.'

'Very good, Sister.'

There was no goodbye, just the turning of her attention to some papers and a stiff nod from Margaret towards the door.

'Who was Magdalene?' I asked Margaret, whose feet continued to fall heavily on the linoleum corridor floor and would have woken a country.

'The old cook. She wasn't black like you, but she'd been to Africa. She was a nun on the missions and she fell in love with a black man and they found out and they sent her home. She stopped being a nun then and she called herself Magdalene. She used to make us African stew with a load of oil, eggs and mince in it. Do you make African stew?'

Her face folded up when I said I did not, she stood stock still, bringing her bowl-shaped eyes up to me.

Magdalene's uniforms were all that would fit me. They were sweat-stained from her time over the stove. But there was a comfort in the smell of another woman, whose scent, I could tell, had not been put down by life and would continue to adventure into her unknown days.

Margaret showed me to the door and did not

close it until I had my way down the drive and out of her sight. On down the hill I went, all the while looking forward. If I looked back I would not have been able to go there the next morning.

16

Them Together Again

Myrna sat at the kitchen window and watched the small figures of Eddie and Carmel on the beach. Them together again, as if they had never been apart.

Why, then, the unease at their coming together? Why did she see dark shadows dance all around them and in and out of the day? Why did her old skin prickle so when they were near and together?

Noreen came to stand beside her. She pointed at her daughter and her daughter's love.

'I know,' Myrna sighed. 'I feel something wrong, but they're happy for the moment.'

Noreen smiled and put a hand on Myrna's slight shoulder.

'Would the young ever grow old if they knew what we know?' Myrna asked.

Noreen shook her head.

★   ★   ★

When I came through the door my mind was set in a trap of tomorrow and what I had to do for money for us all. I made tea and I scalded my tongue on it. Noreen left and Myrna took up the cards and began to shuffle them on the kitchen

133

table. I did not pay any mind to Myrna's muttering and twisting of the cards.

'What will come of this?' she was asking them. 'What is being hidden from me?'

'I just got the job,' I told her. 'And I am called Mary.'

She was not listening. Through the window she was watching the pair on the beach and a long, slow tear trickled down her cheek, an overturned card in her hand.

Later she came to my room and sat on the bed.

'You are to go to work there,' she said. 'You are not Mary. You are Sive. They cannot change that.'

Then she left the room speaking soft words, which I could not hear. But they come to me now for their shape was formed in this house and remains as all words do in the place where they are spoken.

'And we are the ones to be left behind and without.'

In her hand the card of Three Shadows and the card of Beginnings.

'Who are the shadows?' Myrna asked the night. 'When will the shadows make themselves known?'

17

Laid Bare

The following day Margaret was waiting at the gate for me and through all her chatter I did not take my eyes off the house of St Manis or make a sound of my own.

'You'll be on St Michael's ward. That's the worst of them all,' she began gleefully. 'Just to let you know, that's all. How much are you getting paid? Your sister is Sister Saviour and she's, like, the worst slave-driving old wagon you've ever met. But she looks after the men. Sister Mauritius hates her because she looks after them too well. Mauritius just wants them all to die quickly so she can fill the beds again. And she gives out. Your sister, Sister Saviour — '

Margaret stopped advising as I made to walk in the front door, the heavy door.

'No! Not that way! Staff go in through the side door, Sister Mauritius doesn't want the front door opening and closing all day. She says it lets out too much heat. Anyway your sister, Sister Saviour, she just wants everything clean all the time.'

She asked again how much I was being paid for the work, and this time I could not avoid telling her.

'Is that all she's giving you? It's because you're

part dark if you don't mind me saying so. She thinks you're still a slave or something.' Margaret's feet flapped furiously as she tried to keep up with my quickening steps, her imagination fuelled by the pace of them.

'That's why she put you in St Michael's, you'll definitely be a slave there. Are you from Africa or Arabia? You look like both. Do they have harems still in Arabia? Where is Arabia exactly? I know where Africa is. Did your mammy get shipped out to one of the harems?'

No answer from me. We pushed open the side gate and walked the long corridor with no doors off it and turned at the end into a small cloakroom where I hung up my coat with those of people I did not know. I felt all their separateness and their common end in this place. Margaret watched me all the while and would not take her eyes from me and she spoke hushed now.

'Just so as you'll know. You'll be working with Joe O'Reilly. He's a full nurse only he got the sack for stealing drugs and selling them. Sister Mauritius pretends she doesn't know but everyone else does and she got him, fully signed up at nursing, for half nothing, for a carer's wage — ' She paused for breath as we left the cloakroom. 'You just come to me if you need to know anything — I know everything.'

When I reached the ward, Margaret did not leave. She was quiet now, but her voice was still in my ears. There was a smell of sleeping, a stale smell from men whose lives had grown stale, a smell of men who found it harder each night to leave sleep behind.

The night staff had gone home and the day staff had yet to arrive. Sister Saviour was seated at a table in the small kitchen off the ward. A woman of straight features dressed in a spotless nursing uniform. Her hair was hidden but for roots which showed it to be as white as her short, nun-nurse veil.

She looked up from her paperwork with eyes that did not expect me to look away, or down. I could see her kindness was well-guarded but still present. She smelt of carbolic soap and her face had the tightness of endless hard work and more still to do for the men in her care. She was not tender. She talked in proclamations about necessities.

'A good big girl! I hope you will pull your weight! Sister Mauritius tells me your name is Mary! Not Mary you say! What is it then? It is Sive? Good so, Mary Sive you are! I am Sister Saviour! Slack work is for sick minds! I see Margaret has already found you!' This proclamation carried a note of irony. 'Well we'll let her introduce you to the men! She knows them all better than they know themselves!'

She checked her watch, which was pinned to her lapel, and said briskly, 'Pay no mind to Margaret's tales! They're taller than she is herself! Make sure you present yourself here in fifteen minutes! Plenty to be done!'

Margaret's square chin set, but she soon recovered herself with the joy of revealing the secrets stored in each of the beds. Secrets that were stolen and presented as common knowledge to the stranger I was to them.

'This is Liamy. He used to work in England, too. Came home to the farm. Fell down a well and was up to his neck in water for two weeks before anyone found him. Softened all his bones it did. Then he got Parkinson's, then he got a stroke, now he's like this.'

This was a gaunt man whose face was all cheeks and chin and all that remained of his eyes were lashless slits. Hair wisps under a cap the brim of which was no longer than his chin. He moved his curled up hand out of the sleep state as I drew near, the movement was sharp and had warning in it.

Margaret stepped back, 'Watch out! Used to box he did. Watch out for the punches! Shush!' Margaret warned me with glittering eyes as if I was the noisemaker. 'You'll wake them all and then you'll have to deal with them all.'

Margaret went on.

'And this one is Mr Black, with a temper to match and that one is Young Brian, because he's gone mental and thinks he's still forty. He was forty when they first put him in here all right. Now he's really sixty.

'That's Dennis, used to be a priest but they kicked him out and now he's a strokie — they're all mostly strokies — had a stroke like — and he's a right pain in the hole, a big snitch and a whinger. Don't do nights or he'll have you pestered for sleeping tablets.

'That's Ted — he's got loads of money so Sister Mauritius is up his hole most of the day, which is why her face is so brown. But she can't give Ted the private room at the end of the ward, because that's Peter's.

'Peter has the private room even though he hasn't a shilling. His daughter pays for it. He shouldn't even be in here, there's nothing wrong with him. This is a hospital-home for people who need medical care. But his daughter, she shoved him in here as soon as he had a stroke, even though he can still walk and dress himself and do everything.

'The rest are all vegetables, most not as cooked as Liamy, mind you. That's a colonel and the only way to get him on to the commode, now he's gone senile, is to say 'hut, hut, hut!' and up he goes like a rocket at take off and then you've a job trying to get him off it. He locks his knees and you have to tickle behind them, Joe says, and the stink of his old lad's poo would make you want a peg on your nose.

'But most of them don't even do number twos on their own — you have to give them the enema and that's Joe's job. He's the nurse, he says, so it's his job. Like you need a nurse to go up after shite.'

And Margaret laughed and laughed at that.

I learned the lives of ten men I had never met before that day. They were the ones whose bed curtains were open. I did not learn anything of the one whose curtains were still drawn.

'The one behind there is a piece of work. He's work and plenty of it. We'll wake him, will we? The rest of them will work you too if you don't know their tricks. If you give in the first few days they have you. You have to ignore them. Clout when they clout you, scrawm back when they scrawm you. Give them a good pinch and walk away quick if they don't do what they're told.'

Margaret spoke in a loud whisper to me about the men, as if they were too beyond to hear. But the men heard. The men knew they were laid bare before me. They chose not to face me or greet me. Some closed their eyes. Some stared far away beyond us to a place where they once had a choice in who they would meet and who they would not meet, in who they were and where they were.

Margaret was called sharply by Sister Saviour.

'Margaret, you're wanted on your own ward!'

Margaret skittered off, lighter for what she had imparted, but grimacing with the disappointment of not having managed the final introduction to the life hidden behind curtains.

Sister Saviour came to stand beside me and barked that the time for introductions was over and the time to work had come.

'Your first job can be to sort him out!'

And she pulled back the curtains with a swish that almost took the rail off the wall. She did not look once at what she was revealing.

'Strip the bed! Strip the patient! Dress the bed! Dress the patient!'

She opened a large cupboard and pulled out a plastic bottle and a rag.

'Clean the waterproof sheet with this! Put it back on the bed again! Sheets down the hall!'

The chemical cleaner was strong, but not strong enough to mask the smell of urine-soaked sheets, which caused the man in the chair to look down and away from me. He had slept upright in the chair once the night staff had moved him. He had called for a bottle. It had not been brought in time.

He wanted to talk to me, to say that he did not make a habit of this. But he did not talk and I did not look at him. Since his head was bowed I could see only his twisted shell, his white hair was as full as his young days and would have been as white as Myrna's had it not been stained yellow. I thought at first that it was urine he had poured over himself. Carmel had done this to put out her heart fires. I did not know that the dayroom smoke choked him and his hair. I had no eyes to see beyond what he was.

I cleaned the bed and took the soaking pyjamas off. They were not his because his body was too big for them, even in his wasted state. Long ankles stared mournfully at me, long wrists, one curled unnaturally, held by what could have been a proud, fine hand used to work. Now the nails were ragged and uncared for, the dirt underneath them grey. He hid his twisted arm like a secret, using a strength in him where pride once stood. The striped top and pale blue bottoms of the new pyjamas bore the nametags of men who had not known this man and had been smaller than him in life. Fitting the pyjama top over the twisted arm brought a grunt from him. No other sound. Margaret came back as I was dressing his feet in socks that did not match or fit, but would keep out the cold. His feet had been bare and blue up to this.

'He won't do anything for you. Never talks, this one.'

I had not yet seen his eyes.

The day was long and the work was hard and by the early evening when I was free to go I was glad that my walk home was downhill.

★ ★ ★

When I came in the door that night Myrna and Carmel were sitting at the table.

'How was the place?' Myrna's eyes did not leave me.

'I don't know. I just washed the beds and the floors and the walls, the toilet bowls and the dishes and the old lads and then I came home. I know it's clean anyway.'

I drank warm sweet tea which brought me back to myself and away from the man dressed in things not his own. I had remembered my own days and life spent in cast-offs.

The doorlatch lifted and Eddie stepped in out of the cold.

'Should I have knocked?' he asked, catching sight of my face.

'Might as well walk in,' I said. 'Might as well make the place your own, the furniture's yours anyway.'

Carmel and Eddie said they were going for a walk, as they said every night, as they did every night. I sliced bread and buttered it and moved into the chair beside the fire to chew it.

Myrna came and sat in the chair opposite. She said nothing to me or I to her for a long time.

142

Though it was still early she stood to go to bed. I raised my head and she saw what she wanted to see in my eyes.

'We might go for a walk of our own,' she suggested. 'I would like to walk on the shore. I have not walked on a shoreline for a long time.'

★ ★ ★

We walked to the beach down the thick, brambled way and on to the grey stones and then on the grey sand that smoothed the path between stones and sea. Myrna walked slower than time passes.

It was a warm evening on the edges between winter and spring. The sky was thick with the rain that had not yet fallen. The air was expectant. Myrna turned me away from her, towards a dark pewter sea.

'Look — all can be seen here, not like in London. There is always a building in the way. When I was a girl I lived by a lake that was as big as a sea to my eyes. I thought I would never want to leave it and I had to. I travelled the whole world and I never found the same vastness or space that I had found in that one place.'

'Would you never have gone back?' I asked.

'By the time I got there it would have been somewhere else.'

Though the sky grew darker still, Myrna sat, so slowly the youth in me wished to push her down.

'We'd better go back,' I suggested. 'You don't want to get wet.'

But the truth was I did not want to find my way up the brambled laneway to the house in the darkness. The light came on in the kitchen of the house by Noreen's ghost hand, an answer to the growing night.

'No, let's not go back just yet,' Myrna said. 'The rain can wait and the darkness is a friend, Sive. We'll come to no harm in it.'

'I'm glad you think so,' I sat beside her. 'I can't get used to the noises it makes — and the shapes it makes.'

The wind shaved the waves on to the shore and swept what it had gathered in spray over us.

'Now,' Myrna smiled. 'That's a freshness I haven't felt since I was a girl.'

She put a finger to her face and lifted a salt-water pearl to her lips.

'How was your work today?'

'The same as my cleaning work at home yesterday,' I said, watching the sea.

Even in twilight the white-capped waves were visible and could be heard calling to each other. Myrna gathered her skirt about her.

'It took me a long time to sit down and I suppose it will take me a long time to stand. Can you help me?'

I placed the crook of my arm under her shoulder and bent my knees to take what was left of her weight. I lifted her easily.

'Professionally done,' Myrna raised an eyebrow and looked at me as I put her on her feet.

'I learned today,' I said, with a little pride. 'From Sister Saviour. It stops your back straining when you lift the men.'

'I have been lifted in such a way in the place I was kept,' Myrna said. 'On and off potties like I was a battery hen laying eggs. 'Come on then,' the nurse would say. 'We haven't got all day for you to do your business.' 'You have,' I said. 'If you don't want to see my business done somewhere you don't want it done.' '

Myrna picked her way carefully over the same stones that Carmel's feet had skimmed over on a day gone by.

'Now, Sive,' Myrna squeezed my arm. 'You are in the same work as I have been in for many years, making men more comfortable.'

'The men up there can hardly get out of bed, much less think about the other.'

'You have not done the other with anyone have you?'

'Once,' I said. I pushed the men who climbed over my thoughts and memory away. 'They make sure they get what they pay for.'

'They do,' Myrna agreed. 'No matter what way you make them happy, you earn what they give you. In this St Manis Home you will not have to do anything to the men you don't want to do. I promise you that. But you want to do your job well, Sive?'

I nodded.

'Then listen to me. This is for all of your life and especially the life that is with you today. Look beyond what is broken. There is always something whole. See where the mends can be made in the broken. Find what is whole and true.'

'How do I do that? I don't want to be giving it

to the men. I want that behind me.'

'Do you think that is all I gave the men I went with?' Myrna asked me, the setting sun now two flames in her dark eyes.

'I don't know. I only know I did it once and that was enough.'

'There are ways of doing things that make sure you give nothing of yourself. I gave the men nothing but themselves to be happy with.'

'How?'

Myrna did not answer until we had stopped at the end of the laneway and gathered breath and strength for the walk up it.

'You are turning into the wind, Sive, make good with it.'

'Make good with what?'

'With all you have and with all that's coming.'

'What sort of . . . '

She put a finger to my lips and turned to the sea again.

The sun was going down on the horizon, in Myrna's eyes it fell until it disappeared and left nothing but blankness.

'No more tonight. Your curiosity is a good tool,' Myrna smiled. 'I am also curious to know what we can do with the same bread and eggs we had for breakfast.'

'The same as we did with them the night before,' I sighed. 'I would love chips now.'

'I would love anchovy paste on rye bread,' Myrna fantasized. 'And apple juice. I could eat a tub of ice cream. They make good ice cream here, so Eddie tells me. But it comes in vanilla or not at all.'

146

We went on trading food longings and by the time I put a hand to the latch of the kitchen door, the darkness had grown around me and I had not been afraid. It was the first opportunity to grow used to the night that now makes me so welcome as I do it.

18

This One Never Talks

Joe O'Reilly took up where Margaret had left off in the telling of tales. Joe wore his hair long and uncombed with sandals on his feet no matter what the weather. His grubby T-shirts bore loving slogans of the sixties, which had all grown stale.

When Joe was alone with me little was said, but when he and Margaret were together they bickered with a childishness the outside world would not tolerate.

It did not take me long to realize that all the staff who had rooms in the home were as tied as the ones they tended. Each one had plans to leave, Joe O'Reilly wished to go back to London where he had trained as a nurse.

'You've been going for fifteen years,' Margaret would gibe.

'And what about your famous trip to America?' he would lash back. 'Let us know when you have the ticket, Margaret. Sure we'll make a banner for you and give you a little send off. Then we'll all wait around to welcome you when you sneak back on the next plane.'

Each called the other a live-in, as if their arrangements were temporary. This was what they fought over when we had lunch, the same lunch as the men ate. Food with no love in it. They were birds pecking at each other for the crumbs of my attention. For I was the thing that tight worlds are starved off, novelty. Then my newness wore off and I became part of the walls and the day and part of all that was endured in this place. I became known for my silence in St Manis just as I had been known for it elsewhere.

It was not all bad. The work with the men offered me their grateful appreciation. Since Myrna had spoken with me I had looked at them differently. I saw Young Brian's passion for any kind of motor vehicle — the home's ambulance, the cars of visitors. Young Brian would watch them all from the dayroom window. Put his hands to the glass and Mauritius would catch him and cry, 'Brian Justice, paw prints! Leave the glass alone!'

Young Brian would sit, like a trained bear and bring his big hands on to his lap and stare out at the cars as they came and went. I took him by the hand one day and brought him to the ambulance. He put his hands on it as if it were a jewel. I took the keys from my pocket and Young Brian sat in the ambulance and put his hands on the wheel and adjusted the mirrors and ran his hands along the dashboard. He looked, smiled at the road ahead and his heart took a trip down it.

'What are you at?' Margaret poked her head out the side door. 'Your lunch is ready.'

I didn't eat it and from that moment Young Brian and I used my break times to sit in the ambulance.

'He used to be an ambulance driver,' Joe

149

O'Reilly told me, like I didn't know.

In Mr Black, with a temper to match, I saw a man who had once drawn women to him. Loved too many and left too many and then no one was left to love him. His anger was against himself and the foolishness of his belief that he would die as fit as he had lived. Diabetes had cut a man who acted half his age in two by taking one of his legs. A stroke left him in a wheelchair.

With Mr Black I flirted with the fine fit man lurking in the corners of his eyes and the life was brought into him in those moments when he responded.

'You do my heart good, Sive, what's left of it.'

Dennis, the former priest, was one I never warmed to. His wheelchair rammed my ankles once too often to take the too profuse apologies offered. If he thought he could make you run, he tried to. It was all he had left to do in the way of ordering about. His whining was his anger turned rotten and it piped out of him in tortured ways. No sleep and less waking.

I managed him by seeing things he needed before he saw himself, by offering a clean shirt, new towel, fresh socks before he asked. It did not make him ask less.

Ted Leyland believed Sister Mauritius to be the finest of women. I did not try to dissuade him from his belief because he was the finest of men. He was courteous to all of us. When he saw me coming he would open doors, tucking his stick under it so it would not shut.

'Off to Mass.' He would say. 'Off to walk.'

He would fill his days with trips to here and

there. Never out the gates. Ted told me his wife had loved flowers. Each week I found a small bunch, homes are full of them, and put them on his window sill. At night he would close his eyes after looking at them.

Peter, too well to be housed in a home, was one who did walk out the gates, though Sister Mauritius did not encourage it.

'She doesn't like us to stay fit,' he whispered to me with a wink.

He walked to Scarna every day and sat with the fishermen and counted boats and boxes of fish and came back smelling of it. Sister Saviour would give out with a smile, 'You smell like a kipper, Peter, or is it cod? No wonder, all the cod you give me.'

He was Sister Saviour's favourite. She could not help having one because she loved a man who could help himself. Peter helped to clear away dishes and stripped his own bed.

'Wouldn't it be nice, Sive,' he would say, 'if we could have a nice party? I used to love them. Even at Christmas we don't have a proper one, with proper drinks and women. Too bad those days are done.'

Peter was well enough to stay in the town, but the home rules were bed by eight. So he abided, out of having nowhere else to go.

I kept it in my mind to give him his party. Sister Saviour and I made sure he got overcoats if they came in and warm hats and gloves from the stock of dead men's things that were regularly delivered to us by charities.

'Make sure that Peter doesn't get these,' Sister

151

Mauritius told Saviour. 'It'll only encourage him.'

'It will,' Sister Saviour agreed and passed them on to him straight away. She never disagreed with her matron in anything but her actions.

Liamy the vegetable's only voluntary action was pulling on a cigarette, I discovered as I gave the old senile Colonel his in the dayroom. Liamy smacked his gums together loudly, over and over and eventually I heard what he was saying.

'Would you like a try?'

He gummed the cigarette with delight and coughed and spluttered and smacked some more and the Colonel shouted 'Hut Hut Hut!' because he wanted it back so.

Once the Colonel got an unlit cigarette and ate it and I laughed to see him spitting it out and brushing it off his jumper. And he taught me, by looking sad and long and with both eyes and saying, 'I don't understand.'

I understood then that to light his cigarette and hold it for him was as much a part of my job as wiping his old bottom. With my new eyes I saw the men's unbroken spirits rise out of their broken bodies to greet me.

★   ★   ★

The carers watched me with suspicion, even Sister Saviour, but since I got my cleaning work done before attending to other tasks she would not admonish me. Out of the carers came the fear of living their own lives; hiding behind ones already lived, they did not understand that the men needed looking after, because they needed looking after themselves.

I had been there a while before I asked of the one who never spoke, who sat in the end cubicle without looking up.

'This one never talks,' Joe said on the day Sister Saviour asked him to show me the correct way to turn hospital corners. We were making the bed, which I had cleaned on my first day. The man was asleep in his wheelchair.

'Don't bother trying to move him, leave him to me. He's a big lad, even with what's left of him. He won't try, that's what's wrong with him. He's younger than he looks, took a stroke at seventy.'

'And his name?' I asked.

Thomas Cave.

My memory called out to me, but I could not place the name. The flesh of Thomas Cave had already begun to rot before his heart stopped. His thick shock of white hair matted and stained yellow with room smoke, where they left the men to spend their waking hours with nothing but each other to look at.

'We don't go in for the beauty treatments,' Joe said when I reached out to touch the hair. 'Don't go feeling sorry for him.'

He raised his head at my touch. I had not thought of what I had done, it had just seemed natural to do it. He put his eyes on me. No one had looked at this man; he looked at no one. He ate his meals with his good hand and he slept or stared into space.

As I took my hand away from him, Thomas

Cave raised his head further and looked at me. I saw that he would frighten and awe those who truly saw him. I saw blue-black sapphire eyes and I saw that their piercing nature had not changed, in all that had happened.

Joe piled on lists of rules and instructions that held the men to their conditions and the staff to their routines and I stared at Thomas Cave and he at me.

I felt death in the look, not the creeping nature of it but the fierce battle that raged with it. Everyone was dying in this place including the no-marks that ran it. Everyone was running away from dying, or cowed in the face of it.

This man's eyes said he was different. This man's eyes said he was the only one who welcomed death. So it laughed at him and took others who should not have gone before him.

And he felt my knowing of this. All changed for me and for him. Once he had looked at me he would not stop seeing.

His eyes told me that he had been powerful. His rage was the kind that had turned in on him and had eaten him slowly. In this place he had no option but to kill himself that way. There were no dark corners or sharp implements, no independent movements.

'I have watched men wrapped in sheets in early morning,' his eyes said. 'And I have wished it was me wrapped in whiteness and gone into it. Have mercy on me, bring me to an end.'

A need grew to put miles between myself and the smell and sight of that man who I knew now to be the photographer from Sergio's Café. He

154

did not know me as anything other than one who had taken the time to look.

The pull to come back the next day was even stronger. He took my sleep from me and his eyes followed me home to where Myrna watched and asked me what the days had brought to me.

'The photographer, the one from the café years ago. You told me to watch for when he came through my door. I came through his. He's there and you would not recognize him. His eyes won't leave me alone. He's fighting all around him.'

Myrna looked out at the day sky disappearing into night.

'Thomas Cave. He will come through your door. The cards say it.'

'If you saw him you would see how impossible it is.'

'What happens in the darkness? Where will it bring us? We do not know. This is the time of day the old know best. The unknown is creeping in. The old have a harder fight than anyone. They have to let go of life. They are the ones to voyage to the unknown. You have only seen the ending of the old before. Now you are also sensing their beginning, my beginning. It's upon me too.'

'But you are not like them' I told her sharply. 'You are free to come and go.'

'Not much further than they do. These old bones give me only death to consider. I have no lasting home but a grave and even then I do not know where that will be.'

Myrna did not hide behind the words. She looked at me. I saw eyes that had already lost their shine. She was putting her life into me and I would take it because that is what had always been done.

I had complained of living, resenting the burden she had brought me in herself and all the while this old, grey, twisted woman was quietly giving me her soul with a smile.

'I would never ask you to leave here,' I said softly.

'No. And death will want me just the same.'

'But this man is different, death does not want him, he wants death. It won't come to him.'

'Then he has something else to live for.'

Myrna ended the conversation by bending over the fire to begin its lighting. 'And one of those things is walking through your door and I will be here to witness it.'

Later that night she came back to the words as if we had never left them.

'The place where you are now,' Myrna said. 'The old of St Manis journey in an alone way. That is the only way to leave the unknown and come to the known. You will learn a lot from them when you have the heart to.'

★   ★   ★

When the night happened, still I did not sleep. In the late evening of the following day my eyes were heavy. Carmel spoke of the wild flowers, which would come soon to Killeaden headland and the hum that would be heard from the hungrily feeding bees.

Myrna smiled and said, 'It is good to be in a

country place for spring again.'

I did not answer, I had no knowledge of spring in the country. I did not know then that all can be mended by spring. Night brought me the first dreams of Thomas Cave.

I thought I had woken, but sleep had taken me further on and deeper to a place that felt like waking. I stared at my wall, at the shadows and longing cast on it. Then he came to me with what he had been. I watched my bare wall and listened to the life of the one who never talked. The movement of time and people with it had been all around him. He shared in none of the tragedy and none of the celebration. It had not touched him. He had watched too much and many to risk doing the same.

And I knew Myrna was right. It was not the end that he searched for, but a beginning.

So I found myself the following day, walking the hill before dawn, heavy with the need for sleep and peace and an end to all new knowing for a while. But I was not to be granted such luxury.

I worked that day away from him, though his thoughts screamed. My head was bursting with his one single demand.

'Can you give an enema?' Nurse Joe O'Reilly asked me over dry biscuits and strong tea. 'You're not a nurse unless you can give an enema.'

He talked the tools of his nursing trade. He talked circles around his frustration and softened its edges for a while.

I asked him of Thomas Cave.

'You'd think he couldn't talk, but he can,' Joe O'Reilly advised. 'No, he's choosing not to talk that one, anything to be difficult, like them all in here.'

After hours of the same — Thomas Cave screaming help for my ears alone — it stopped as suddenly as it had begun. He sat, still and silent, reeling in the hour of his lost death, alone.

Don't go near him, Joe O'Reilly advised. Don't go too close is the first rule of a good nurse. There's only trouble in that. But I had to go near. I sat on the edge of his bed.

Come closer, he pleaded. I leaned towards him.

'I stayed silent a long time too,' I told him. 'You must speak words. I know you have them.'

'Bring me something tomorrow,' he whispered in his real voice.

It went deep and dug a permanent path with its gravel tones. He was the first man to find that way and he did it with a voice that scraped and rubbed against the softness in me.

19

Thomas Lives Again

Thomas Cave found his way to a dream place. He woke with a start and a scream.

The night attendant rushed to him before the other sleepers were wakened and he found Thomas Cave shivering, wet and stinking. The attendant wrenched him out of the bed and put him back in his chair with a blanket and left the bed to the day staff.

But the night was to give him no more nightmares. He had the first pleasant dream since he had woken up from a great blackness many months before and found his body twisted and cold. When you have not moved much in a long time your blood stills and turns to coldness.

In the dream his blood was honey-warm and flowing.

Thomas woke, but he kept his eyes closed and cherished the warmth and did not wish to open them and face the grey surroundings.

After a time he realized his movements were not his own. He squinted down, not wishing to disturb the girl kneeling at his feet which were placed in her lap, where she rubbed life into them.

He believed on that first day, when she had dressed him with a tenderness he had never felt,

159

that she had come to release him, to give him the tools to die soon and without further suffering. But as the days went on he stopped calling and it was then that she sat on his bed and leaned closer to hear him, though he had thought never to speak again.

'I stayed silent a long time too,' said the girl with the green cat eyes that he felt he had known and the cat walk. 'You must speak words. I know you have them.'

'Bring me something tomorrow,' he spoke with a voice grown hoarse and stale with non-use.

Now she knelt at his feet and she fixed the cat eyes on him and she said with a soft purr that stirred him, 'I brought proper socks and a pair of slippers. They came with the last delivery of clothes. Your feet are like blocks of ice. At long last we have something in the way to fit your feet. Like canal barges they are. A man must keep warm to live.'

He cried silent and warm tears.

He had thought her to be death's sweet messenger and instead she brought a sweetness of life with her that was too tantalizing to taste. To make him swallow what he had not the courage to while young, now, when all was lost? Cruel life.

He saw not her but all that went with her, surrounded by figures too shadowed for him to determine. And the smell of her! Citrus fruits and fresh cut flowers. Her hips moved easily, like water, and would have moved more easily if it were not for their straining against the uniform, cut for another shape.

He could not have imagined a more beautiful woman and her beauty had come to wake him. She had not come to put a spirit to rest, but to move it restlessly in a body that had lost movement.

In that moment Thomas Cave was lost. Life had won.

★   ★   ★

This is how the wanderer that was Thomas Cave came to be stilled.

In the darkness of the boxroom Thomas Cave had studied the pattern of the curtains. In the course of his nonliving he tried to patch up the pieces of his memory that remained, but lost track of the time, as you do when you are faced with eternity.

He exhibited his past as a series of photographs, which he hung carefully in his mind. Photography was how he had made his living. He had no great love for it any longer, but it was how his imagination worked.

His imagination did not hide truth — many of his recollections were uncherished. Some were glimpses of lost times that could not be restored because there were no pictures, but undeveloped images. Out of the darkness came not even shadow but a suggestion of one that darted and danced away from him.

He could make out other pictures, but could put no story to them.

Grey, early morning and the bare shoulder of a woman dressing, the captured and fading

161

coolness of an iced drink in draining heat, unknown arms holding a young child wriggling with expectancy. He was left with nothing more than a sense and an ache to know what had occurred in those times. He was left with the memories of a stranger.

There was one thing in the gathering of memories that Thomas Cave was certain of. These pictures were of the times of other people and not his own times. They were happenings that he had watched and did not belong to.

This did not stop Thomas Cave from wanting to retrieve all he could.

There were gaping holes now in the lost commonplace — where his knowledge of other languages used to be. Now they all merged into one confused tongue that he dare not speak. And that tongue, once also an educated palette, was half frozen. There was a twisted hand that had once curled naturally around the body of a camera and allowed him to survey the world of his choosing.

Thomas Cave now knew that all the choices were fate's prerogative. His own body, his own mind were not his. They belonged to the callous events of the moving world.

He was not a fool before this. The indeterminate nature of existence had not escaped him. It had simply never claimed him as victim. He had spent his life observing human experience — the edges of it that most eyes hid from: the movement of a recently severed hand removed for theft in the same crowded marketplace from which it had stolen; the

162

clouded, fearful eyes of a gypsy girl put into a marriage at twelve; the silver spread of terraced rice fields and the colourful dots of humanity owned by the land.

Thomas Cave had seen and photographed life against every backdrop the world could present — mountain people, valley people, desert people, ice people, plains people and city people. And life had never come to him. He kept it at bay, as a series of journeys, tasks, darkrooms and published material. He had remained a stranger to all but the work. Now the lives of his subjects were the only ones he had known and their lives were denied to him.

Still he could not give up. His body had been broken up and his mind had been broken up. Each day he spent in the dark boxroom, denied the irregular shape of the world, he wished for life to end.

So out of his brokenness came the heart-driven task of piecing together the map of existence and the world it had taken place in. The curtains were his Asia — their shape presenting shadows and patterns, which, if he stared hard enough for long enough, would offer something in the way of memories. The ridges of the beige candlewick bedspread became the ridges of desert in the worn, old land of Africa and the many lives it offered. Lives in lush jungle, on open plains and lives on relentless sand. The three separate walls were bare but for the memories he had hung on them of India, the Americas, the frozen reaches of the polar caps and Siberia and Central Asia.

All this world he had lived in and not belonged to.

Footsteps could be heard. Thomas's fear rose and he felt the ache in his frozen side as he twisted and shifted to fit himself into the corner furthest away from the door.

'Father,' Jonah Cave's long shadow entered the room before him. He threw back the bedspread. 'You have soiled yourself again.'

Since Thomas had lain in the dark boxroom his bowels had almost ceased to work. For this Jonah punished him. It was Jonah's considered task to spare his father no shame. Jonah wanted his father to remember all that he could not remember, all he had not been there to witness: the growing of Jonah, his child, the stretching of his bones towards the sky.

They had been fatherless bones. Jonah had grown tall like his father, so his small spirit rattled around inside a tall emptiness. When he moved there was a hollow echo in the cavern beneath his ribcage, which his father now heard.

Thomas did not weep when Jonah made the pain come, for even now he was not a man given to emotion. He cried single tears not for what his son inflicted, but for what had been inflicted on his son in his absence and because the time to put that right was long past. He found in the box of feelings he had opened that regret was the first to jump and grab him.

Sometimes Jonah would decide to turn on the main light, the bedroom light, which was not welcomed by Thomas, who did not like the ruin of his own wasted body — the skin had turned

164

grey without daylight. Sores had formed on all points that rested on the bed, and when Jonah pulled back the sheets to survey this, the smell rose and Thomas closed his eyes.

Jonah's face did not light up at the sight of his father's wasting, he stared at it and occasionally he would nod as if to say he understood it, as if he were an artist studying a work in progress for clues as to where it might lead.

Thomas made efforts not to catch the eyes of Jonah, eyes that were not like his, in a face that shared no similar feature to his own. He saw plenty there of a woman whose face he had purposely forgotten.

The food that Jonah provided on a daily basis was serviceable. It served to keep the father awake and alive to the son. The son gave bread and the father ate bread, dry with a slab of dull cheese, the life processed out of it.

He dreaded Jonah's violence less than his tears and he dreaded Jonah's tears less than Jonah's emptiness. It was a void he had helped create as carelessly as he had once coupled with Jonah's mother and married Jonah's mother.

'Love me,' Patricia Cave née Nolan had said, and he had loved her with his eyes on the wall.

'Don't leave me,' Patricia Cave née Nolan said when he had found her under another man's heaving. He had not been hurt, the feeling had been one of relief, one of a way forward opening that did not include her or Jonah. The child who was not even his own but might have been.

Jonah was two when Thomas left. The ring that he took off on that same day had not made a mark. Thomas made one or two visits in the first year after his departure. But as Jonah grew so did the knowledge that he was not Thomas's son.

He forgot the boy who was not his own and simply sent money to Patricia and Jonah once a month and entry forms for good schools and fees.

Jonah was five when Patricia wrote.

'Help me.'

When she drank she wrote and when she dried out she wrote. No mention was made of Jonah's progress, or name.

'Your son needs new shoes, your son needs a uniform, your son needs money for a school trip, your son needs . . . '

Thomas forgot the boy's name and soon his existence, only the standing order that still left the account each month reminded him that Jonah still lived. Now he and regret visited many places together, including the short-lived days of his marriage.

For Thomas, then, there was no question that he had not behaved honourably. Even when Patricia died of her drinking, he had continued to send money to Jonah. The child had done with the money what the mother had done with it because the mother was the only one there to teach him.

Thomas Cave had reached seventy before he had learned his deeds were not honourable. Then the day arrived to teach him about that and much more besides.

166

It was a month after his birthday, a birthday that he had marked alone in his small and comfortless cottage in the emptiness of a western townland.

His chosen emptiness and isolation had near killed him when the white blindness and burning pain had shot through him and the cold numb after it. There was no one around to hear his cries but the black crows that answered them.

He lay unconscious for a long while and when he woke there was a bright sky, then a dark sky. Then he saw no sky, but heard only the sounds of his life disappearing into light that he did not find peaceful, but in time all he could do was go with the whiteness and he left the body behind. But the postman found it while it still breathed in the grey-white dawn.

The postman prided himself on his role as link between outside world and forgotten people of the countryside, had delivered valuables and letters and, on one occasion, even a baby. After that he decided to do a first aid course.

So it was with great interest he stumbled on the whispering shadow of a human being turned blue with the lack of breath. And he knew how to pipe air into the losing lungs and splint the broken wrist. He lifted the twisted form into the back of his van, though it took a long while to shift the giant. To leave the man for any length of time was to let him die.

He transported Thomas Cave in his green van, on sacks of undelivered mail, to a hospital

167

twenty-five miles away, whistling cheerfully in the knowledge that he would surely secure the Postman of the Year award for services above and beyond the duties of mail delivery.

★   ★   ★

So Thomas Cave was carried on the whinges of men and women who did not get their post that day, or for three days later in the year when the postman travelled to Dublin to receive his commendation at a special awards ceremony presided over by the Minister for Post and Telegraphs himself.

Thomas Cave was a known figure, a winner of many meaningless awards.

So a picture of Thomas, bedridden, was published in the papers alongside the smiling and rigid snap, badly composed, of a proud postman and a bored minister with his mind on lunch.

'Photographer saved by Postman', the clippings would not have a chance to gather dust in the postman's scrapbook, so often would they be taken out and shown to canvassing politicians and door-to-door collectors and deliverers.

Those clippings brought an unknown man to Thomas Cave's bedside, an unknown man who told him he was his son. Thomas knew on first sight that Jonah Cave was not his blood son, but he was the son of his experience. For both of them were tall and both of them had the small, rattling spirit of non-feeling.

The hospital was only too delighted to sign the

care of the surly patient, after some months of no improvement, over to his only living relative, who took pleasure in transporting him to the nameless suburban dwelling of 45 St Peter's Road. It was the house that Thomas had left Jonah to rot in, Jonah told Thomas as he pushed the wheelchair through the gate and up the garden of weeds and neglect.

Jonah closed the door between Thomas Cave and the world.

20

The Same Love

The same love Thomas Cave felt grew in me, though I had no name for it. I knew a horrendous excitement that robbed me of sleep and knew a calm that could help me dream standing up.

I did not know what to do with all that I was feeling, just as he did not. The tasks of caring for him in my daily work were tasks of loving. I had his hair cut and I found him clothes that never fitted but at least brought living back to him. I grew used to seeing jumpers that came only to mid-arm length and so did he. We would laugh about them.

'Look at me, poking out here,' he would smile. 'There's just too much of me.'

'There is,' I would laugh, and want to cry at the same time. I would want to ask — how come you came with no shoes, Thomas? Where are your clothes? You speak like a man who should have plenty of them and good ones at that. What has happened to you?

But I felt the thin line of pride that was in him was all that he had. I could not take it from him with questions of how he came to this. Though I did not know it, he looked at me and thought the same.

Whatever we had to tell we would tell in our own good time. We were silent and the silence brought the questions and the questions brought more interest. My last act each day would be to fold down his bed and to straighten out the little he had on his locker.

He would thank me for it with eyes that looked away as I was doing it. A man, I knew, who had never had a woman do for him. I put a picture on his wall. A sad and tired thing left sitting in a cupboard, which featured ill-drawn mountains and a careless sea. But he looked at the picture like it was a masterwork.

'Thank you, Sive,' he said without a smile, 'for bringing something of outside to me.'

The things I did for Thomas were not noted as unusual. I did the same for the other men.

In the dayroom Mauritius only allowed each man three smokes.

'One for morning, one for afternoon, one for bedtime.'

The men had grown in a time when smoking was a way of life. It was the one pleasure they had left. Drinking alcohol was allowed on Christmas Day and Easter Sunday and on the birthday of each resident. Those that did not smoke were given chocolate. Three squares. As soon as their visitors had left Mauritius made it her personal business to gather from the men everything that was not allowed in the way of luxuries. These were kept in a ration cupboard and doled out by the matron herself. No other hand touched them. The men complained regularly about this, but she would reply, 'What

171

would you prefer — to eat and drink this in one go or to have it as God intended and recommended. Moderation in all things!'

And her soft, sensible shoes would carry her away on noiseless determination while the men grumbled and said, 'Half of it will go missing.'

The men got a small allowance each week, but there was nothing to spend it on. Each month Sister Mauritius organized a tombola, for which the men bought tickets. The prizes were religious objects, left over luxuries from residents who had died before getting through their rations, personal effects that relatives had not claimed. The allowances tended to be squandered on this one event, which offered the only spontaneity in the lives of the men. Most of the men had a religious object in the cubicle. There were more statues of Mary and various saints to be won than bars of Cadburys and packets of Players or Sweet Afton.

One day I saw Mr Black press money into Peter's hand and Peter refuse it.

'I was told if I was caught again bringing things in I would be sent out. Now I can't risk it. I'll give you one of mine,' he said, trying to placate the grimacing Black whose good hand clenched the wheelchair and whose twisted mouth spat back, 'That cunt Mauritius says I can have no more ciggies till I take my chance at the fucking tombola. I've won six Virgin Marys in a row and they're not even good-looking ones. I can't go another day without me fags, Peter — I'm gumming. I'm dying I am! I'm a forty a day man. What can I do on three smokes a day?

172

I might as well smoke them with me arse.'

Peter shook his head and carried on out the door.

'I'm sorry. She said she'd take my room off me and give it to Ted. She checks my pockets and my drawers and lockers to make sure I'm not sneaking the things in. She says . . . '

'Ah, she says, she says, my hairy hole! Are you scared of an old dry cunt like her? I'm not. If I had me legs I'd be out of here.'

'Well, you don't,' Peter lost patience. 'You've only one and I have both. The walk into town is my only outing. Without that I might as well be dead.'

'Ah y'are anyway!' Black sighed. 'Give us a bit of your chocolate then. Or a sucky sweet.'

'You're allowed neither. You're diabetic for God's sake.'

'And if I had one of my needles now I'd jab it in your arse instead of me own,' Black roared at the fast-departing Peter. 'What use have you for legs? You run round in circles with them. If I was a fitter man I'd be gone from here. Not hiding scared like you ye . . . '

I came up to Black and put my hands on his wheelchair handles to take him into the dayroom.

'What're you at? Leave me where I am!'

'What do you smoke?' I asked.

There was a short silence, then an urgent request for Players, untipped, as many boxes as I could manage.

The next day three of the men found their way to asking for a box of Liquorice Allsorts, tobacco

173

and papers and the *Racing Post*.

I did not go to town myself for the requests, because word would get out that the black one, as I was called, was bringing stuff to the men up above in the home. Sister Mauritius would have heard in turn. I got Eddie to go in once a week and get it. The men hid everything like prisoners of war.

The downturn in demand for tombola tickets on St Michael's ward was noted, but could not be pinned on anything. The discovery of chocolate in the sluice cisterns, caused the plumber some consternation. Alcohol supplies were delivered to the locker of Ted Leyland, who took them gladly, being partial to the odd drop of Powers whiskey. Mr Black organized it with him.

'She's such a lick arse to you, Ted, she'd fire one of us out quick as look at us, but she'll never search your locker and if she did she'd only say 'naughty, naughty, now' and pour it down her own throat, lush that she is.'

So it was that the spirits of the men in St Michael's ward lifted for no reason at all. When Sister Saviour was asked about this by matron and Joe, she smiled and said, 'Spring does it. They know they're going to get a nice spring cleaning, too. It's the time of year for it.'

Joe and I went to bed with aching backs after one week of buffing already polished floors, cleaning clean beds and bathrooms and disinfecting the sluice room, on the floor of which you could already have eaten a four-course dinner.

I didn't mind the work. I didn't mind the bad

pay. I didn't even mind the pointless cleaning. St Manis, a place where most had it taken away, had given me purpose, most of it contained in blue-black eyes that watched and called me all day long.

* * *

You are here now, Thomas, opposite me, fixing me with a shared look. You are my Beloved and I am yours. You called me and I answered because I could do little else but come to you.

How did you come to love me? I asked you once. There was something in my eyes so much a part of a different world. An old and lived soul in a young body. Yours an unlived soul in an old body.

You could not die once your heart found the way to beat strong and sure again. But it was agony for you, an old man in a crippled form with his eyes on a girl-woman. You knew the girl-woman called Sive had found a way into you and you did not know that I could do this because love called me too.

We answered that which was unanswered in each other. I reached for the kindness that was buried within you; you reached for the warmth buried in me. No other had seen that in us.

And the day came in St Manis when Joe O'Reilly was poorly and Sister Saviour said, 'You'll have to do the baths today!'

You watched me fill the bath with lukewarm, safe water with which to soap you down and you wished instead that my hands knew your

175

body in the lover's sense.

'Please, make it hot,' you said. 'I have had enough of these tepid hospital baths.'

I turned off the cold water.

The night before you had called to me because you did not know I could answer. You reached for me in the dreams you did not know I entered.

'Unless you come I will die.'

Over and over you whispered it until you fell asleep with the makings of a dream on your lips.

'Unless you come I will die in my own despair,' your dreaming self told mine.

'Unless you come my heart will howl all this night at the moon and persecute these broken shells of being, strewn in careless beds around me, into ordered early graves. Why was I born so many years before you?

'I have drunk wine older than you, slept with and beside women who saw fifty years of living you have not seen, lived through times as a grown man your mother has not even seen. Yet I have this wanting of you that will not listen to the body I am in. I want you with this twisted, battered body and this emptiness behind my left eye. I want to kiss you with my crooked mouth that feels only half of your imagined lips.

'Why talk of kisses, why dream of them when I do not even have the legs to bring me to you! If I had legs that could bring me to you I would go now and meet with you in your place as I once was and could be again, if I could only have you.

'Listen to this tired old rant!' you told yourself. You told yourself that a woman such as me would not only spurn but also mock you with the savage unknowing of the young who do not imagine youth has an end.

'Still, I want you, Sive!' you called. 'Still I say why do you not come to me? Why do you leave me each night to go out into the other world, abandoning me in this one, which smells only of my and other men's inching death? Why do you remain young when I wish you to be old, embittered, pounded and lost like me so I could prove to you it is not your youth that I desire but you and what is in you!

'You are a witch and I wish to know your magic. Yet in all this love of you there is a torment that says I will never know you.

'A curse on my empty life and emptier end.

'A curse on all the life you will live without me.

'I do not mean that, Beloved, but love for you is torturing me into continued life, if only to watch you. Torturing me into death as an end to the watching. Torturing me into the nowhere between the two.'

★   ★   ★

I sat awake listening to your dream words. The strength of your plea caught me and made me afraid, Beloved, afraid and full with anticipation for our new knowing of each other. You had called to me in dreams and I had found dreams to answer with. I could answer as I wished to answer.

I walked the hill road of Pass If You Can

177

quickly that morning, as if it were not a steep climb but a short step. My eyes glittered and my strength was at its height, I knew you were only moments away.

But when I went to the cloakroom, Margaret was waiting to trap me with words and eyes.

I had to stop and speak to her. I knew I had to be patient and I knew suddenly that the moment when we would be away from everyone would be a long while in coming. I had expected just to walk up to you and say I had listened and would answer.

In her talk I found patience and I clung to it, knowing as long as you and I were tied to St Manis we must be apart for more moments than we were together.

When the breakfast was served and cleared, when the beds were made, when the floor was swept, washed and buffed, when Sister Saviour had gone to her morning meeting with Sister Mauritius, I wheeled your chair into the sterile, white coldness and began to fill the bath for you.

The steam shrouded us, clouded the glaring tiles and chrome out of their unkindness.

'You'll have to help me,' I said. 'I cannot lift you alone.'

When you stood with my support you were crouched and bent and shaking. Still you towered over me.

'I was six foot six before.'

You spoke aloud for only the second time since I had known you, using your crumpled mouth. The words were perfect and laid in the gravel tones that had caused me to catch my breath the first time. I knew that Joe O'Reilly had been right, you had chosen silence.

You were thin and wasted. Though your shoulder bones had no meat they were wider than my entire body. I remembered the days when they had meat on them, the days of Sergio's Café.

'A big man can fight small ones even when he is only half himself,' I said aloud.

You smiled at that.

Your broken body gave me strength and purpose. I would make you well. I soaped the tired folds; I soaped the grey away and found living skin underneath and heat underneath the cold.

I took in the nakedness of you and then you took in mine under the clothes I wore.

I took off clothes not as I had done for the unseen eyes of my Soho time. I took them off with shyness and with pride, for I knew what I had to offer you was worth taking and I knew that I had pride in giving it.

The water opened you up and you felt the long ago warmth again flood into the frozen parts of you.

The sight of my young body before your old brokenness brought tears hotter than the water. I did not wipe away those tears for in each one was the ice that had held you to your frozen self.

I sat on the side of the bath and took those tears on my breast that I gave to your mouth and you sucked the comfort out of me and you drank your own tears. You felt your groin-blood pulse and pound against your thinned vein walls and

179

gasped, so afraid it would gush out of you and over me.

But I knew what it was and was not afraid, I felt your blood join mine and I felt your heat and I felt my own and I took the new hardness until it found a way.

Then I placed my lips on yours and whispered into your crooked mouth with hot pearls of breath that moistened your throat with hope and possibility.

'We will be together.'

We held each other and we waited for the coldness to come before we let go.

★   ★   ★

That is how it was the first time. The first of Thomas's feeling, brought back into legs that tingled with anger at the long non-use and the lateness of love's arrival. Each time more, more feeling.

Other men, too, improved with kind hands.

Sister Mauritius's eyebrows knitted. Our job was not to improve the men, but to offer them a place in which to end their days. Fewer men were dying. How was she supposed to account to the Board of Governors for the fact that no beds ever became vacant when they constantly reminded her of the length of the waiting list?

'Too much care,' said Sister Mauritius, 'is wasteful of the time and energy of those who run the home. No,' she told a silent Sister Saviour, 'we give too much care already and it must be stopped.'

180

At this point Sister Saviour, who put her life into working hard and had loved nursing above nunning, felt her faith slide away. She left the meeting concealing her intentions and Sister Saviour had rarely concealed anything in her brisk and upright existence.

Her nursing had taught her to make men well. She took delight in the small progresses made in recent months. Her desire was that the broken senses of the men be restored. Pride first, she thought. The new girl gives them pride before care.

After thirty-five years nursing Sister Saviour had learned something new. The men were to be called by first names and to be asked if they wanted something before it was done to them. This was her resolve and she told both Joe and me.

It caused some interruption of routine, so she had us drop the latter part of the policy as soon as it began. But the signs were all of improvement. Pride made men well.

And Thomas, my Beloved, among them, became well and proud.

★   ★   ★

Sister Mauritius had no direct power to destroy the new wellness. She could hardly complain about it, but she knew she must do something. So she took to calling Margaret into the office, for talks.

The talks involved giving Margaret the best biscuits on the plate instead of no biscuit at all,

181

and a few extra comforts. A new room with a window that opened. A record player of her own. So her eyes and ears could be employed to watch all of us on St Michael's.

Joe O'Reilly was green-eyed too about recent developments.

'You're not a nurse,' he reminded me. 'Mine are the nursing jobs around here, yours should be the skivvy ones. What education have you to be doing this?'

'You are right, Joe,' I would say, and ask questions about how men should be handled and why. The home had worn him down. I did much to placate him by asking advice. It was Margaret now to worry about.

21

The Coming of Summer

The bite of spring gave way to a relentless heat unknown to living memory.

We were not so isolated in our house now the town was drawn out on evening walks to meet us.

The days went on, growing into one another in their hot sameness and the people grew out of their pale selves into tanned faces and bodies. Couples, who had never shown care for each other in public, strolled arm in arm down evening lanes of birdsong. The café in the town of Scarna advertised: 'Iced tea — an exotic from the Orient'. Cold cuts of meat and tomatoes, with potatoes drenched in salad cream were served instead of the usual hot steaming dinners that drove out the chill of coastal life. Life on the grey sea had turned blue and sparkled.

All around there were rolled sleeves and brown forearms and smiles unearthed.

The sea was fringed with the colourful tassels of bodies in little-used swimsuits. Those who had never swum before, swam that summer. In the heat, Myrna's stiffness eased and her tongue with it. There was more talk in a short time than there had been in a long while of knowing her. As she spoke more, so I spoke more.

'Myrna,' I urged. 'Tell me what you did with the men to make them happy.'

'No.'

In the late evenings we were now able to leave the house and walk the laneway to the shoreline, even on to Killeaden headland.

'I am with Thomas Cave,' I said finally, when we rested there and drank the view that offered all the joyful, sparkling sea at once.

Myrna looked at the sea. 'I knew that much.'

I stayed quiet then, with her, without words, until the sea had long since ceased to sparkle and the shadows of night and red gold of evening were growing on it. Then her own voice came again, gentle and strong.

'I have been with men, but I have never stayed with men. I moved quickly through them because the call elsewhere was too great and I followed it. I could never stop these feet from moving once they had started, Sive. There was a world to see.'

'When did you leave your home?' I asked her.

'Long before I was meant to.'

I was sorry to hear it and she said there was no need for that.

'I would never have had the life I got if I had stayed. I would never have known half of what I came to know. All I saw, Sive! I could not regret that.'

I asked how she came to leave her home place.

'War.'

What had happened to Myrna to make her known in Soho, so well known, I asked.

'I was not well known, I was known only to

those who I wished or needed to know.'

'Myrna,' I laughed. 'You were a legend.'

'The nice thing about legends is they have so little basis in truth. The legend I was, or might have been, was most likely based on two or three women's doings, and even then exaggerated. The world has no use for unremarkable stories.'

'Can you tell me what you know about men?' I asked again.

'I can tell you that I do not have the secrets the women in Soho thought I had. I had only mirrors, Sive, plenty of them. Show the man who he is. Use mirrors that flatter as well as reveal, mind. They do not like to see all their flaws at once.'

'You mean I have to get some mirrors?' I was confused.

'No child!' Myrna threw back her head and let out an old woman's cackle. 'Let me tell you the story of the gypsy and the long road.'

★   ★   ★

The card of the Long Road falls between Myrna and me on this night, as it did back then when Myrna told me of it and the gypsy who gave it to her.

'When I left my home, Sive, I was not much older than you were when we first met. That is part of the reason why I took you to my heart. You had a special nature as a child. I talked a lot more than you did. In fact I chattered from sun up to sun down. I talked with the whole of life and it talked back. My world was large, on a lakeside.

'Then it was taken from me, by war. I walked alone out into the world. The story of how is for another day, this is a happy day, not the time for such a story. I fell in with gypsies because they did not ask me to go away when I followed their caravan out of a town and down the long road into life. I never thought to look back or examine the way in detail so I could return along it. I was walking into forever from what I had known.

'Many of the Soho women thought I was mysterious when I would not say where I came from. The truth is I do not know, Sive. It was a place by the lake and I left it young.

'The gypsies gave me the room to grow into a woman. In the years coming up to that I learned from them about the herbs and then the cards. The woman who showed these to me let me sleep curled up beside her. I stayed close to her in the days, too, and she treated me like a daughter. None would harm me with her about, Sive. She was a fierce woman and I do not remember a day of that time when I went hungry.

'Then the girl left me and the woman-time came. The fierce woman turned the cards for me and the card of the Long Road fell. She said it was mine and that it meant I would find no place until the very end of life. This caused her to cry because she had imagined that I would marry one of her own. But even the gypsy caravan was too much settling down for me, Sive. I had

186

thirsty feet and eyes.

'The next day I left because the woman said the shape that was on me meant she could no longer protect me from men's eyes. She gave me the cards and they have been my constant companions, my longest friends. She gave me the eyes for ghosts and taught me not to fear seeing them. 'Fear the place where there are no ghosts,' she told me. 'For there are no people living there either.'

'I got on the road and I went as far as my feet would take me without sleeping. I walked on after sleeping and I slept out for many nights until I came to a town. At the edge of it was a house of women. One found me asleep in their garden and had me carried, still sleeping, into the house. When you sleep after days and weeks of walking, Sive, and little food, you sleep like the dead.

'When you wake, you have a hunger that will not let you speak until it is satisfied. I woke on a soft bed with the eyes of three curious women on me. All I could say was food and all they could do was get some, for I would say no more until I was fed.

'They brought it to the bed, and with it came an older woman who watched me from a chair in the far corner of the room.

'I ate like there was no food left in the world. The women watched and when I finished they waited for me to speak and still I did not.

'The gypsies had taught me to be wary of people who slept in beds under the one roof in the same place. They get, the gypsies said, so as they would do anything just to keep that one spot.

'So the women took to asking me questions. Why were my eyes black? Where did I come from? Why was I alone? Where was my family? What money had I? How had I travelled here?

'I did not know, Sive, and so I could not tell them. I could only say I had been on the long road for a long time. They pulled at the bedclothes and they pricked the blisters on my feet and they brought hot water and put my feet in it.

'The older woman told them all to leave and they left as quickly as she asked. They seemed to hold fear for her. I did not. She was as fierce as the gypsy woman but no fiercer, so I knew how to be with her. The woman lifted off the nightgown the women had put on me and she looked at me long and hard and I did not feel ashamed, but I was shy and tried to cover myself.

'She got fierce with me and pulled my hands away to look more and as she looked she asked, 'Have you anywhere to go?' I did not and so that was how I came to stay there. 'This will be your room,' the woman said and she told me her name but I do not remember it now.

'I liked the room, Sive. It had dark green walls and pictures of places I had never been to. It had a soft bed, as I said, and the woman opened the wardrobe and there were four dresses. I never had more than one before that time. There were creams and powders and a dressing mirror. The woman said, 'With the black eyes and pale skin

188

you'll go well. But we'll get you ready first.'

'She taught me, Sive. She taught me first by getting me to look through spy holes while the other women worked with the men who came each evening. Sometimes two women worked together but she did not let me look because she said, 'You are one who works best alone.'

'That has always been the way, Sive. She put her hands on my body to show me what I would do with the man and how. She showed me many ways and she gave me only kind men to begin with. But when I had been there for some time I learned this was a place where the women grew old while young.

'I was shown many ways and I will tell you what I was shown, Sive, shown to satisfy the men who felt as if they loved me. There are other ways in the work, Sive, and I do not wish you to know them. You can have a life and a place, Sive, and love. I would have liked all three but I did not have the feet and the eyes for it. In my day the only way to have freedom was to do this work or the work of God. But God did not seem to want me.

'The woman and I parted ways when I had been with her for five winters. I left with the spring as I had arrived. I did not want to stay and she said it was as well I went for, to tell you the truth, I was too good at the work for that small place, Sive. The other women grew to narrow their eyes at me. I was best, as she said, working alone. I always did from that day on.

'Now, what you have wanted to know, I will tell you.'

Myrna said this before she said anything else, sensing my impatience to know only what was relevant to me, my wanting to have the old woman part of the story out of the way. It was only in later years that Myrna's story rang back to me and I was haunted with questions I wish I had asked. Instead I heard only this:

'Sive. Feel like your fingertips have eyes. Use the eyes to see all parts of a body and then the body will fall away and you will have only eyes and spirit under the fingertips. Massage will tell you all you need to know, as will time. Never rush, Sive, even for the one who wants it all quickly. The time will rise the blood in them and it will tell you all you need to know.

'When he asks for something, do not give it to him twice. Vary each movement and make him ask again and again. Still do not give him what he asks for. That is the way of women who work with men. For a woman who loves a man I would say do the same, until the point where you wish him to know you as you know him. Open to him only when he has been to all your openings and explored. Tell him your deepest heart in the moment when he has given you all he has. Match his giving and you will invite more. Never give too much. The man will lie back and expect and in my work that is what they pay for, but in love there are two working together.

'Hide parts of yourself as if you do not have them and they will be forgotten. When you love you must reveal or you will lose yourself in love to all that he reveals. He must know who you are to love who you are. Pray for quiet days with rain

190

and for days of sunlight, pray for cold days and days of warmth. In all these days you will know him in different ways.

'Do not hide the woman in you. A woman is all you are. Show him possibilities and he will take them. Encourage his tears and you will hear his laughter. Take the whole of him and do not look for anything else. To do otherwise is the one sure way of killing love.

'Last of all, Sive; do not lead the way. Do not let him lead the way. Let love do that. It has all the experience and you do not. Let the one you love know the shadow in you and he will know the whole. You cannot speak for him. Speak of yourself in love and walk away from any man that tries to do it for you. Walk and don't look back. But there are moments, in union, when you can have one voice.

'This is a new world, Sive. I watched it grow. This is a world when a woman can love a man equally and you are in it.'

'I feel all of that as you speak it,' I told Myrna and the night growing round us. I could hear her smile. 'Even with all I feel, I feel the call from him stronger. I hear him at night even. He is not young, there is hardly any life left in him.'

'It is the same love,' Myrna said. 'He does not feel it any less or more than you do. But he has lived longer than you without love. He feels desperation. The last years are on him and he is given this to contend with. Poor man.' She clucked her tongue against her teeth. 'Lucky man. You are wrong to say he has no life, Sive. He has plenty of it. Plenty there waiting. It is the life in him that loves the life in you.'

I felt afraid that she might say what we did was wrong, to love in such a way.

'He is old, Myrna. Is it wrong?'

Myrna reached for my hand and held it to her, 'The old can be young and the young can be old. He is who he is. You are who you are. You will have the time together that you are meant to have. Then it will be over.'

'Do you watch us with your cards and eyes for ghosts?'

I was fearful, suddenly, at the thought that our moments together might not be our own.

'No, Sive!' Myrna laughed. 'You are living for one thing and you have your own way to go for another. I know you as I would know my own daughter. I have the eyes and ears and heart you have, though they are not what they were.'

She shifted her hips off the now wet grass and I heard the dry creak of them and put my moist hands on them and they softened under my touch.

'No,' Myrna said, giving my hands back to me. 'Don't waste this on me.'

On the way home I was silent, as was she, but there was no easiness in the lack of words and we did not see the magnificence and violence in the death of the day, in the blood-red sunset. We did not look up, only down at our feet and the next place they would land on the walk home.

We did not hear the high and free sound of my mother's laughter in the wood.

At the door of the house Myrna placed her bony hands on my shoulders before meeting my gaze with hers and planting her thin, dry lips on my forehead.

'We should call this place by a different name,' she whispered. 'For all new things are happening here. Solas.'

Though it was the hottest of summers, in this house with its thick walls full of secrets, it could still be cold. We had tea and sat by Myrna's fire. The flames licked me to sleep.

It was not until Carmel burst in with high colour on her cheeks and Eddie behind her, that I woke and felt the pinch of the creeping cold. For the fire had long since gone out and we were in the middle of the night.

Myrna woke too and more tea was made and a conversation begun, though I could not help but think of my early start.

Eddie stayed as he stayed each night, on blankets by the fire. Though he could have gone in beside Carmel. He had asked Carmel to marry him and she had grown down and silent at that. It had not been mentioned again.

We knew my mother's fear and the reasons for it. We knew she had only seen one marriage.

22

As It Was in the Beginning

'As it was in the beginning so shall it be in the end.'

Jonah whispered into the ear of his stranger-father and wished, with all of his strangled heart, there was a way of knowing if what he said was heard.

For every time Patricia Cave lashed out at her son she told him why it was happening.

'This is because your father left us.'

Often.

When he went hungry, he was reminded it was his father's absence which left them without a provider.

When he missed school so much they forgot who he was and filled his seat with a more financed child, his mother wept and said it was his father who had sent orders for him to go to this school and she could not afford it.

He was sent instead to one that did not demand fees, closer to home, and he was sent home for having no uniform and for his lack of hygiene, homework and schoolbooks.

Jonah Cave, sad, strange, tall, ghostly, unwell Jonah Cave, was the one everyone could hurt. It stopped when they realized to touch him was to land a week's coal tar scrubbing and soaping from the hard hands of irritated mothers, who had to rid them of nits and the like.

It was best to leave him be, and leave him be they did — only their shouts covered the distance between them and the thin bag of bones and eyes that Jonah Cave grew into by an early age. He never lost the look.

When he came home from school his mother Patricia Cave was either passed out on the floor or well on the way to it, or wrapped up in a blanket and staring at the television and talking to it.

He would search the house for money and find coins with which to buy his own food. One day a block of Calcia cheese caught his eye, the bright, healthy girl on the bright healthy blue box. He imagined if he ate it, he ate her happiness and her eternal summer sky. This is what he ate — the girl's happy cheese — and imagined her inside him, bringing bright blue to him.

Happy melted on white bread, happy chunks with bread and milk, there was not always enough money for happy unless he got to it before Patricia's foray to the same corner shop. The shop's supply of vodka spirit and Calcia cheese were reserved almost solely for the bony inhabitants of 45 Peter's Road, a house the newly formed residents' association complained of as their first act of togetherness. Its lack of order and maintenance let the whole road down.

So the council sent letters and the letters were ignored until one day the residents marched *en masse* to the house, armed with paint, trimmers and strimmers and lawnmowers and the like. They got busy in their rightness and righting — they worked, painted, chipped, primmed and preened at the front until it appeared to be like all others. All the while not a sound from the inhabitants, though it was a Saturday afternoon and the television was on and they had to be home.

For an entire decade they neighboured and laboured while Patricia Cave spat blame on the long absence of Thomas.

When the neighbours found her lifeless body they tidied it up quickly.

★ ★ ★

It was a solitary funeral without flowers, and the lost body of lost soul Patricia Cave was put into a grave marked with a white cross that only Jonah visited.

All this Jonah told Thomas and Thomas heard, but chose not to speak. To reply that he had faithfully sent money in the place of love for almost forty years was no reply at all.

'Why did you marry her?' Jonah asked. 'Why did you take her on? Why did you have me? Why did you leave me with her? Why did you never come back?'

Thomas did not answer that Patricia had been pretty and she had been an actress. He had met her at parties and she had always been gay at them in a brittle way, her eyes always bright, too bright now when he looked back. His eyes had always been piercing and that made some afraid of him and others distant. His own mother and father were cold to him and warm to each other.

His father was a bank manager who painted and visited galleries at weekends. Thomas had gone into photography because it offered a training wage straight away and because he could not paint but wished to please his father into noticing him. His father noticed only that photography was a poor imitation of painting.

His father noticed that Thomas had not got a job as a bank manager and would never be able to live respectably. Thomas's mother shook her head sadly because she agreed with her husband that their only child should be respectable.

So Thomas had grown tall and mournful.

He reached thirty and had not loved and was not aware of being sad, only of being missing in some way from the world. Patricia's lips were glossed to a wet inviting. He took her picture; she kissed him softly in thanks. She took off her clothes and walked naked into the bedroom. He did not follow. She came back out and found him, sitting, staring at his own hands. She called his name and he looked up and came to her.

At the beginning it went well.

This woman poured over him like cream on tart and he loved the easiness about her. He did not realize that her easiness hid a similar aloneness to his own. He was an innocent and he did not know her golden honey smile was for many a man and came from golden whiskey that she drank neat.

Shared melancholy brought them together in a frenzied way at the beginning. The new reality came only when she had given him her all softness and he landed on the hard edges of her despair. She would go missing and come back and weep and he would look at her and not know what to do. She could never say why she was crying and he could never ask. They did not live together. It was not respectable.

Thomas knew that Patricia was not respectable, but he did not think less of her for that. He was glad to have a woman who had come to meet him, since he could never manage to go to a woman.

Even with her tears and disappearances it was still good to have comfort.

Then she fell pregnant, though he had been fastidious in his use of French letters.

He married her because he believed he had taken something from her. And he expected he would not meet any woman he would love so what was the harm in having a wife and child? They would be company at least.

After they married, with no parents present, hers dead, his disapproving, they lived on as they had before. He visited her in their home for his dinners and for a bed when he was not working and he had no say in the home or its running. She cooked and someone else cleaned and they got along until she grew big. With that she grew demanding and he was at a loss.

So he tried, and she grew more demanding still and one day she was lying belly up, swollen stomach pointing skywards, blind with drink and tears.

'I married a stone,' she said. 'I have a rock for

a husband all right. A stone he is.'

He had asked her to come, please, out of the cold and she had not come until he pulled her in, screeching her lack of love for him and how it was not his baby she carried at all, but a bigger, braver man's.

The next day she woke and did not remember. There was no talk between them in the days that followed.

Her pains began and she bore a child, trembling cold, sickly with the need for milk mixed with whiskey. The doctor had words with him and the nurses tut tutted and he looked at them all with his piercing eyes and they avoided his and could not tell him what to do.

He asked her to stop drinking so much and she drank vodka so he could no longer smell it.

He got a commission to photograph a war and he went and when he came back she did not even bother to hide the bottles. But the paid help minded the child like her own and Thomas paid her for the kindness.

She left when Thomas Cave left Patricia.

In two years, Thomas could see well that Jonah was not his but had the look of another man he had often seen in the party days. So he decided it was more honourable to leave than to stay and hate a child. He could provide for him at a distance.

So that is how it was. Now the effects of that provision had been made apparent in the small boxroom of 45 Peter's Road where Jonah Cave had slept and grown without a father.

Patricia Cave had shown Jonah a picture one

day in the newspaper.

'Your father,' she said, 'took this. He is very good at what he does.'

And a half smile came to her lips and Jonah reached up to touch it. She put the paper between them and turned away. From then on Jonah Cave looked for his father's name in old newspapers and magazines from the Calcia and vodka shop.

He kept ring binders of his father's work and pasted the press photos in and waited for the day when he would turn up to take him away from her.

But over the years he had learned, Thomas Cave was not coming.

★ ★ ★

Thomas would have liked to put a hand on Jonah. He would have liked to say to Jonah that he was not his father but should and could have been, and nothing could be done about it now.

Sometimes Jonah took a long time to come to the room and Thomas thought on those occasions that he might be able to die without further incident. But Jonah knew when to return, how to keep Thomas on the same thin point where life and death are one and the same.

Jonah had never felt more alive. He kept Thomas alive and gave him the Calcia cheese and told him it would always be like this.

Then the standing order stopped. Thomas had always renewed it yearly and increased the amount according to inflation. Now, without

Thomas to sign there was no money for happy cheese. Jonah would have to let him go. Jonah made preparations as to where — scouring the surrounding areas for a suitable hell for the once active man, a chance to live among those similarly desecrated.

Thomas was glad to give Jonah all he had. In return a deal was struck with the money-conscious Sister Mauritius of St Manis. Jonah found it a miserable place for an errant and absent father. Thomas Cave lost everything he had and gained a set of ring binders with his work pasted in them.

Just before Thomas was loaded into the ambulance, Jonah had said to him, 'I will come and visit.'

23

The Beginning of One

The card of the Rivers — the joining of two and the beginning of one.

My mother's whole life now was Eddie, waiting for him, imagining when he was not there that he had left her. Eddie was a simple man, sometimes he felt he was swimming in a bottomless sea with no sign of land, so strong was her need.

Yet she would not marry him. She would only love him with everything she had.

They walked and walked wide and far now, as if by walking they would walk away from themselves and what had happened and just have each other. Carmel now a shadow woman.

Only on the walks did the world of before surround Carmel and Eddie. Carmel's ways were odd ways and Eddie could not stop himself from feeling afraid when the Scarna people saw them. He took his fear and turned it into proposals. He wanted to be inside her life and not out of it, so as to keep her truly safe.

'If we married, Carmel, we would not need to be apart,' he said in the long summer after a long time of not mentioning it. 'You would not need to spend hours at the end of the laneway, waiting for me to come.'

For that is what she did, even though he had told her the night before what time he would finish his work and what time he would come, and she had nodded her understanding. The next day, soon after breakfast, she walked to the end of the laneway and waited like a faithful dog for the sighting that would gladden her heart.

'I think it is this place has her this way,' Eddie said to Myrna while Carmel slept on the old bony couch. It had been too cold to walk that evening, an evening that had brought with it a bite that had been missing since the first days of summer. It was all the harsher for being unexpected.

'I think she's the way she is because of all she has suffered here, it must be full of memories for her,' Eddie whispered, as he looked for reasons to take her away from it to his own place which he was missing. It had more comforts than this. It had a television and sports results and all the things with which he had filled up his solitary life while Carmel had been gone. It had been a lonely and comfortable life.

Myrna took herself up out of the chair by the fire and came over to put a hand on Carmel's forehead, stroking it. In the soft light the worn lines fell away.

'She will not leave here,' Myrna advised Eddie. 'It is where she belongs. In the town she will be broken in no time.'

'Well,' he flustered. 'We can't go on like this.'

He felt uncomfortable in Myrna's presence then and went home before Carmel woke. When she did wake and he was not there Carmel walked out into the night, wordlessly and without heeding Myrna's urging to remain, to wait for him. I found her when I came home from work.

'He might be back yet,' she explained to me.

'It is too cold for him to be back,' I answered with shortness. I wanted to be in out of the cold and I wanted Carmel with me.

'I might call on him,' she said. 'I might go into the town and meet him.'

'We'll get you a jumper first.'

I knew well she would not go, for she had never gone into the town since she had come home.

Later, when Carmel was in bed, I was sharp with Myrna for leaving her out on a night like that. The next day the summer was back, unrepentant for its short absence, which had left us unguarded in thin clothing. Eddie and Carmel went out as soon as he called.

Carmel came back alone, in a high, flushed state and wanting me.

'Eddie says that we have to get married.'

She stared at me, so little of her left and most of it eyes, lines and bones.

'You may as well, then. Marry him,' I said without looking at her. 'You may as well make sure of him.'

'I am afraid of it, Sive. I cannot live in the town. He will not live here.'

'Have you asked him?'

'I did ask him,' she said after a long time. 'Would you want him here?'

'I don't mind if you want it.'

'I'll go so and tell him. I'll go to the town.'

Carmel did not go to Eddie but to the end of the laneway. She waited for seven days and nights and he did not come. On the seventh night she began the walk into town. Myrna and I watched her go.

'Will I follow her?' I asked.

'This is something between her and Eddie,' Myrna insisted.

So we went to bed and the next morning she was still not home. I went to work and all day I could not eat and moved quickly through my work. Thomas asked me what was wrong. I told him it was home trouble and he did not ask me again but in his eyes I saw the questions, the wondering of what nature of home I had and what nature of life I led away from this place.

When I returned Carmel was still not back. I imagined her lying lifeless somewhere, or wandering, or following Eddie while he ignored her.

Myrna by now had lost her usual calm, had got her cards out and turned them over and over to distract herself. Then, all of a sudden, her face cleared of expression and set again with a sadness that never lifted.

'What is it?' I asked.

'Every beginning means an end.'

I knew I would gain nothing from questioning but my own frustration.

We waited. The dog's warning bark outside brought us to our feet.

We sat with Carmel and Eddie at the hour of midnight. They announced their intention to be

205

married at the earliest opportunity. A calm had come to my mother, which she had lost before I had known her. She was a stranger to me. Her eyes shone and Eddie's look was contented enough.

'I can move in me television,' he offered.

'No,' the women spoke together.

He sighed.

'Well, there's always the wireless.'

The sadness was still with Myrna which, when we raised our steaming mugs of tea to toast the new intentions, could not be driven away from her black eyes.

But that night was all of us together and all of us opening rooms in the old house that had been closed for many years so that we could fit in our new family member. Behind each door we were expecting to find ghosts. Only Myrna saw them.

We found nothing but the spiders' webs filled with the dust of the times before even Carmel had lived here.

'This is a place where life went on before death took hold,' Myrna said. 'This is a place where life can begin again.'

24

The One Who Watches

The One Who Watches is a shadow in a doorway, an icy breeze on a summer's day, a sudden mist when all around is clear. The one who watches is one to be watched. The One Who Watches, say the cards, can be feared or loved.

I loved one who watched and I feared one who watched. They were father and son. They were different and the same.

*   *   *

When I walked through St Manis's gates on one of the last, bright mornings before winter, I saw a tall figure full of intent move towards me. He leaned on a stick but you could see that it obeyed his wishes.

The closer he came the more real he came, his left arm still tucked up neatly in its frozen state told me it was Thomas.

He kissed my forehead and said, 'I have wanted to walk to meet you. The chair had to go.'

He had waited each night until everyone, including the night attendant, slept and he began by rising out of his bed and standing with his

207

stick, until he could stand sure and then walk sure.

When he fell the watching moon made no attempt to pick him up, but her light was clear and steadfast and he learned to pick himself up, until one night he could walk far enough to go outside and meet her. On that night she praised him in her fullness, shining from a cloudless sky. He did not sleep that night, waiting for the time when I would walk through the gates and he would meet me.

The doing it alone was not only to surprise me, but also to prove he had still the power of himself.

'Do not kiss me here, Thomas,' I whispered and stepped away from him, looking for Margaret's eyes. My hard words hid my rising heart and hope. To see him this way made me gladder than any gladness I had known.

'They will see that as a grateful kiss,' he assured me. 'Those eyes behind us. They know how much you have done for me.'

'I don't want to them to know all I have done with you.'

His face hardened. I did not stop walking while I spoke.

'Now we'd best get in before Margaret fills in Sister Mauritius and I have no job and no opportunity to see you.'

'I want to leave here,' Thomas said. 'I could leave here if I had any money left. But I will think of a way. I will find a way, if you think you would want me outside of here. I am not an easy man, and I am not asking you to be my nurse. I am not even asking for us to be together until I die. I know I would hate to take away your happiness.'

'You have not taken it away, Thomas.'

The joy in having him walk beside me and talk of leaving his cage. He seemed to have swallowed the sunshine of the day and for the first time I saw a smile on his grave face. It rested uneasily, bringing fresh creases to the deep-wrought furrows carved from the alone times that had passed over it.

The heat in me went out to him and I could see it took all he had not to put a hand on me.

'I am ashamed of myself,' he said. 'Being like this with someone like you. I will be seen as a dirty old man.'

'We must get in.'

He followed me in the door.

'I am not used to following,' he said.

He did not see my smile. I walked ahead of him.

* * *

Inside, the summer air held the men by the throat, as many of the old windows had seized and swelled and could not be opened. Thomas went quietly back to his corner cubicle and I found Sister Saviour in the kitchen.

'Should we not bring the men outside, Sister? It's such a hot day,' I asked.

'The men are never brought outside!' she exclaimed. 'There's never time to bring the men outside!'

'It would not take long to wheel them. The fresh air will do them good. I can get the ward straightened while they are gone.'

Sister Saviour frowned. But the thought of unhindered scrubbing was too inviting. 'We could get on with a lot of work all the same!'

'I hope that does not mean I get to spend all day cleaning while she stays with them!' Joe O'Reilly had appeared behind me.

'And what exactly do you mean by that?' Saviour enquired.

'I'll be glad to do the cleaning, Sister. Joe can take the men out.'

As I scrubbed I heard them laugh and call to one another. I even heard the deep tones of Thomas in amongst them.

Margaret found her way to me more than once during the day and watched me.

'You do great work,' Margaret said reluctantly, 'for someone on slave's wages.'

'I'm glad of it.'

'I could give you a hand, but I'm not stupid.'

She danced away with her shrill laughter and raced outside when she heard the sound of a strange car in the driveway.

A pearl-blue Jaguar pulled up and a tall thin man stepped out of it. Margaret was the first to greet him.

'If you have come to see anyone in particular?'

'Thomas Cave.'

'He's outside with all the others, having a sunbathe.'

The tall man's face was pale but for two high spots of colour which flushed deeper. Margaret stared at them openly, but the stranger did not appear to notice. He was already on the move, through the front door.

'Not that way . . . '

Margaret had to push the front door as the stranger tried to close it on her.

Jonah Cave did not approve of his father being in sunshine. He had not seen him for nine months and had imagined Thomas to remain in darkness. The threat of a visit, Jonah had thought, would keep him there.

In the nine months his father's money had been spent well on improving Jonah's life. He had a fine new house and a car that purred like a satisfied cat at the slightest touch. He had many women interested in him and keen to know the source of his wealth. He had been drinking and feeling bright. 45 Peter's Road was sold to the highest bidder. By rights that should have been the end of it all with his father.

But in Jonah's dreams, Thomas Cave rose up to admonish him, side by side with his wife, Patricia. In dreams they were united, as they had not been in life. As his mother reigned blows on Jonah, Thomas stood tall as a grown tree above him and shouted with the voice Jonah had never heard. The voice carried all the weight and might of thunder and Jonah was being driven into the ground by both mother and father. Then, Thomas would walk away and not look back and his mother held him. She would laugh gaily at his screeching and wailing.

The further Jonah went into sleeping the more the dream came to him. When he could sleep no longer he had to visit Thomas.

The ring binders were Jonah's father. He had thought only to shame Thomas in presenting them to him on the day the ambulance had come. But they would also keep Jonah safe, he realized now, from the stranger-father and the known mother. The father of the ring binders, unseen, was the one Jonah had known and taken comfort from, expecting his arrival at any moment.

This was the father who had spoken to the son, through the careful selection of photographs and the world he had shown the son through them. This was the father who might one day decide to return. Not the old, broken stranger-father Jonah had found in a bed in a Galway hospital.

Jonah had not discussed the world he had searched for and grown to know in his father's work with the old silent man who had lain in his boxroom for six months and more. He had only felt anger towards that weak and crumbling creature.

'They're out the back,' Margaret said. 'You'll have to walk out this way, through St Michael's ward. I'll show you.'

She got no thanks from the tall and well-dressed man whose pale brown eyes had disappeared into black hollows.

'I'll show myself.'

Jonah dismissed Margaret with a tight smile that said he did not see her as noticeable in any way. The smile made her afraid and caused her to lag behind him.

212

Now he is here, with us, part of the story's spine. The storyteller faces the story she would rather forget.

As it was with Joseph Moriarty so shall it be with Jonah Cave. There is truth waiting here for him and it will be told without him if he so chooses. Or it will be laid in front of him.

A part of him will never leave me. How did Jonah Cave see me? The part of him that is still inside me tells.

Jonah Cave almost passed me by, but then he caught sight of my movement.

It had a rhythm he had not seen, a rise and fall like a slow wave over an empty beach. He wanted that easiness to be put against his own jerking and jolting — his own movement that he seemed to lose control of and then was unable to start.

He needed a drink now, he needed the benefit of golden whiskey that calmed him and gave him the right movements. He wished to put his hands on either side of those hips he watched.

He could not stop the wanting there.

I did not need Jonah Cave's hands on me to know what I saw.

I saw a man who time had made old; a swallowed child peered at me through the slats of his ribcage. I saw a ravaged face and desolate eyes. I saw a drink-dampened evil that had begun as innocence. I saw a thin line of a man almost rubbed out and nothing but loss and failing in the places where he had been. His fine clothes did not match his face, for it had the look of hunger about it.

His impression on me more fearful than any other I have formed. His reality more fearful still.

★ ★ ★

Jonah said to me, 'Thomas Cave, where does he sleep?'

'In the corner cubicle, but he's outside if you're looking to visit.'

Jonah made his way over to the place where his father had been hidden from the world.

He pulled open the tin locker and wardrobe with a savage snap and saw what he was looking for under the assorted dead men's clothes his father dressed in for want of anything else.

'If I could ask you to stop that,' I said, standing over him as he crouched to pick up ring binders. I had to repeat myself before he looked up at me.

Jonah's eyes had little colour in them but pale mud. The red veins in the whites of them all the more prominent for this.

'If I could ask you not to touch those things. The man who owns them is not here,' I repeated.

'And what is the man's name?' Jonah spoke, soft and menacing laced with a thin smile.

'Thomas Cave.'

'And what is my name?'

'I have no idea.'

'Well, you can gather that I must be a relative. His son. I am here to collect things which he does not need or use.'

'You cannot remove someone's belongings.'

'I am doing this for him,' he hunched down to pile up the folders and turned his back to me.

A shadow passed over my shoulder and on to Jonah's face. I thought it was Margaret, returned.

'Jonah.'

The man in the hunched figure of Jonah slipped away, menace gave way to fear, a child stared through his ribcage. Thomas put his hand on my shoulder and in that hand I felt all that he was holding back.

'I'm taking what is mine,' Jonah said in a voice that could not rise.

'Take them gladly. I have no further use for them.'

'You do not want them?' Jonah asked by way of a whisper that lost itself in the emptiness all around. The truth struck him deep and he could not rise from under it. He remained hunched.

'They are yours, as everything else I have is now yours,' Thomas said, not gently.

Jonah Cave, like a crouched unborn, in full view of us.

I moved out of Thomas's grip and went to Jonah and put my arms around him and gave him the comfort he was in need of. He sank his teeth into my shoulder and dry racking sobs tore him up. I held the shreds of him in my arms.

Margaret had arrived with Sister Mauritius.

'When you have finished here, Mary Sive,' said Sister Mauritius, 'I will see you.' And she departed.

Margaret watched on. Thomas barked at her.

'Move away. There is nothing more to be seen.'

'Get off her now, Jonah,' Thomas said, still standing, when we were left alone.

Jonah held tighter.

Thomas gripped the fine tweed of Jonah's jacket with his one hand and his one hand was enough to peel Jonah off me, for there was no weight or substance in him. Jonah flailed like a cat falling through the air, clutching for any part of me.

⋆　⋆　⋆

'I do not ask, or pretend I wish to know what was going on out there.'

Sister Mauritius began a lecture that I had waited for an hour outside her office to receive. Sister Saviour had been obliged to wait with me and was not best pleased.

'We have so much to be getting on with,' she muttered. My shoulder ached with what Jonah had put on it.

'But you seem to be very involved with those two,' Mauritius continued. 'Sister Saviour has advised me that this is a good thing, since Thomas Cave has been a very difficult patient from the word go. I am aware already that his son is — ' she paused and pushed her thin wire glasses up the length of her nose, 'also a difficult individual, but he is a very generous one to this home. He readily appreciates the work we do and has donated over and above what it costs to keep his father.

216

'Sister Saviour tells me you have brought Thomas Cave on. I am telling you, do not bring him on too far. If you want to know why, consider what has happened here this morning. This has all occurred because the patient has become too rowdy and that is because of you.'

Sister Saviour made to interrupt.

'I do not wish to be challenged on this, Sister Saviour! I only wish to give an express order that must be adhered to so this ridiculous situation does not arise again. Mary Sive is not a nurse. She is not to be given nursing work. She is to clean and she is not to be too involved with the patients. The ward has not been the same since she came to work on it.'

We were both dismissed then. But before we left Sister Mauritius drew Sister Saviour's attention to the fact that the men were all still outside.

'They are littering the lawn, move them inside and quickly.'

As we made our way back to the ward Sister Saviour spoke in a tight voice, 'She is not my Mother Superior and I will be seeing my Mother Superior about this! We are a nursing order. That woman — ' The talk ran on inside her.

Thomas was outside again, not with the men but apart from them. Jonah gone.

'Why do you not sit with the men?' I asked.

'Because I am not like them, I am not happy to stay here.' He spoke like a child. 'Why did you do that with Jonah?'

'It was all that I could think of to do. He is upset. He is your son.'

'He is not my son.'

'He has your name.'

'That,' said Thomas before he turned his broad back to me and walked away, 'is all he has.'

25

No Joy

There was a sound of laughter in another room, laughter unshared by Eddie and Carmel as they spoke to Father Malone.

It had gone badly for Eddie when he realized that they were not to see the curate. The curate was taking Father Malone's appointment, for Father Malone felt he had to see this couple, given the circumstances.

Father Malone had pointed this out to the curate over their boiled eggs (Father Malone got two, the curate, one) at breakfast in the priory.

The curate was required to run through his list of tasks for the day at the table. Eddie Burns had asked specifically to see him.

He explained this to Father Malone when Father Malone suggested that he take this particular appointment, but this only seemed to fuel Father Malone's determination.

The curate was not allowed to finish his tea and bread fingers before the housekeeper came to clear away the dishes. When Father Malone finished breakfast the day began for both of them.

In a few years time the priesthood, as it was presented to him in Scarna's parish church of St Alphonsus, would break the curate. He would cause outrage by leaving the priory to move into the Greeg's pub with its proprietor, Mrs Greeg, a woman widowed only a year, her husband buried by the curate. Life was not much different in Greeg's pub, he did as he was told there, too. Father Malone still disapproved of him.

But this was all ahead of them, for now it was up to Father Malone to see Eddie Burns and Carmel Moriarty.

It was evening and Eddie's arms ached from cleaning all his regular shop windows after a summer storm and three freak days of rain had left them muddied.

Father Malone's housekeeper had brought them tea. Eddie had drunk his in two gulps, as the cups were dainty. Carmel had not touched hers. Father Malone sipped. The longer Father Malone's cup lasted the more embarrassed was Eddie. His throat ached for another cup. He did not ask for one.

'You will not be able to consummate this marriage.'

Father Malone was talking to Carmel and Eddie as if he was thinking of Carmel and Eddie after they had departed the priory.

'Otherwise it will result in a child and, I'm sure you've realized, neither of you is in a position to bring up a family.'

The dangers of childbirth for the older woman was an issue he had never had much opportunity to raise. He was glad of the opportunity to do so with Carmel.

'You already have a child?' he asked her, as if she spoke a different language.

'She does, Father,' Eddie broke in.

'Can she not speak for herself?' Father Malone's eyebrow was raised to its quizzical and kindly position. It was a position the curate knew to be nervous of.

'She can, Father, but she doesn't talk to many strangers.'

Carmel was looking at Eddie. The more she looked at him the more his jaw tightened. She put a hand out to Eddie, who brushed it away, embarrassed.

'Well,' Father Malone watched all this and the more he watched the more he knew. 'Can you tell me how the daughter feels about her mother taking up with someone else?'

Father Malone had heard all about us. We had not even darkened his church or priory door since we had come back to the town and certainly he had received no invitation to darken ours.

'Well, the girl's her own woman, almost twenty, Father,' Eddie said. 'She's not depending on Carmel any longer.'

'And the girl's father?'

'Dead, Father.'

'How?'

Eddie had trusted my word on this and did not know how the father had died or when.

'Sive, the daughter, told me.'

'And Carmel didn't?'

'No, Carmel's sick, Father. She doesn't say or do much. I just want to look after her, Father, and I'll look after her better if I am married to her. She deserves that, Father. You know who her father was.'

Father Malone had been a curate himself when Joseph Moriarty had been alive. He had told Joseph's wife to go home to him more than once. She could not control him, that was all, or the child, Carmel, who had grown and remained strange.

'It sounds to me it is a good hospital she needs, not a husband.'

'I am able to look after her. Will you marry us?'

'I will,' Father Malone began and Eddie had the ghost of a smile. 'If you can produce her husband's death certificate and if we see you both for the next six months at Mass. For the banns to be read out. I see you there all right, Edward, but I have not seen Mrs — ?'

Carmel found some words, 'I wasn't married before.'

'Have you confessed your sins lately, Mrs — Miss — Moriarty?'

Carmel looked at Eddie. Eddie stood up.

'Will you marry us or not, Father?' he trembled in voice and body.

'I would ask you to remain seated, Edward. This is not a bar you're in now. I would ask you if you have considered that Miss Moriarty's spiritual condition is not great. Even great sinners who repent find forgiveness. Christ Himself looked for it. But Miss Moriarty,' he pointed steadily at her, 'Miss Moriarty, by her silence, indicates she is above it and, indeed, above marriage up to this point. Now,' he paused. 'Why change the habits of a lifetime?

222

Have you asked yourself who you have chosen to marry, Edward? You have not asked enough questions, Edward, that is all I am saying.'

'If you ask me, Father, you have asked too many,' Eddie said, as he and Carmel left. They walked briskly along the coast road.

'You will not be talked to, or about, like that again I can promise,' he spoke into the quiet of her round shoulder. 'We will live in sin and to hell with them all.'

But part of Eddie was thinking of the windows that he had to clean and the talk he would overhear through them.

'We've no need for papers, Carmel, we know how we feel.' He said it softly, as if the watching people were with them. 'We're a pair, Carmel,' he put a smile on her face with his warmth. She was happy when he was happy. She was anxious when he was anything else.

'Sure, we might as well be married already.'

★   ★   ★

That night over a boiled dinner, Father Malone had an argumentative stomach, the curate asked how it had gone with Carmel and Eddie.

'As well as could be expected,' Father Malone eyed him coldly and went back to severing his bacon fat from the lean in a most particular fashion.

26

To the Dead and Back

I thought of my obligations, my need for my job.
I did not look at Thomas for weeks. All the while
his eyes pierced into the back I kept towards
him. He did not make an attempt to put a hand
on me. His son was between us.

Once or twice when I left in the evening he
walked down the driveway behind me and did
not utter a word to stop me from going through
the gates.

Down the road of Pass If You Can I felt eyes
on me that I thought were his.

Thomas began to write letters to me. He was a
man of few words so he did not send them. But
I read them in my dreams and there were words
of love and promise that drove into the heart of
me and could not be taken out such was their
determination to stay.

Sister Saviour and Joe O'Reilly were delighted
with the now talking Thomas. He would offer to
help them, finishing his food first at each
mealtime and rising to collect cups and dishes,
then sweeping the floor. He made his own bed
and stripped the sheets off others with his one
hand.

Sister Saviour asked to speak to him.

'I see you are helping us, Mr Cave. Very good!

If only we had more of that we would have our work done in no time and plenty of time for other things!'

He did not like her shouting tone, but he nodded just the same.

'I wondered if perhaps you could be better preoccupied doing other things!'

Sister Saviour found the shortest way in conversation to be the best.

'Doing what?' Thomas asked.

'You are not spending much time with the men, Mr Cave! This is your home! You will have to learn to get along with those who share it!'

'I am not the same as them.'

'Oh, but you are!' Sister Saviour brushed invisibilities from her lapel busily. 'You are every bit one of them, Mr Cave! These men are every bit as good as you, Mr Cave. Do not attempt to put yourself above them.'

'I am not doing that,' he said quietly. 'I should point out, however, that I am not here because I chose to be here.'

'That makes you exactly the same as everyone else,' Sister Saviour returned. 'These men are every bit as proud as you, Mr Cave, they have just been here longer and learned to be less obvious about it.'

'What do you want me to do, Sister?'

'You are clearly an intelligent man, Mr Cave, you clearly have done a lot of travelling. They would certainly wish to hear about it and they might even share something in common with you.' Sister Saviour followed the remark with what she thought was a smile.

225

Thomas walked the grounds and came into lunch with his eyes full of thought. After lunch he retired to his cubicle, took up his pen, wrote a short letter to an address in Galway. It instructed a former colleague as to where he was and it wondered whether that former colleague could access some of his possessions.

Thomas explained where the key was hidden. He did not explain the situation with Jonah, except to say that he thought his son would have been too busy to handle this. He also wrote that he had no money with which to reimburse the former colleague.

The former colleague was John Coughlan and he had been the closest thing Thomas had had to a friend in his self-chosen life. Certainly he had admired Thomas, for all his aloofness, and certainly he would go to the cottage and see what remained of his collection and his equipment and personal possessions.

★ ★ ★

John Coughlan found he did not even need to use the key to get in, he found the cottage Thomas Cave had lived in exactly as it had been left over a year ago.

There was no reason for it to be otherwise. Though Thomas did not own the place he had paid ten years rent upfront. The sum he paid would have bought the property and left some change, but he had never owned a house and did not want one.

John Coughlan parcelled up Thomas Cave's

existence and drove to Dublin with a carload of possessions. He was surprised at how grateful Thomas Cave was to see him. He was surprised what almost two years had done to the man of before.

Thomas Cave had changed utterly. Dressed in dead men's clothes that were too short, he had the look of the mad, his body curled around a thin stick which before would have snapped in two with the bulk of him. Lines of loose flesh stretched between bones all too visible.

But the height and the hair were still there and a shadow of the old demeanour clung enough for John Coughlan to say, 'It's good to see you, Thomas.'

Thomas and John made hard conversation and John knew then that it was only the outer man who had changed. Thomas was still silent. He moved quickly, to bring the end of the visit nearer, filling Thomas's cubicle with remnants of his past, leaving him to sit among them as he hurried away with busy promises to return one day when he was up in the Dublin area again.

Thomas Cave looked at him with the noiseless stare all the ones left in these places give occasional visitors. A stare without small talk, without talk at all, which says they know it is a promise that will not be kept.

It came to John Coughlan only after he left the dark stretch of the midlands and the lights of the western city, which was home, came into view. John Coughlan knew that all he had acquired was worth giving away if he could simply have more time to be fit and whole and with his family. He felt a strange exhaustion that made him cold despite the blazing heater in the fine and comfortable car that cushioned him against the night and road.

He resolved to take an early retirement.

'Thomas Cave,' he said out loud as he pulled into his own driveway and saw the light pour out of his opened front door and the welcome outline of his kind wife in the middle of it. 'Thank you for going there before I did.'

★　★　★

I walked with the birth of the next morning against a sheet of driving rain and wind that carried with it the crying, dying leaves of autumn. My legs burned with the effort of pushing up the hill. It was as if the day knew what was to happen and it sought to turn me back from it.

But I had in mind to see Thomas and somehow to lay a new and touching hand on him, so that he might see I had not abandoned him. The more I pulled away from him the more I felt the pull towards him.

I curled my head into my chest and watched my feet take each slow step. I did not see the car until its headlights were almost upon me, their menacing shine spread over my shoes. I was in the air and it seemed the whole world was wailing and reeling before I felt emptiness.

I woke and I found myself on the back seat of a car. The taste of salt-blood in my mouth. I could not speak, my jaw clamped with a dull aching.

Jonah was sitting in the front seat, lighting a cigarette. Blue clouds of smoke filled the pale beige space. I stirred to shake the mist out of my head. Jonah turned, his muddy eyes were clouded.

'You,' he pointed a long and sharp finger at me, 'were not looking where you were going.'

I moaned. I could smell the stale whiskey now, under the fresh smoke.

'What will we do?' he asked me. 'What will we do now?'

I managed to make a noise like, 'Home.'

He brought me to Solas. He knew where to go. He had been watching me all the while.

I took the invitation of blackness.

★   ★   ★

I woke and found Carmel and Eddie sitting with me.

'She should be in the hospital,' Eddie was saying.

'Myrna says no need,' Carmel spoke in a scraping whisper. She was hunched up in the chair beside me, like a piece of discarded clothing. I could see she was weak with the need to sleep. When Myrna came in her eyes had shrunk into deep sockets. I found myself moving. I was still whole.

Myrna saw my eyes were awake and she placed her thumbs over them and leaned down to me and whispered known words into my ear that caused life's heat and movement to return.

'Welcome back,' she said, as she stood up and smiled with an unhidden caring.

Eddie and Carmel moved to see if I was the same person who had left my body seven days and nights ago to go to a place I could not remember anything of, except it had been a long way off.

In the intervening week much had happened.

★   ★   ★

Myrna opened the door. She looked at Jonah. He shifted and gabbled like a turkey about the wet of the day and not being able to see in front of him. He did not mention my name so she was left to form her own assumptions which caused her to push past him and wrench open the car door and cry out.

'How could you leave her there? Why did you not say something at once?'

She made to pull me out of the car, but had not the strength to. Jonah had to lift me out. Together they carried me into the house and put me down on my bed. Myrna felt me.

'She has grown cold already.'

She peeled off my stained and torn clothes and she felt Jonah's eyes watching.

'Go. Do not come back in here.'

Carmel and Eddie found a pearl-blue Jaguar parked outside, and inside the house a strange, all-eyed man sitting at their table.

'Upstairs,' the strange man said. He did not look at them.

They found the room filled with a smell like burning liquorice, and Myrna standing over my body, which was still but for the streaming of blood from my head and the rising of bruises that stole the shape of my face. She was sponging me with liquid from a bowl.

'What's the smell?' Eddie asked.

'Life fighting death,' Myrna spoke.

'I'll go for a doctor,' Eddie suggested.

'Too far gone for that,' Myrna snapped. 'Too far for doctors to reach her.'

Downstairs, the all-eyed man was gone, into the dark and dreadful day.

Myrna sat beside me for the days and nights I slept. And downstairs Carmel braved fire and made it serve a purpose by making food on it, which sustained Eddie and her into the long nights they kept watch.

★ ★ ★

The fourth day after the accident had already turned to evening when Jonah returned, with flowers. Myrna was sleeping for a while and Carmel had done the same, both exhausted. Eddie answered the door. He told Jonah to leave or to expect the police at any moment. Jonah saw that there was no phone and so took his time to explain to the small and angry man that he was not at fault in this. The girl had been in the middle of the road on a wet day and he had no time to stop. He had brought her here because she had asked for here.

'I know Sive, she takes care of my father at St

Manis Home. I was on my way to visit him.'

'At seven in the morning?' Eddie enquired.

'My father is very ill. I see him whenever I can. Could I please see her? I only want to give her the flowers.'

'She's no need of them now, she's out cold still.'

'Should she not be in hospital?' Jonah asked.

'That is what I said. No one ever listens to me around here.' Eddie sighed. 'I suppose a minute will do no harm. A minute, mind!'

'We should be bringing her to the hospital,' Eddie said on the way up the stairs. 'But they won't let me. They say wait. I'd hate to see what would happen to me if I got cancer. They'd probably give me an aspirin and a hot-water bottle.'

Jonah said, 'What do we know about women?'

In that moment, Eddie took a small step back into the man's world he so missed, felt the welcome logic of a sex he understood, even if this man was a strange example of it.

★ ★ ★

Jonah peeled back the sheet to examine the form that had caused a savage wanting in him. Since he had first seen me, he had watched and followed, staying far away, as he had learned to stay.

But he knew the time was on hand to draw near and claim what he had waited for all his life. He put his hands on me.

In that moment he felt a cold blade held

232

against his neck. He turned to find no one. He went to touch me again and the blade was there again. He moved away and out of the room. The ghost of Noreen Moriarty stood behind the door he had just closed, her eyes were such that, if he had seen them, Jonah Cave would have left for good and not come back.

But he did not see. When I woke, he resolved, he would speak to me and win me with the promises of all the things I could never have in this damp and old place.

Eddie was waiting downstairs with a whiskey bottle on the table. Jonah had been much longer than a minute.

Long hours passed in the kitchen until night had grown deep and dark. The ghost of Noreen Moriarty went and rose Myrna out of sleep. She would not let the old woman rest.

'Why should I get up? It's night,' Myrna groaned.

Noreen nudged her with an insistence that did not pass. Eventually Myrna, having looked in on me, came to the top of the stairs.

Jonah found himself standing at the sight of Myrna. As she came down the staircase he once more felt the cold blade against the back of his neck, the hollow echo of his disappearing spirit. Myrna saw the two silent men and a half-bottle of whiskey on the table between them, and without a word she opened the door and asked both of them to walk through it.

Jonah went to the door, but not before her eyes held his. In hers he saw all the emptiness he had known and her intention to bring him back to it if he returned.

Carmel woke next and when Myrna told her what had happened Eddie was not let back into the house. He spent a night in the barn.

'He's to be kept away, Eddie.' Carmel spoke to him in anger for the first time the next morning. Eddie had vanished down the road with Jonah in his pearl-blue Jaguar. A lovely car all the same. Jonah told him he had a good job when Eddie asked after what line of work he was in. Jonah paid for all the drinks.

Eddie did not see what was wrong with him at all. But he did not say that to Carmel. He said instead, 'It was an accident, Carmel, he told me what happened.'

Jonah had told Eddie several times, until Eddie had put his hands over his ears and said, 'Don't tell me again. I know.'

'We will have to wait for her to wake to find out,' Carmel said, filling a basin with hot water. She took a cloth from the linen press and went up to give it to Myrna.

'He does not seem a bad sort, Carmel,' Eddie called after her, then sat in the stew of his own anger and hangover.

When she came down, Carmel went to the kitchen and filled a pan with beans. She cut up some bread to make toast over the fire and poured hot tea while Eddie used an old wire coat hanger to do the job of toasting. As they watched the bread go golden brown, the moment did likewise. They grew warm to each other again and the food tasted well. He held her in his arms and they lay on the rug and drank steaming tea and kissed until her eyes turned to the stairs and who was up them and she rose to go and check.

'There isn't a stir out of Sive,' Carmel trembled with the cold of the upstairs. 'Myrna won't come down either. I said we'd take tea up to her.'

'I'll take it up, Sive will wake soon enough. She's strong that girl,' Eddie whispered, and put his arms around her.

Myrna came to the top of the stairs and called, 'She is waking.'

When I did it was with the fiercest hunger I have ever known. I ate the whole of a dozen eggs collected from the reluctant hens that had gathered around, acting as if they owned the place. I drank hot tea while the soda of the bread and the salt on my eggs sharpened me out of the sleep.

'Where did I go?' I asked Myrna.

'A long way off.'

She had a new weakness in her and something dark about her. The long wait had worn her.

27

The Voyages of Other Men

It was only after I was wakened that Eddie thought of going to see Sister Mauritius to explain I had an accident.

'You are lucky her position is not filled,' Sister Mauritius said. 'When will she be fit for work?'

He said he did not know but that I was wanting to come back soon.

★ ★ ★

Thomas was at his wits' end. His dreams had lost their colour and the sense of me in them was fading. He could not sleep when such bleakness awaited him. So he paced the corridors. He drank coffee with the night attendant who had handled him so roughly in former days and played cards with him.

Then he walked the gardens until the steel light of dawn crept up again. At the gates he stood, afraid to find in the wider world what he had truly become. In St Manis he was a well man, beyond he would translate into a sick and weak one.

'Have you left me without a word?' he whispered, after my disappearance down the long hill of Pass If You Can.

Sister Mauritius did not tell anyone of the accident. She wished first to get to the bottom of it before taking me back to work.

Two weeks passed without sight of me. St Michael's ward had been concerned at first and then all talk of concern faded when it seemed I was not coming back.

Thomas did not let this put him back to where he had been when I met him. He forced himself to go on and in going on he found himself poring once more over the details of his forgotten life. The images he had tried to piece together back in the little boxroom now were on hand and full in their display of life, colour, suffering, joy, darkness and death.

He opened the boxes, all labelled by assignment, country, year, a copy of each of the published articles relating to his work, clipped to the original material. He had been meticulous. Jonah's ring-binder efforts seemed patchy compared to this catalogue.

He marvelled at the blindness of his eyes and the hard nature of his heart.

How could he not have seen the whole world in the toothless grin of an old tribesman, his face too lined to go back in time and so many reasons for wanting to?

How could he have taken the photo of a young girl with a younger brother or sister bound by one piece of cloth to her back? How could he have taken it when her eyes told him not to?

He sifted through the years. He found not one trace of his humanity in them. Not one trace of him, even in the personal albums of small black

237

and white prints. These mounted on cream paper, captions underneath in copperplate handwriting: 'With the Jenkins in the Transvaal', 'With Declan O'Connor in the St George Hotel, Beirut', 'With Declan O'Connor in the Holy Land', 'With Sister Margaret Nolan on the Kitale Mission'.

With acquaintances and colleagues and subjects and with all parts of the world and with no one.

He had left a world without his mark. He wanted to rush out and advise the young about the terrible secret of the old. In a world that has grown indifferent to them they are not to be spared the pain of emotion. They can fall in love with all the feeling of their youth and none of the possibilities. Their clarity housed in decayed bodies that cannot hope to bring their thoughts to fruition. He found himself wishing to say what the old say many times over.

'Do all you can while you are young.'

But he knew, too, the young think they will never be old.

The eyes of another interrupted Thomas's thoughts and he turned to find Mr Black, known for the blackness of his moods and fag bumming.

'Is that Tunisia I see?' A gruff voice.

'It is,' Thomas replied.

'The ruins at El Jem?' A thin seam of excitement.

'Yes.'

'I was there, merchant navy, 1958. Through the Suez I'd just been. That was a wonder, that Suez. I took some photos myself but I had the camera stolen in Carthage,' Black's words rushed. 'Got any more to show me?'

Thomas had and by the end of the day Tony Black had seen many of them. Tony Black had been to many places.

'That's what I went around the world for, looking for a place to live in. Never found the one I wanted, so I went on.'

Thomas nodded. Tony Black tried to give him a smoke.

'Don't touch them? Well, no reason why you can't start now. All I can say is they got me leg,' he looked down at his stump, 'and they can fucking well have the rest of me. I'm not giving up my fags for no one! Mind you, since Mary Sive disappeared they've been harder to get hold of.'

Thomas did not answer.

Black picked up another album, asking with his eyes if he could look through it.

Thomas nodded.

'That reminds me of a girl I knew.'

'I was once in a place where . . . '

Then Thomas came to the last albums, alone, the men all gone to their tea and separate thoughts. One of them held the story of Soho women. Carmel and I waited with our shared green eyes.

'You,' he said. 'Grown.'

He put a thumb on the child's brow and watched the green eyes, grey in monochrome, but a green remembered. He stared at the green until the lights went out and then his memory stared on.

239

28

Myrna on Her Way

From the time of my dead sleep Myrna and I had not gone outside. I would not and she could not. She moved from bed to chair and from chair to bed. She held her cards against her chest and she muttered long words into the fire and they were carried out on the air. On her way.

She called me to her, crooking her long bony finger.

'Sive, Sive, listen to me now. When I was young I had a tall straight father who had white blond hair and a big fishing boat which took him out into the water. The water found him and his boat so fine it wanted them and it took them, leaving my mother and me all alone. And she died on the birth of another child while wailing for my father. Then the war came and I walked the world. I was alone in my wanderings. When I found you, Sive, I knew that you were already a woman, you had grown in ways I had never grown. You were alone from the first moment and you survived aloneness,' Myrna went on. 'But now is the time you will be tested most. All around the air feels close; I can barely breathe. It is filled with warning, Sive, and we must listen to it. Don't be alone, Sive. Take company over aloneness. Be close to protection.'

She was fading and I could not leave her.

* * *

Carmel came to me many days later and said, 'You need to get out again.'

I did not answer her. Eddie had helped Myrna to bed, in a downstairs room that we had made up for her, since she had grown too weak to climb stairs.

'There is no weight left in her at all.'

Myrna was disappearing before our eyes. There were shadows where life had once been.

'How can I leave Myrna?' I said to my mother.

'If you don't get back to work you'll have no work to get back to!' Eddie came in on us. 'We can't all four of us live off window-cleaning money.'

'I'll mind her,' Carmel promised. 'I'll look after her well.'

* * *

I made my way up the hill slowly, my ears and eyes searching for signs of Jonah. None.

The gates were a welcome sight for once; my body had lost strength.

Thomas was different. I found him talking easily with the men and I found him dressed in clothes of his own and the fit of them said he had grown into himself. He had put on weight and he had begun to use his bad arm.

I found the pain of missing him turn to a kick

241

of joy, which took the wind out of me. I could see his eyes fill with delight before he hardened them and turned away to continue his conversation.

Said Joe O'Reilly, 'That was a long holiday you had. We were not certain you were coming back.'

'It was no holiday.'

I went to Sister Mauritius.

'You took your time. I had a day or two more in me and then you were no longer employed here,' she said. 'You will find Sister Saviour gone to the missions. I am looking after your ward personally for the present.'

Her eyes said that whatever fight had been, Sister Mauritius had won it.

I went to Thomas then, who was lying on his bed.

'Have you Sister Saviour's address?' I asked. 'I would like to write to her.'

'I have, in the drawer there, help yourself. Could you pull the curtains round my bed?' he asked. 'I need to sleep.'

I did and remained inside them. He stood up and put his hand on me. I turned into him and he pulled me into his chest and I put my lips to it and my arms around him and we rocked slowly back and forth.

'Where have you been, girl? Where have you been?'

He wanted to tell me that he knew me, but when he moved back to look at me, he saw a sore turning to scar on my temple and he put his fingers to it.

'What happened to you? Where did you get

this? Who did this?'

'Nothing and no one. I fell.'

I did not tell him. I thought of the father and the son and the need for peace between them. I knew that the peace could not be reached if I told Thomas the truth.

'Thomas?'

'Yes.'

'Are you still of a mind to leave here?'

'More mind than ever,' he whispered.

'What are you to do about Jonah?'

'There is nothing I can do. He is the way he is,' the softness gone out of him now.

'And he was not always that way. Thomas — I want you to leave with me. But there is . . . '

'Sive?'

'Yes?'

'The café in Soho — what was it called? I have no memories of these things — only supposition.'

'Sergio's.'

'Sergio's, I do not remember at all. But I remember your eyes.'

'That,' I smiled, 'is only because you know them now.'

I heard the movement before I saw the broad feet at the edge of the curtain and knew Margaret was close at hand.

'You will have to rest now, Thomas,' I said loudly. 'We'll sort this out again.'

In the few days that followed we had no time to finish our conversation. But we had silent times together in the bathroom and it was all that we needed to know one another again.

243

Dear Jonah,

With all the chances I had to get to know you and not used, I don't know how this letter will be received. I only know the need both of us have to talk.

I am not asking you to do anything that you do not want to do. But if you would visit me we could at least reach some sort of agreement. I am sending this letter via the solicitor who facilitated the signing of my assets over to you. I do not know where you live now.

Yours
Thomas

With each passing day Thomas grew stronger in the knowledge he wanted to leave St Manis and make his way into the world again. Still, he knew he would not go empty-handed to me; he would make having him worthwhile. He would find a way for that.

29

Not Ready to Go on —
The Card of Passage

The hours Carmel had spent roaming were now put into Myrna. Eddie was left to fill in the times she was not with him.

It was something the years of window cleaning had trained him well for, to witness a world on the other side of the glass, a silent world which, when it spoke words, produced no sound at all to his ears.

He watched the woman he had always cared for. She treated the old and worn Myrna like a shining jewel. She spooned food into her and washed her with the love a mother shows for a child, took the shame out of the straight and unbowed Myrna's losing strength.

And Myrna thanked Carmel for her kindness.

'This is life,' Myrna said softly. 'Where one fades, another grows. You grow fine, Carmel, finer each day.'

'Don't leave us,' Carmel whispered.

'No intention of,' Myrna smiled.

When Carmel came to bed each evening she was bone tired. Eddie held her. In her stillness he felt the memory of the young girl come back to him and he pressed his lips to the hair that had lost its shine to all others but not to him. Though not aflame it bore the shadows of the flame that had once risen within her. He kissed the white skin of her shoulders, which in youth had the appearance and texture of pearls and in middle age was clouded pearl, sweeter for all the suffering it had endured and for all the love it was still capable of.

Sometimes she would murmur names and fight to put out flames which, in her sleeping, she insisted were consuming their bed. The dream flames had taken a little more of her by morning. She grew finer each day and she grew more tired.

'It is caring for Myrna has you worn out,' Eddie said to Carmel as she carried the breakfast tray into the back room, which Myrna rarely left now.

'It is not,' Carmel said.

'It should be Sive looking after her, you're not able.'

'Sive has looked after us all. Leave her have her time away from us.'

And that was how the talk went each morning. By evening there was too much tiredness to talk. The weeks turned to months.

At night I would sit with Myrna, sleep on the bed beside her. We did not speak, but the dreams passed between us and when I woke each morning I expected her breath to have left her. Then Carmel took on the caring the days required.

We three had established a rhythm of our own which Eddie could not follow. The rhythm of those who know all there is to know about the ones they travel through life with, the rhythm of lost souls preparing to lose one of their number.

While Carmel slept heavily one morning Eddie and I should have gone out the door together to work. But he chose to stay behind to let Carmel sleep and to spoon soft egg into Myrna's mouth. I was grateful to him and I felt Myrna's eyes on me as I left, eyes that reached through the stone wall from the back room and I did not turn back because what I wanted was ahead. I had now to see Thomas or my day had no brightness.

He had told me, in whispers, that he had known me. I nodded and smiled and watched who I was.

'How could I not have known you immediately?' he asked me as if I would know.

'We were to know one another again in a different time, and one day you will meet the woman who said that,' I promised. 'That will be when you come through my doorway.'

There was not time for anything else. Margaret's curious, bowl-shaped eyes were continually on us. Even our bathroom time was all looks through mirrors and not at each other.

Eddie broke pieces of white bread and made to give it to Myrna with the egg but she said softly and firmly, 'I will feed myself if I need feeding.'

'You need to eat. You don't eat if we don't feed you. You need strength,' Eddie replied.

'I have enough strength to go on for as long as

247

I choose to go on for,' Myrna smiled. 'But I could use a cigarette. I know you have one of those.'

Eddie weighed up Carmel's or my anger against Myrna's pleasure and lit up two cigarettes. Together they sat and smoked and Myrna even managed to drink hot sweet tea that brought a flush to her cheeks.

'Has there been any sign?' Myrna asked.

'Of what?'

'The man, Jonah.'

'No sign of him.'

Eddie felt ashamed to remember his inviting the man into the house at the end of an evening where he had paid for no drinks.

'I'll talk to the girls,' he had promised. 'They have to listen to a man sometime.'

He had been glad there was no visible sign of Jonah taking him up on his offer.

'Keep him away, Eddie,' Myrna broke through his thoughts. 'You must promise to keep him away, always.'

'I will. I will.'

He thought to do what he could, maybe have a word with Jonah's father, the next time he was in St Manis on his window cleaning, ask him to keep the son away from the place.

They sat quietly together. Neither heard Carmel stirring.

'It looks like rain today,' Eddie said mischievously, looking out at the unrelenting blue sky in a week that had been filled with grey ones. 'I might stay home.'

Carmel appeared in a half sleep and came to

248

sit by Eddie, taking his hand in hers, a smile just for him.

'Well, that's me decided,' Eddie said. 'It looks like it's going to lash all right. Will we go for a walk in the lashing rain, love?'

Carmel frowned and took a sip of his tea. The moisture on her sleep-hardened tongue was welcome.

'What about Myrna?' she asked.

'Myrna's much more herself today, aren't you?' Eddie winked.

'I am.'

They laughed all together. Carmel said, 'Were you smoking at this hour, Eddie?' and she went to get dressed.

Myrna took hold of her blanket and pulled it around her knees.

'Eddie, please could you get my box?' Myrna asked.

They left her shuffling the cards and they walked into the cool, crisp air that put a freshness on everything, although its fine blaze of red and gold was already browning, preparing to be stripped bare by the harsh and bony hands of winter.

They had not gone long when Noreen Moriarty came, wearing her sunflower hat at a determined angle. She took up the chair beside Myrna.

'You have an air about you today,' Myrna said as she shuffled.

Noreen nodded.

'Could you not just enjoy yourself in the other place and not trouble us for a few days? You seem to mean work for me lately.'

Noreen smiled.

'I have lived through times,' Myrna said in a voice that gave away all her years. She spread the cards on the table and one fell to the floor. Noreen picked it up. Myrna turned it over. The card of Passage.

'I am not ready to go on,' Myrna's hands shook as she pointed at Noreen to stress her insistence. 'I cannot go until I give that girl some sense. I know it is coming. She needs more sense and I will go then.'

Noreen continued to smile at Myrna. Her eyes said, 'These are not your concerns now. It is time to come away.'

Myrna grew angry, 'I would think that you would understand. She is your flesh and blood. You should protect her.'

Noreen rose and left by the door. She looked back and her eyes said, 'The next time, there will be no asking.'

* * *

Jonah read his father's letter and would have done little about it if the prospect of meeting me, away from the cold-blade eyes of old Myrna, had not come with it.

Jonah wondered whether his stranger-father meant to contest the financial arrangements. The solicitor assured him they were incontestable.

He could still feel the flood of soft strength that had run into him when I held him, the

250

protection it offered against his father's indifference. Now his father was writing lame and badly worded attempts at reconciliation and Jonah was not interested in those. He was interested only in the warmth that came with me.

There was plenty of money now; he could look after me now.

He poured himself a drink. It was almost lunchtime but he did not feel hungry. He worked it out.

If I had lived and woken it was a sign that he was meant to have me.

★   ★   ★

In my dreams that night I felt the one who watched me wanting to join me. All around black walls sprang up and I had no choice but to face his watching. I woke, wet with sweat, and went to Myrna's room — faint shadows all around her. She was sleeping like she would never wake. The breath so faint she barely breathed at all. She would be gone from me. The alone time was coming.

★   ★   ★

I heard the purr of the car coming towards me and I held my breath.

It came to a stop beside me. I continued to walk.

Jonah shouted, 'Please let me talk to you.'

He drove beside me at a snail's pace. He talked on and on about how he had not seen me,

251

how he had not meant to harm me.

I stopped then and turned to see his white face peering out. The boy lost in it. The wind snapped harder, I thought that if I got in I would help that boy. The wind lashed my legs together, pleading with me not to do it.

The back seat still had my bloodstains.

'I'll be getting it cleaned,' Jonah promised, as if he believed it was the car I was concerned about. He was overcome with happiness. He had found me on the road, before even reaching the home. More than a sign, it was a decision made.

If I had not got into his car to go the mile up the road I would not have taken the road marked out to this night.

Then I saw it only as a means of beginning the work I knew would have to be done between Jonah and Thomas. He talked. How well off he was, how well-regarded he was, how his life had only settled lately but he knew exactly what he wanted to do now.

I did not look at him. I stared out of the window and I watched the road-lining brambles as if they might never break and reveal the high stone pillars of St Manis's gates. My fear was still in this car, its markings on the back seat. I felt them call out: 'Get away!'

My head was pounding. The roar of ten drums in it. Even as the car snailed along I felt the wave of sickness and asked him please to stop and got out as all of my fear came out of me in a rush. The wind caught it and covered me and the side of his car. He came along beside me and cried, 'What's wrong with you?'

'I'm not used to cars.'

'Why did you get in if you felt sick?'

'You have other stains of mine to clean up,' I said, wiping my mouth.

I walked on and he sat in his car and watched me all the way until I had turned the corner and gone through the gates. I heard his car roar past, carrying all his anger with it. I went into the patients' washroom and sponged my coat and Margaret found me there. She gazed at me without blinking.

'Have another accident, did you?'

'It's nothing.'

I draped my coat on the heater, the steam rose off it and the air was filled with the strong smell of damp turning to dry.

Thomas came in, carrying his shaver and soap, it was not the scented kind of soap but it had its own distinctive smell of Thomas. He nodded to both of us and went to the mirror to lather up. I caught the lines of his back and I could not stop looking or wanting to look. Eventually Thomas barked, 'Can't a man shave in peace without two girls watching him? Does a man have no right to privacy in this place? Have you no work to be getting on with, the pair of you?'

Outside Margaret said old bastard and I agreed.

Joe O'Reilly was arguing with himself over who would wash out the sluice and bathroom and I said I would do it. I went into the washroom as the men sat down to breakfast and I found him there, still scraping at his chin.

'Well,' he smiled. 'That is the slowest shave I have ever had.'

I closed the door and the air was filled with the scent of my damp coat and I began to cry because it reminded me of Jonah and the fear. I did not know how to say it to Thomas. He came to hold me and I cried tears until they stopped.

'All this beauty and these tears wasted on an old man. Too much on your shoulders,' he whispered.

He knew who I was, but he did not know what went into making me. I had more than him to carry. Later in the day I found him with Black going through his pictures.

I saw the care that had been put into preserving these pictures and that this was the care that had restored Thomas to himself, a care he had no idea he possessed.

'You know, Thomas,' said Black. 'I would like you to take my photograph before I die. I would like you to do that. Take a picture that says I used to be good-looking, not a carcass.'

Thomas said he did not take pictures any more and Mr Black went quiet and the corners of his mouth were dragged down towards the death he knew was coming.

'It's a shame,' he said. 'When a man no longer does what he is good at.'

Later in the day I took up one of Thomas's photo albums for myself. The first picture was of a beautiful woman eating a strange fruit.

'It's dragon fruit,' Thomas told me. 'The Vietnamese eat it because they believe that it gives them the heart and the courage of a dragon.'

'What does it taste like?'

'Like a sweet and spongy nothing with seeds in it. It's the only way they can persuade themselves to eat it in my opinion. But they are a very brave people. If Black is right about me, then I need to get some dragon fruit.'

I smiled at him and turned back to the book of photos.

A thin black woman as long as life, wrapped in white cloth, her hands held up to her face, to shield herself from the light. She looked at me through her hands and I knew her as only those who have been to death and back know each other.

'She had a fever which had lasted six, maybe seven days,' Thomas told me. 'It was a sickness. All of them were dying. But the help didn't come. The people piled the bodies and burned them at night. The stench was terrible, and across the Mara you could see these bonfires and hear the people wailing all the night long. When I came to the village she was well, then she grew sick and during the whole of her illness I followed her, for a picture story to show what happens when the outside medical resources do not come. I thought that showing one would make more difference than showing many. We expected the last picture to be her body being placed on the bonfire. Her family were lucky, they had a shroud still, others had lost too many. They had already wrapped her up when I woke. She had become still and cool. They thought the death would be soon. The others had all had a sudden cooling before they died.

'But she was a strong woman. Her fever had broken and she walked out of her hut like this,' Thomas pointed to the eyes squinting through hands. 'The sunlight blinded her — she had been in the dark so many days. They said it was a miracle. They wanted me to take pictures of all their sick, to save them from death. They believed the camera had saved her. I pretended to take the pictures. They all died.

'I won an award for this picture,' Thomas said softly. 'I never saw this woman again.'

He cried because he had discovered that somewhere inside himself he had indeed carried them all, all those he had photographed.

I put my arm around him and his shoulders shook. Sister Mauritius found us that way. I was called into her office once more and she said, 'First I find you with your arm around the son. Now it is the father. You are on your last warning. If you do not behave appropriately then you are not fit to work here.'

'He was upset, Sister. I comforted him.'

'We are in the business of looking after, not comforting.'

When I came back to the ward Jonah was sitting at Thomas's bedside.

30

Paid Twice to Look Once

Jonah was staring at the albums, asking his father where they had come from.

Now the son had come to his bedside the father could find no words to say to him.

'I asked you where you got these?' Jonah repeated.

'From a friend who had kept them for me,' Thomas finally spoke.

'What else have you hidden away?' Jonah said, standing above him.

'Well, that would be my own concern,' said Thomas. 'But I will tell you that you need not worry about money. You have every penny.'

'Where is Sive?' Jonah asked. If Thomas knew about the accident he had not mentioned it.

'She's with the matron,' the guarded note in Thomas's voice.

'I gave her a lift this morning. Did she tell you that?'

'What were you doing around here at that hour?'

'Coming to see you, Father, but she vomited all over my car so I had to go and have it cleaned. She's not used to cars, did she tell you?'

'She did not. Leave her alone, Jonah. I am warning you. Any trouble you bring should be brought straight to me.'

'Oh, I do not want to be any trouble to her,' he smiled.

'You can't help it. It's in your nature.'

'But this is not the way to talk to your son, Father. This is not the way to talk to a son you write a letter to, asking to see him, to talk.'

Thomas got out of his chair and sat on his bed, offering Jonah the chair. He did not like his son towering over him.

'I wanted to explain some things.'

Jonah drew himself out of the chair and sat on the arm, so his gaze was level with his father's.

'Plenty of time to discuss things again. I mean to visit a lot more than I have done.'

'I am going to leave here soon, make a home elsewhere. I do not want you to follow me. I do not want you to think I have anything more to give you,' Thomas could not help but speak. 'I want you only to know that I will never come after you for what you took from me. It is yours and you are welcome to it.'

Jonah looked at his father a long while. Then he said softly, 'I would prefer it if you stayed here.'

'You have no say in what I do.'

'I have plenty of say. You have no money. I pay for you to stay here and without that money you are on the street with nothing for company but the creaking of your bones.'

Thomas smiled at this.

'For all the son you claim to be you do not know me. I am plenty more than my money.'

Jonah rose, did not leave Thomas enough room to rise.

'I have my reasons for wanting you here. If you do not stay you will be worse off for it. I will find you.'

And he was gone, saying, 'I'll just see if the girl wants a lift. She must be heading home soon.'

'You leave her alone, Jonah.'

Jonah could not find me. I had hidden when I saw the car.

'Why did you not tell me he met you this morning?' Thomas knew where I would be; in the washroom.

'Now is not the time to talk about this, Thomas,' I pleaded. 'Sister Mauritius has me on my last warning.'

'Keep away from him, Sive!' Thomas's voice rose. 'He is dangerous.'

'Do you think I do not know that? That's why I asked you to speak with him. But you only make things worse between you. He is your son and you make things worse between you.'

'He is not my son. How many times do I have to say it?'

Thomas's eyes held an aching, an aching to hold me and to put the wrong he was continuing to do, to rights. But he saw I would not come to him and he left me to put on my coat, which had hardened with the day on the radiator.

I walked home through the fields, to avoid the road. I took the same way to work the next morning.

★ ★ ★

259

Jonah waited on the road for two hours the next morning. No sign. He drove up and down the narrow twisting road. He killed a sparrow, its tiny heart gave way as the pearl-blue monster with the shining eyes swallowed it up, mashing its heat and feathers into the cold and uncaring road.

Jonah parked his car by the gate and began to pace and smoke. He had not been able to sleep that night. He had thought of all the possibilities and had decided there was only one way with me, the right way.

He would become perfect for me. He would not make mistakes. If I was fond of his father then his father could be brought to live with us and he would make all of this work for me, make all of this right for me.

He knew he would have to work hard to win my trust. He thought of the shape of me and of the smooth skin that held that shape. He could buy clothes for my fine shape and dress me up and take me to fine places where I would be treated like a someone, instead of someone who slaved for those who were beyond thanking me for it.

He took his last cigarette and crumpled the empty packet, throwing it to the ground, and turned to shelter his lit match from the wind. I walked across the lawns, from a gap in the hedgerow. The flame burned towards his fingers and caught the tips of them and burned on and he did not feel it.

He stared at me disappearing into the building without a glance to left or right and he knew I sensed him and he saw the fear in the sensing. He got into his car, drove a short distance up the drive and parked it in full view of every window. Margaret was inside the door of the porch.

'You are not allowed to visit now,' she said. 'It's after ten o'clock the visiting starts.'

'Then I will wait.' He smiled a thin smile and asked her, 'Do you have cigarettes?'

'In the tin shop-box, but that's not open until ten either, when the men go to the dayroom and the sister comes with the key.'

'Will you open it now?' he asked, waving a five-pound note at her. 'And keep the change.'

Margaret took the money, found the sister, got the key, opened the box and scampered back with the cigarettes with all the joy of a dog that has learned to retrieve.

'Well done,' Jonah smiled and Margaret looked away, nervous of that smile. 'Would you like one?'

'Don't smoke,' Margaret sat on the bench beside him.

'What do you do here, then?' Jonah asked.

And Margaret told him. He nodded for the several minutes it took her to tell him and he asked if she would like to earn more money. She said yes, because the wages were shite in here.

Then he told her how she might earn more.

'I have to go now,' she said, 'wait here till ten,' and she laughed so her teeth and gums were bared and she danced a little and said in a whisper, 'Paid twice to look once. I can get rich at this.'

31

Like Old Times

It took me some time, when I came through the door, to place the two strange women sitting at the table with Carmel and Eddie. Myrna was in a chair by the fire, roused by the visitors' appearance from a bed she had not left for weeks.

'Well, how do you like that.' The one with the bright dyed-blonde hair said to the one with the black-dyed hair. 'She don't recognize us.'

'Well,' the dark one said. 'I wouldn't recognize her. She's gone different. She's got like a proper woman.'

Lulu and Fanny. In our kitchen.

'You might,' Fanny said, 'give us a hello. We come a long way to get it.'

Eddie looked like he was about to fall through the floor. Lulu had her knee and thigh pressed against his. He was not sure if it was rude to move it away. I embraced them. Lavender sweets and cheap scent and cigarettes were still part of their lives. Lulu did not smell of the vodka she drank from small bottles kept in a handbag, still pristine patent leather, still with plenty of pockets to hide a life's contents.

'You look as well as ever,' I told them.

Their hair colours were finding it harder to

hide the grey. They seemed paler. Lulu was putting on more make-up now. Fanny's blonde hair was new, at odds with the worn look of her clothes. She saw me looking.

'I got it done special. I said to Lulu, 'I have their address and I expect they'd like to see us after these months going by.' We sent a card. Well I wrote it, Lulu sent it. Didn't you, Lou?'

Lulu sniffed at Fanny's obvious annoyance that she had not got around to posting it. She picked at her nails and grinned at Eddie in a way that made his ears burn. 'Got a light, lad?'

She shoved her cigarette into his face. Fanny talked nervously.

'So sorry for turning up unexpected, Sive. We thought you would meet us at the bus. Well, I thought you would meet us at the bus. I gave the dates up and all on the card . . . '

'They look like they fuck their brothers and sisters in this town,' Lulu said.

Eddie's neck burned now. Carmel looked down at her hands.

'Easy, now, Lulu, in front of Carmen's chap,' Fanny said in a pleading tone.

'Fancy Carmen having a fella and a big house,' Lulu continued as if it was polite conversation. 'You never know with the quiet ones, do you? They always do well for themselves. Though this place could do with a lick of paint. It's nice, mind. I never liked the country meself. City girl me. Leeds and London, me.'

Lulu's voice trailed away, then, 'Got a loo?'

'Outside,' Carmel pointed.

'Lovely,' said Lulu, raising her eyes to heaven.

'We'll have an inside one soon enough,' Eddie promised. 'I'm getting around to making one of the upstairs rooms into a bathroom.'

This was the first Carmel, Myrna or I had heard of it. Eddie, up to this point, had seemed to like his tin baths in front of the fire and his long trips out to the toilet.

Fanny took Lulu's absence as an opportunity. 'I kept your address in my purse all this time. I didn't want it to be the last we saw of you. Lulu's had her fair share of trouble since and so have I, I need not tell you. Lulu did a little bit of business for a fella. Her own wasn't going so well you see. More girls coming up all the time. So she did a bit for this man. Messages. Got a bit sticky and she almost got caught. So I says, 'Right — time to go on a little holiday and let things settle. Time to go and see our friends in Ireland.' '

Fanny pulled at the bread slice on her plate. There had been no biscuits to offer them.

'Everything is more difficult these days. You girls would not recognize the place. Full of business people doing it all big. It's a good job that I'm near pension age. Still,' Fanny raised her cup with tears in her eyes. 'It's good to see the old girls doing so well for themselves,' she looked around uncertainly. 'Though, like Lulu, I'm not country material. Nearest I get to country is a trip to Bethnal Green to feed some ducks, only there weren't none. Ha.'

When Lulu came back from the toilet with brighter eyes, Fanny went, asking Carmel to come for company, 'I'm scared of the outdoors.

What if something bites me?'

Lulu made a beeline for Eddie, but he was up and out the door, with an excuse to mend or buy or fetch something. Lulu sat at the table, opposite Myrna and me, facing us.

'I didn't want to come here. That's why I didn't send the card. But once she was coming I couldn't let her go alone. I live with her now you know. She drives me mad with her talk. Not one of those girls she had stood by her. The first two let off at her for being on the game. The third one ran off to get married to a fella you wouldn't piss on.

'The last one, Sive's age, wild she is. Fanny wouldn't let that one out of her sight these past months. She's bold as brass, gone into all sorts, drugs and what not. I don't mind telling you I'm glad I hadn't a child. Not one that lived anyways. They treat you like shite, but for Sive here. Sive's a good girl aren't you, Sive?'

I made sandwiches.

'Here, they looked at us like we were circus animals, getting off that bus. They never see a good-looking woman before?'

Lulu laughed at herself, and took out her compact. She put on lipstick with shaking hands, tutting with annoyance and dabbing the mistakes out with the corner of a hanky.

Fanny and Lulu settled into my room and I slept in the bed beside Myrna.

Getting washed and ready for bed was an affair. With so many women in the kitchen Eddie said, 'I'll rinse me neck under the cold tap outside.'

'I might try that.' Lulu went to totter after him. But Fanny held on to her skirt firmly. Later that night I heard them arguing upstairs. Like old times.

★ ★ ★

Fanny and Lulu made the house seem brighter and smaller. It was my weekend off and Eddie, Carmel and I took our guests into Scarna to show them the town and the town's eyes near fell out at the sight of them.

'A fucking dump, this is,' Lulu puffed smoke and pronounced. 'My old mam was right to leave Ireland.'

'Your old mam had no choice,' Fanny reminded her.

We had just left the drapery where Lulu had left the proprietor purple with rage having tried on everything in the shop and pronounced every item a rag.

'It depends,' said the proprietor, with her face stuck firmly in her accounts ledger. 'On what sort of person is wearing them.'

'I wouldn't wipe my arse with this,' she said cheerfully to the proprietor who went to Mass each day before opening up and took confession twice a week.

Eddie and Carmel went to wait outside.

'It depends,' Lulu smoothed her hair and waistline in one practised movement. 'On whether you have a waist or not. I happen to have one and that makes everything in here the wrong shape. Barrel shaped everything in here is, wouldn't you say, Sive?'

I wouldn't and hustled Lulu out.

'That one,' Lulu said smartly, 'has been humping herself on pokers all her life. She should try a hot one to warm her up.'

'That one,' I reminded Lulu, 'is Mrs Scully and Mrs Scully is the mother of five children. Her shop is one of two places where we can buy our clothes. After that performance there is only one place where we can buy our clothes.'

'Good so,' Lulu insisted. 'I'll go there next.'

Fanny and I followed at a pleading distance and Eddie and Carmel said they would see us in the Harbour View Hotel.

In Rose's Fashions, Lulu charmed Rose with a commentary on the quality of her garments. Rose, who looked no different to the thick-waisted Mrs Scully and sold clothes no different to Mrs Scully's, blushed deep and long.

'I dressed in Paris stuff all me life and this is Paris stuff. I'm telling you,' Lulu wagged her finger at Fanny and me, 'these are the clothes to buy in this town, a lot better than the rags at that other place.'

Rose nodded her head, because she could not say it, it was not good business practice, but she knew it to be true.

'You.' Lulu pointed at Rose so violently her handbag tipped off her wrist and over her index finger and on to the ground; the naggin bottle quickly stuffed back by Fanny who bent down to pick it up as soon as it fell.

'You!' Lulu repeated louder, 'have the eye for fashion in this town. Sive, this is the place to come for your clothes. This woman can look after you. I know a good outfitter when I see one. Mr Chanel himself looked me over for fashions. I'll be telling all London about this shop.'

Then Lulu left without buying anything.

'Sorry, Sive,' Fanny said quietly as we followed Lulu down the road to the Harbour Bar. 'She's always lively in the mornings. She'll be ready to sleep by tea time. I thought if things had worked well for you here that you and Myrna might have Lulu for a bit. I'm just not able to manage her as well as I used to. She insults anyone who doesn't know her well enough to know she doesn't mean it. Don't worry, Sive,' Fanny saw my look. 'I can see it's not the thing to leave her here.'

We walked into the lounge area to find Carmel and Eddie in easy chairs on either side of the fire that was lit all year round. The Harbour Bar lounge had always had a fire in the lounge for the lady drinkers, regardless of whether it was July or January. Noreen had stood around it with her small wedding party while Joseph Moriarty had repaired to the men's domain.

When Lulu pulled up a chair between Carmel and Eddie's, Eddie immediately got up and said he was going to the other part. Lulu immediately went after him.

'You can't,' Eddie lost patience and turned on her. 'It's no women in the bar.'

Lulu stood rooted to the spot as Eddie made his way through the gents, which had a double entrance into both bar and lounge.

'Well, we will see about that,' she said and set

off in the same direction.

'Lulu!'

Fanny called idly after her, sat down and sighed and pulled up both feet to rest them on a table.

'Well I'm buggered if I'm following her in there.'

Carmel, Fanny and I sat quietly drinking a pot of loose-leaf tea and waiting for scones that never arrived. The noise of male laughter and a shrill female whinny came from the bar. Carmel asked, 'What is she doing?' and Fanny said she had no idea.

'No dragging her out of there,' Fanny said resignedly. 'Best be off and let her follow.'

We had been home at least two hours and had Myrna chuckling with recounts of Lulu before Lulu arrived home with Eddie.

'He's a good boy, your Ed,' she said to Carmel. 'Told me all about you two on the walk home. A windy walk if ever there was one! Told me you were childhood sweethearts. I wish I could look mine up. He's married. Mind you, he was married when I was his sweetheart.'

Eddie went to sit beside Carmel who took up his hand.

'I met an acquaintance of yours, too, Sive, a Peter, said he lives where you work. Lovely man. Lovely man.'

When Lulu had passed out on the chair, Eddie told us how she had told the customers of the Harbour bar about her singing career in London. She had given anyone who wanted one a song and sat on their knee while singing. When

Eddie had tried to remove her Lulu was not the only one to protest. The Harbour bar regulars on a Saturday afternoon found this better entertainment than the company of themselves.

Lulu hadn't to buy a drink all day.

'I believe the manager was after me for a spot,' she insisted to Eddie who had walked her home before she needed carrying. The regulars were wondering how long she was in the town for.

'I told them,' Eddie insisted, 'that it was a one-off performance.'

He looked at Fanny.

★ ★ ★

The following day I felt the air in St Manis was lighter.

'It's Sister Mauritius,' Margaret filled in. 'She's away for the week at a conference of her order. Didn't tell us so we wouldn't know.'

'I bumped into your Auntie Lulu in the Harbour bar,' Peter came up to me in the ward kitchen. 'Lovely lady, real lady. Sang 'Hello Dolly' better than Barbra Streisand. Lovely lady.'

Peter walked off, whistling. I shook my head and poured jugs of water into the tea urn and turned it on, ready to brew up for the men's breakfasts. When Joe O'Reilly found me he had a clipboard. Sister Mauritius's departure gave him matron status, being a full-trained nurse.

'There's a problem with tonight. The night help just phoned in sick. That leaves a problem with tonight.'

I took time in offering. To show enthusiasm

would raise suspicion.

'You're a grand girl, Mary Sive. You can sleep for most of it once the men are put to bed.'

I had no need for sleep. At home I asked Lulu if she'd like to come to where I worked for a little party.

'A little one, Lulu, with no noise. Otherwise I get the sack.'

'And what about me?' Fanny demanded. 'My party girl days are not over I hope.'

'Fanny,' I smiled. 'They are only just beginning. Follow me up the road an hour after I leave.'

★ ★ ★

St Manis Home at night was quiet from eight onwards. On St Michael's ward the men had been put to bed regardless of age or condition. Even Peter and Thomas, the most able-bodied of them, were ordered to be under the covers. Most evenings, Thomas would slip out to play cards with the attendant, or into Peter's room to talk about the few things they had in common. The conversations were shorter than the ones he shared with Black. Thomas was with Peter in his room.

'Peter. That party you said you wanted. It starts in an hour.'

In sixty minutes his room had a record player, a small selection of scratched favourites, a couple of bottles of whiskey, cigarettes, chocolate and some crisp bowls. Peter's bed was pushed against the wall and Black had been roused, none too happily, from his sleep, as had one or two others.

The men were assembled in their dressing gowns, but their hair had been combed and Ted had kindly let them all have use of his aftershave. They were as excited as the children they had once been and long since forgotten.

I walked down to the gates to meet Fanny and Lulu who arrived clutching at each other and screeching at the slightest rustle of wind.

'No fucking lights, 'cept for one car that nearly took me legs off,' Lulu raged. 'You might have told us! Fanny has her nails dug into me arm bone.'

'I have not! What about you leaping into my arms when the car went by, bloody great Jag it was!'

I went still and cold, but there was not sign of it now.

'Come on, girl! Lead us to the drink and dancing,' Lulu marched ahead.

I took them in the side entrance, on strict instructions to be quiet.

'We know how to be that when we have to be,' Lulu said, and moved quickly.

Fanny pulled at my sleeve.

'How do I look, Sive? A long time since I went to a party.'

'Well,' I fixed a bright hair lock behind her ear. 'You're as nice-looking as I've ever seen you.'

Fanny and Lulu and all the girl inside them that had never had the chance to come out, walked ahead of me. I looked up at Margaret's room. No light. Asleep at the same time as the inmates, as Joe would be.

They tripped over each other and giggled and shushed. I wondered whether it was a good idea at all, having them there.

Then I saw the men's faces as I opened the door to Peter's room and I knew it would be all it was meant to be and more, in those hours after dark when they played music and took turns to dance with the female company. After the whiskey was gone I made tea and they drank it like it was whiskey. The noise was kept low. They knew what the rules were. Lulu draped her silk scarf over the harsh light from Peter's lamp, 'for atmosphere'.

Thomas and I danced. I asked him if he remembered the two women and he shook his head and they shook theirs. I got his album and showed Fanny and Lulu. Everybody was so young they said.

Everybody was young now. It was a night that lasted a long time and when I packed two women through the gap in the hedgerow, to walk home through fields and tear their tights and curse me as they ground high heels into soft earth, the grey light of morning was already on us.

★ ★ ★

We saw Fanny and Lulu to the bus stop, Carmel, Eddie and I. Myrna had given them a long goodbye and a present each, wrapped in cloths.

'Enough for both of you,' she smiled. 'But don't open them until you're on the ferry.'

'We will come again,' Lulu promised. 'If we're

welcome.' Fanny added.

'You're more than welcome, ladies,' Eddie spoke. 'Next time we'll have an inside toilet.'

Lulu turned away before we saw the tears, Fanny had no trouble with us seeing them. Inside the bus they got a seat together and as it pulled off I saw them open their cloths. Working women have been trained to examine contents long before a giver intends them to. Both mouths opened. Then they rapped on the glass and showed us — two rings, with stones larger than most.

'Costume jewellery?' Eddie asked.

'Must be,' I said, Carmel and I looking at each other.

32

Blood and Hair and Fire Flowing

Without Lulu and Fanny the house grew quiet. My mother went into a long silence. The last thing Lulu had whispered to her had been, 'You should marry that Eddie, or someone else will. Not many men like him.'

Carmel took to walking on the strand, with nothing to keep her from the growing cold but a thin piece of cloth, which the wind snapped at. The autumn was well in. The sky filled with the Vs of departing birds and panicked swarms of starlings that called to each other: 'Where will we go to hide from the cold?'

Receiving no answer they clung to the ivied gable end of the house. In the late dusk they screamed and chattered high alarm and not one of them with a mind to do anything about it but be close to the next one.

My mother did not cling, but went out as she had done in the days of before. When he came home from work, Eddie had his dinner alone most nights now. Carmel was off just as soon as she put it on the table in front of him. The sun was setting earlier each day and she went to the beach to be with it in its dying moments and then she would not come home. Sometimes Eddie went to look for her and more times he

275

did not, for she could not be found. He listened to his radio and read his paper and sighed.

I knew what was in my mother's heart. She knew that life had stopped and was moving backwards and she feared that. For the past was filled with people she did not wish to meet. The ghost of her mother was often with her and she cried out to her in the night air of the woodland, 'Keep them from me.'

But Gomez and Joseph were not far, their blade eyes cutting into the back of her. She went to the beach for the heron and it did not come and it did not give her the stillness she needed, the life she needed.

Carmel Moriarty, alone still, after a life of alone time.

I asked Myrna why it was happening and she told me the walls between worlds are thin. There are places where the past still exists and the future has already begun and ended. I did not like what Myrna said. I asked her to give me the cards that I might determine what would happen. I might have the power now to push my mother out of the madness and guide her to the peaceful.

'The cards are the last thing that I will give you.'

Myrna spoke sharply, her spit was dry and formed in white beads at each corner of her mouth. 'Not yours until I am gone.'

'I only want to help my own mother. How is that harmful to anyone?'

'Leave the cards to their work and you get on with yours.'

But while Myrna slept I took them from their box and went to sit by the fire I sit at now. I turned over the first.

It was nothing but red. Blood poured out and over my hands and on down over my clothing and blood poured from my temple and I screamed but no sound came. Then the strands of red hair the same colour as my mother's came and twisted around my fingers and entwined around my arms and made to encircle my neck and choke the life out of me. Then thin licks of orange flame sampling my fingertips, turning them black, and still my scream could not find a way through.

I cried out to Myrna and my cry was heard. I heard her moan and open the door with a slowness that must surely mean I would die before she came. But she came and she wrenched the card from me and spat on to my hands and the fire and blood and hair shrank and disappeared without trace.

I trembled. She spoke with barely a voice at all, 'You were told. How can I teach you when you will not learn?'

'But I have learned! I have learned about Carmel, what you knew all along and kept from me.'

'I know, child, and I know there is nothing to be done, nothing I can do.'

'Who will do this to her, Myrna? Who? Answer me.'

She put a hand up.

'I cannot answer because I am bound up in this ending too. The cards can't tell.'

And it came to me then. It came to me why she would not have spoken to me of this.

'It is not you that brings this death. It is me. It is Jonah Cave who will cause this.'

'It is not told. The cards say only that Jonah is the one who watches. And his eyes are everywhere.'

'I will not see Thomas.' I was not listening to her. I was lost in my own talk and thoughts. 'I will leave St Manis, leave this house. We will go to live in Eddie's house.'

'Your mother will die there just as surely as if you had killed her yourself. She belongs here. This is her place. She will never leave it, even if you take her away, she will come back.'

I listened and knew what Myrna said was true. I had no power to change my mother, only to look after her.

'If I do not see Thomas, then Jonah cannot harm us.'

'Sive,' Myrna used my name, her black eyes now turned to a clouded grey. 'Your mother has been with men worse than Jonah. It could be one of these comes to get her. Dreams can be as bloody as reality. We cannot know which comes for her. The cards do not say. But you are bound to Thomas Cave. The cards say that. Your mother's death may come from her aloneness, from the dreams and fire of before.'

She came to me then, whispered softly, 'It is not possible to change your mother's heart, any more than it is possible to change your own. You must walk your own way, Sive, go where the heart follows.'

278

Myrna then went to rest. So little left of her. I was taken by longing and rushed out into the night, calling for my mother. No sign of her. Eddie looked out of the window of their bedroom.

'What are you at? You know she's off. Quit the noise! I have to be up in the morning. Get to bed!'

'I will not get to bed, Eddie! You get up and go find her. You help me find her.'

He got his trousers on, and his bad temper with them, went off into the night pulling on the coat I threw at him.

'I have had it with you all,' he warned. 'I need to go back into the town where there's peace!'

'You'll go no such place,' I shouted after him. 'You'll be with her night and day now and make sure nothing happens to her.'

I went back into Myrna's room. She sat up in the bed looking at me, her eyes half closed with a tiredness that never left her now.

'I have thought of a way, Sive,' Myrna whispered. 'A way to bring Carmel out of aloneness. What is her heart's desire?'

I looked at the old woman and the kindness all around her.

'She wants to be married to that little man, more than she wants anything else,' Myrna answered her own question. 'I can give her that, still. It will help her, Sive, I am sure of that.'

I believed Myrna, because I wished to and because she would never lie.

★　★　★

When Eddie came in he had Carmel by the hand and she was talking the talk of all the time she had stayed quiet.

'She has the ear bent off me,' Eddie smiled. 'She leapt up on me and I walking down the Gamble's wood way. She had me out of my skin!'

I knew it would be different now. Myrna called for Carmel and Carmel went.

Carmel came out of the back room.

'We can be married, Myrna says. She will marry us.'

'With a wave of her magic wand,' Eddie muttered.

He stoked the fire and put on more sticks to start it up again.

'We might as well get up before the rest of the world. Put on the kettle, Sive. I'll grab what eggs I can from the ladyships. If I am to be married I will need some breakfast, as will my little wandering wife!'

★　★　★

Carmel took the walk as if she had not taken it before, as if each thing so familiar was new and unseen. She walked slow from the back of the house, up the sloping field and into the woodland and I walked with her.

It was autumn and Carmel's fire was all around her and the blaze of the trees was answered by her in the high flush of her cheeks and they were young girl cheeks once more. No longer white and without life or interest.

She had been this way since the night before, since the news that she would marry Eddie. He had felt the heat of long ago rise in him too. He knew this girl that Carmel had become again better than any of us and the ripe expectancy of her. It had not occurred to him until she returned that he had missed her so and that every day that he had spent with the shadow woman, was a reminder that she was long gone.

The girl hid behind the lost lines in Carmel's face and the worn lines of her body, she taunted him with the occasional, teasing glimpse or movement that had once held all suggestion and love. The younger woman had loved him with her fullness, the older woman loved him with an aching.

On this day it seemed all of this aching was behind them. The high hope of the young ones had returned and made the bodies marked by ageing glad of it and, for now, able to bear and even forget what time had done to them.

Carmel Moriarty. Autumn was hers. She had lost years but she had the riches of surviving them, in this day, as her reward.

She was called, now, to her woodland, her familiar, and she answered that call. It was as if the vibrant nature of her hair, the wildness that had been stolen from her, had been offered to the trees and they had taken the offering and held it close to them and called to her: 'We are grown old. We are soon to be stripped bare. We fill the air with our blood-seeped leaves and we cover green and earth for you as a welcome back to us.'

The wind issued the invitations, lifted its skirts and ran calling through the woodland that the girl was come back, one of their own. And the wind called that the small, dark man who waited for her return just as the woodland waited, he should be welcomed too, as her chosen one.

And I walked behind my mother, Carmel, up through the high, sloping field where I had learned to hear so well. A heron perched on a rocky outcrop came to rise and fly when it saw Carmel advance in a pale cream dress, bought that day in Rose's Fashions. Her feet bare and her head bare but for the last of the roses we had pinned in her hair. The last roses, a deeper red than the darkest blood, to crown her.

The heron flew over the path of Carmel's progress, its shadow fell across her and she raised her eyes and shielded them against the brilliant sun. She stopped and turned to make out its flight and descent. It flew to the beach of beginnings, over the sea and far from sight.

On she went, followed closely by me and I asked her softly if she was glad that this was her wedding day and she smiled.

'I am not a pretty, young bride. But I am a happy one.'

Our party walked through the rustling trees, to the clearing and the oak under which Carmel and Eddie had come to know each other. It was there that Myrna and Eddie waited for us. Eddie, wearing his one suit that he had worn on single days spaced far apart from each other, since his eighteenth year. He had not put on weight, for he was an active man who worried.

The tall frame of Carmel came towards him, sure in her step, and his eyes filled with the tears no man of his kind dare shed in company. But he shed them now, in the company of women and woodland. She so thin, more a shadow than ever, but the vibrancy of old times was in her eyes and the trees knew her real beauty and they showered their leaves on her like confetti and she smiled.

When Carmel came into his open arms and leaned into him he cried more and she was like the willow that reaches down to gaze at the moving water, and in his eyes she found her own reflection with the years taken off her. Restored in him. Restored.

And for Eddie Burns, Carmel Moriarty was all she had ever been or could be. And for Carmel Moriarty, she had all she ever wanted.

Myrna sat in the chair that Eddie had carried for her from the house, before he had gone back to carry her. She was light now, lighter than air. All bones and eyes.

Now she stood. Eddie had wrapped her woollen blanket around her shoulders and I had pinned it with a silver brooch of hers. I had brushed her long, grey hair out of its coil and it ran like moonlight on night water over thin shoulders.

Myrna raised her arms, trembling. She was the dead come to life, so pale the sun shone through her bare arms making the bones visible. She could have been a dead one were it not for her wet lips and the moisture pearls appearing on her forehead.

She spoke and we knew her voice, clear and

sure, without the tremble her body had taken on. The wind quieted to hear it.

'In this place,' Myrna said, 'they came together. Beneath this tree they knew each other. The place knows Carmel and Eddie and they know the place. They are part of each other. This, then, is a match in nature's eyes. Let us say you are married and let no one say different. Carmel and Eddie. Married now.'

Myrna sat then and Carmel and Eddie embraced and I was witness to the union under autumn sun and under kinder circumstances than my mother had ever known. I embraced them.

Eddie gave Carmel the same ring that had been his mother's. We talked some time there and the wind talked with the trees and the trees with the sun until we noticed that Myrna had grown silent, she was sloped in her seating and whiter than she had ever been before.

Eddie made to lift her, but Carmel said, 'We will all carry her.'

She was so little weight she was none at all.

Eddie laughed and apologized to Carmel that she would not be the first woman he would bring over a threshold. The dogs that were ours now barked loud and long and rushed to meet our arrival. Myrna came around at their barking and whispered hush to them and they quieted.

Before we were halfway down the sloping field, Myrna asked us to stop.

She looked at the sun making its way into the sea, the deepened blue of that sea, the grey sand and behind us she glanced at the darkened woods with the fields cut out of them and then she looked on to the house that is Solas. She breathed in the air all around us, a breath that took all of ours and made us faint.

We took her across the threshold.

Myrna did not speak during the meal I had prepared and served. She did not sing when we sang, when Eddie told stories she did not hear.

★ ★ ★

Later that night, when Myrna was in bed and I slept, Carmel and Eddie went to their room after a moonlit walk and they opened their windows so that the same moonlight they had lain under so long ago in the woods could come again to them. And she opened to him again, as she had to him as a girl. Though he did not move inside her it was as if he had. She held him in her hands until what had not happened in a long time happened.

'If we die now, we die happy,' Eddie said to her. But she was already sleeping.

33

Bound to Go to Heaven Now

I ran up the hill of Pass If You Can, in the first of the light. I ran so Jonah would not catch me and I ran because I wanted to carry the news to Thomas that even if the whole world does not wish it there is nothing to prevent two who love each other from being together.

I heard the sound of Eddie and Carmel's love even in the dawning of a day that was as grey as the day before had been bright. I was eager for the love sounds of my own. I found him by the bed of Black.

'She's an early bird, that one,' Black raised his hand and a smile. 'Are you the worm she's after, Thomas?'

Thomas laughed.

'Good morning, Sive. The day has not begun so well. He has a bad pain in his chest and he will not let me call the nurse.'

'Nurse Joe. Pah! I want to be left alone; I don't want none of the examinations. The examinations are what kill you!'

I asked him, 'What would you like instead?'

'You're the girl, Mary Sive,' Mr Black grinned a toothless and decayed grin. 'You're the Last Request Girl.'

'Black, the world will be a better place without

you,' Thomas said gravely.

'I would like whiskey, Mary Sive,' Black ignored him. 'And one last cigarette. Quickly mind.'

I took the untipped Players from his drawer and I took a nip from the bottle Sister Saviour had kept hidden in a pot in the kitchen for emergencies. Black sighed.

'This is a good smoke and the best time of day to have it. Kills the tastebuds before I have to eat the muck they serve up here.'

He eyed me, then Thomas.

'Don't think I don't know what goes on. And fair play to both of you for it.' A hacking cough, then a spurt of words.

'This is it, Cave, man. No drum roll, no last words. No woman crying. No family. Just the smoke and the nip, the eternal, faithful friends, eh? Twenty years I've been living here. No one outside remembers me. I might as well be dead all that time.'

'You're not dying,' Thomas said.

'Then I'll be leaving through the window, if you'll give me your assistance. I've had it, Cave, man.'

'Will I leave?' I asked them.

'Not at all,' Mr Black signalled to me to sit down by him. 'Feed me the water of life, Mary Sive. Feed me whiskey. And while you're at it, show us your lovely breasts.'

I put the glass to his lips.

'A true drinker never loses a drop,' he insisted.

And he did not lose one. Before his last sip he shook the hand of Thomas and on its way back

287

to his side I caught it and placed it inside my clothing.

He lay back against his pillow.

'It's been too long since I felt a woman. Bound to go to heaven now. Fuck.'

His grip on me loosened. His hand stilled altogether.

'Eloquent to the bitter end,' Thomas sighed. 'That was our Black.'

He pulled the sheet over his friend's face and wondered when someone would do the same for him.

After a time, the first of the men rose and those that could began to dress themselves.

★   ★   ★

Thomas followed me to the bathroom.

'I am almost as close to death as Black. I am older,' he said.

'Your dying is far off. We are alive and while we're alive we should be together, Thomas.'

'And your family?'

'They would have no reason to be against you. But we cannot stay with them. We would have to leave, Thomas, get away altogether, whatever problems we would have,' I said.

Thomas looked at me for a long while.

'I am old, Sive, going the way Black has gone. I cannot take you away from the family that needs you.'

'What would you know of their needs?'

'I know that you have to work here to provide for them.'

'You do not know that. My mother is married now, to the window cleaner of this place. And you could work too. Mr Black was ill, Thomas! You are a strong man.'

'We cannot be certain of that. And there is Jonah. He is bound to follow me wherever I go.'

'Then we must go to a place where he cannot watch us.'

'I do have a place we could go to,' Thomas stopped. 'But I cannot take you away from your family. It is a very lonely place, I lived there before I came here.'

'You do not take me away from anyone. I take myself.'

'And you would spend all the time we had together wondering how they are.'

'I will not have to wonder much longer about one of them. Myrna is one you've seen before. She is going after Black. The other two are married now and have each other.'

The sounds of the breakfast trolley and Joe complaining of my lateness came from the ward. I went out to the duties of the day. My first to tell the men that Black had died.

'That's paperwork. Nurse's work,' Joe O'Reilly said. 'I'll notify Sister Mauritius and get the forms ready.'

The men ate the breakfast I served up. But for the pulled curtain in the middle cubicle of the right-hand row of beds, it was a normal day.

I wanted to talk to Thomas again, but he had enough with the death of his most recently made friend, and with bearing Jonah's daily visit, which went on for most of the afternoon.

289

I did not have to see Jonah. I worked split shifts now and had afternoons off. On the rare days when I had to work right through I kept myself occupied and out of his way. He would come looking for me, would talk to me as I worked. I would not answer.

I did not speak to Jonah. I did not walk along the winding road of Pass If You Can because Jonah had taken to sleeping in his car near Solas. Eddie had caught him twice and had reported the car to the guards, who said they could do nothing about it. A man could sleep and park where he liked.

I went to work through the fields.

It was a hard time for us all. It was a time when nothing seemed to happen at all. But we had very little time left to wait.

34

Bound to Go to Hell Now

Sister Mauritius had Black removed to the chapel, not before she asked me to prepare the body. It was not a thing I had done before. But she was sharp with me saying, 'I will phone Father Malone and arrange for the funeral Mass to be said in the chapel. Then he will go into the St Manis plot.'

'The St Manis plot?' I echoed.

'The plot we use when the men do not have enough money to pay for their own plots. Don't worry,' she answered my look. 'His name is put on the headstone. If he had died at sea he wouldn't have had that luxury.'

'What about getting the men to the graveyard?'

'The men don't go. They will pay their respects to Mr Black at the chapel.'

Later in the day I did not go home, as I usually did, between shifts. I walked for miles through the hills and down on to the shoreline. I walked through woods and fields until I could walk no more and the anger had left me.

I went back to do the second part of my shift on a black night without stars. I did not see Thomas waiting at the gap in the hedgerow until I was almost upon him. It was winter. The last of the autumn had been taken by Carmel for her wedding day. The light was gone before the day. The dark season had fallen heavy on us and kept us in its grip.

I was tired and the sight of him made me lively again. But he had his own words for me.

'Eddie was here today cleaning the windows. I went to pay my respects to him on his wedding. He says Jonah gave you the scar on your forehead, ran you over. He said it was an accident. He says Jonah watches you and gives you lifts sometimes.'

'Not sometimes. Just once.'

'Don't take it again, Sive, don't go near him.'

'I know that. But I can't avoid him.'

'Why?'

'He follows me.'

Thomas was so quiet I thought he had stopped breathing. 'You should have told me.'

'You must have known.'

'I knew he had some interest, but I did not think it had developed . . . ' He stopped. 'He will never lay a hand on you again. I will make sure of that.'

'If you do anything to stop him following me he might harm my family, Thomas.'

'Then what do you want me to do?' he shouted. 'Stand by and watch him hurt you?'

'He did not hurt me intentionally. He needs help, he has no one.'

Thomas looked at me in disgust. The leaden feeling dug its way deep into my belly.

'Where does this sympathy come from?' he asked. 'Are you encouraging him?'

'I have not encouraged him.'

Thomas did not listen to the little I said, he cut across me, 'You have encouraged him. With your walk, with your eyes. Why do women behave like this? Do you think it is some sort of game, to bring on the father and son at the same time?'

He had time to say no more. I walked away from him quickly and did not turn my head, even though he shouted my name for a full minute as I crossed over the lawn.

When the men were settled I made myself tea and sat in the kitchen. A notice from Sister Mauritius advised that Mr Black's funeral Mass would be said tomorrow, and he would be buried after it. Already the bed was prepared for someone else. It would be filled within the week. But I would never know the next occupant. I would not get to say goodbye to the men I had cared for.

It was to be my last night in St Manis. I have not been inside its doors again.

★   ★   ★

I put my head on the table, to rest my aching head and heavy eyes. My throat hurt with uncried tears. Sleep came on me. When I woke, it was to feel a hand on my head, stroking my hair.

I looked up and he was there, sad, as I was.

'I am sorry. I am upset that Black has gone. I am afraid of what I have brought on you with Jonah. You would be safe if you had not met me. I am so sorry.'

I put my finger to his lips and hushed him. I looked at the clock, nine-thirty. I should have gone a half an hour ago, the night attendant would come on duty at ten. All the men were sleeping, no television after seven, bed by eight, even the ones who still had minds and mobility fell into step with the routine, for their curtains were closed too.

I sat on the table, held my lover's head against the breast that Black had placed his hand on and I placed my lover's hand in mine. Then I took his hand and I moved it along the long line of my thigh and into the heat that waited for him. He sighed and we stayed like this and I rocked him softly and said, 'Soon, soon we will go away.'

He did not answer, he placed lips to where he could find skin — throat, breast, shoulder, the crook of my arm. All tenderness.

That is how Sister Mauritius found us.

'This,' she spat, 'does not surprise me one bit. Outside now, the pair of you.'

We came into the office where she waited, Thomas holding my hand, my head held high against my fear. My eyes shining brightly with recent love and now anger, my lips red with it. Thomas did not look at me, but his grip was sure.

She looked at the hands and she looked at each of our faces and she said, softly, 'Disgusting.'

We did not answer, which forced her to carry on talking. She pointed with a trembling finger at me, 'A woman who was given a chance to make something of herself and this is what you do with it. Did you give her money?' she asked Thomas.

He shook his head.

'If you want to have a bed to sleep on, you'd better answer.'

'No.'

'Then she lets a man who could be her grandfather, a sick man, do that for nothing. I know now the stories are right about her. Why wouldn't they be, with the mother she has.'

I thought of Thomas and his need to remain here a while longer and I did not speak.

I found our continued silence shameful. I did not know why Thomas would not defend us and I could not speak since I knew he would be the one to remain here. I know now that in our silence we held all dignity. Had we uttered one word we would have said our love needed defending.

The more we remained silent the more Mauritius railed.

'You pair were watched up to this. Don't try to pretend this has not happened before. This little bitch, this little bit of nothing, would turn us into a brothel. Bound for hell she is. And,' she pointed the finger at Thomas now, her brows knitted together, her breath short and bursting out of her, 'no doubt you'll be making the trip sooner than her.'

The years when Sister Mauritius had touched herself and hated the wetness, then hated the dryness which came after desire left her, all this torment came out of her now. So she retreated into sanctimony. She lowered insult and swore never to let me near the place again.

'Get your coat, get out. Tell that window cleaner living with your whore mother to look elsewhere for work. He won't work anywhere in Scarna either, once I have had words with those that I know in the town.

'Go on,' she screamed, when I showed no signs of movement.

'You,' she pointed at Thomas. 'If you follow her you will not get back in here.'

I left the two of them there. He did not follow me. When Sister Mauritius told him he had until the end of the week to make other arrangements he nodded and turned on his heel.

★　★　★

Margaret was pacing up and down the dayroom, Joe slouched in a chair. It was the slack time just before lunch, on the day following the discovery.

The news of the night's activity had been pieced together only from Sister Mauritius's admission that Mary Sive would not be back. Joe was told to assist Mr Cave in the packing of his belongings should he need help.

Black's Mass and funeral were to be put back until the afternoon. An eye was to be kept out for Mary Sive. The caretaker and gardener had already turned me away, on Sister Mauritius's instructions. Cave was to be watched, on Sister Mauritius's instructions.

Thomas Cave had not risen for breakfast. He lay on his still-made bed, fully clothed, facing the curtain that was the only wall he had. The staff had not touched him. He made no attempt to answer their questions.

'A cup of tea, Thomas?' Margaret enquired.

'Will you take your pills, now?' Joe wanted to know.

They had not shifted him. They took pleasure in surmising what Cave had done with me.

'I'm the only one saw anything, I was doing the baths with her the other day and I saw her giving him a job under the flannel,' Joe revealed.

Margaret was eager to match this, 'I was told by Mauritius herself to keep an eye on them. I saw them at it loads of times.'

Around them the men near death, who sat in the dayroom, seemed as if they heard nothing. But they had heard and they all, without exception, wished it had been them.

★ ★ ★

After lunch the Jaguar pulled up in the driveway.

Margaret rushed to meet Jonah, before he entered the building.

'Well, I have the news for you. I want the money first and I'll tell second.'

Jonah was tired, he had been drinking all night and that morning. He had begun to wonder if I was worth his attention, he felt me to be ungrateful. His father bored him now.

He had really wanted a quiet day.

'If the information is good, the money will be good,' he snapped.

'Oh,' Margaret rubbed her hands on her skirt. 'It's good.'

She held her hand out.

Jonah ignored it and made to move into the home.

'It is freezing out here. I want to get inside.'

'No! Out here I'll tell you, not in there. Give me the money first though.'

He continued walking.

'OK,' she looked agitated. 'Show me the money first.'

He sighed, his head pounded; his mouth was dry and stale. He took out a ten-pound note from his wallet.

Margaret told him.

She did not feel much. Just the sensation of falling at first. Then the gasping as the wind fought to get back into her lungs.

He had hit her once, hard, then walked away, then walked back, to punch her, hard again, in the stomach so she would not be able to run after him.

He had to do it, to stop her following him. He needed time to think. He needed to sort everything out. He drove away, without entering the building, without looking back.

★ ★ ★

Jonah parked the car at the end of the laneway. He watched the house. There was no sign of activity, no curling smoke. No dogs or hens about. It was quiet as a grave. He pulled away again and drove along the coast road, parking up to look at the sea. It was a day that spelled winter's arrival. The wind tossed the sea's white mane and gulls called to each other. He smoked slowly. His heart was turning to stone, his mud eyes darkened.

All his plans. All along I had been with his father.

★　★　★

Jonah came to Thomas, found him lying as he had lain since the night before, facing the curtain that surrounded his bed.

'This time,' Jonah said, 'you will not be able to hide behind silence.'

Thomas did not stir. Jonah sat in the chair next to his bed and waited. The old man's breath was so quiet he did not appear to live.

Jonah leaned forward and pushed him slightly, with the tips of his long fingers. The body tensed in an instant at the touch, all resistance. But it did not shrink away from it.

Jonah pinched the flesh on the back of the old man's arm until it turned red and then white and began to bruise under his fingers. Still no reaction, no sound.

He cast his eye around the curtained quarters, sighing, his breath came in shallow bursts of steam into the cold air, air filled with knives. His eyes glistened with the need to begin and the frustration of not knowing how. He opened the wardrobe doors and began to pull out the albums. Flicked through them. Snap, snap, snap. All names, all faces he should be familiar with as Thomas's son. All strangers.

'You will have to move eventually,' he spoke to

299

the back of Thomas. 'You will have to get up sometime. I can wait until you do. I will stay until your bladder is aching. I can stay until you shit yourself.'

Thomas listened.

'Like old times,' Jonah smiled. 'Old times.'

A slight shift in Thomas's shoulders brought Jonah to his feet then. He leaned forward and whispered into the ear of his father, his lips so close he could almost bite it. He covered it in breath beads, so cold was the day.

'You never knew what to do with a woman once you had your way with her.'

Thomas's face, hidden from view, was wet with tears. He looked into the life he did not have and he closed his eyes on it. All morning he had waited by the door. Mauritius had told him if he left the building he could not expect to gain entry to it again or collect any of his possessions. The old and frightened man in him had retired to his cubicle, suddenly afraid to leave his world.

'If I am like this now, how will I be when I am in the world proper? She will be smothered,' he thought, as he waited for me to come and get him.

I had not come. He rose up from his chair and made to leave and instead lay on the bed. The eyes of Margaret and Joe were waiting to report to Sister Mauritius. Even the men were talking. Peter came and whispered, 'Thomas?' and went away when he got no reply.

He tried to reason with himself and reason failed him. If he had been young, like me, he would not have come either to take away an old lover. He was glad for me that I had not come and taken on all that he was. He ached for himself and the public shame of all of this.

Then Jonah had come. Jonah talked on and finally the curtains were pulled back briskly by Joe O'Reilly.

'Well, if it isn't the offspring of the great Casanova here. You'll have to be on your way. The lunch's on its way up. Not that this lad will have much of an appetite.'

'I'll be back soon,' Jonah said. And, just before he left, 'You will have to give it up with her. She is only after what money she thinks you have. You know her type. My mother was one.'

Thomas's voice came then, and it was so that all could hear, 'You will not go anywhere near her or you will have me to deal with.'

There was no reply. Thomas heard the sound of Margaret and Sister Mauritius pursuing Jonah, calling to him. But his footsteps continued out the door.

★ ★ ★

Sister Mauritius sat in the chair, still warm from Jonah.

'You know that man attacked one of our staff? What kind of a family did you raise? I have not called the police but I will do so if you are not off the premises by Friday. The member of staff is looking for danger money now, thanks to you.'

Thomas could not help smiling.

Sister Mauritius stood up. In the middle of the ward she made the general announcement.

'The funeral of Mr Anthony Black, postponed from this morning, will take place this afternoon, at three.'

Thomas thought of where he might go and he found he could think of nowhere. He thought of his friend, Black, shortly to be placed into the ground. He thought of himself as a weak old man who had no clear notion of anything he had stood for. He had passed this on to the son who was not his, the legacy of being one who has always watched and has no right to join the world in its ways.

35

The Last Words of Myrna

I left Thomas with Mauritius and I walked through the gates and prayed he would find the courage to follow me when I came the next morning.

I know now that we had both invited the day of discovery on us. We had persuaded ourselves that we had been hiding from the world. But we had done everything but declare ourselves openly.

All this went through me as I moved through the night air, heavy with mist.

The night was calmer than my thoughts. I should have known it was a death night, unnaturally still. The mist met my warmth and turned to beads of moisture on my skin. My tears linked the beads and together they wove a damp shroud of sorrow and non-seeing. What hope for Thomas and me?

I should have opened the eyes I had not used; I should have listened to all that the stillness was calling. But I was too lost in myself.

★ ★ ★

I was in the door before I knew all that had changed and the change caught me by the throat and took words away. Carmel was sitting by the fire, crying, Eddie with his arm around her shoulders.

'Myrna,' Eddie explained. 'She's taken a turn for the worst.'

'Where have you been all night, Sive?' Carmel's voice was accusing. 'She's been asking for you. Again and again. She's been shouting words we don't understand. Now all her voice is gone.'

'Should we call the priest?' Eddie asked.

'No,' Carmel and I spoke together.

'No need for them here,' I continued. 'We have our own ways.'

I went into the back room, alone. Leaving Eddie to argue with Carmel, in hushed tones.

'If we don't call a priest they won't bury her.'

'Don't talk now, Eddie. Let Sive tell us.'

I closed the door so their voices would not carry.

It was dark but for the lamplight which cast two dark shadows in the place where Myrna's eyes had been. When she opened her eyes they were as black as the shadows that had been placed in them.

She smiled thinly.

'Where is he? Thomas Cave?' she spoke in a grainy whisper, squeezed through a tightened throat. 'I was calling to you, to bring him with you.'

'He did not come with me. I don't know whether he will come at all,' my voice liquid with tears. 'We won't speak of him now. You must save your talk.'

304

She raised a hand.

'Your grandmother is here, waiting for me to come off with her. She thinks as I do. If you can, do not be apart from him at all.'

The mist that had shrouded me in its warning had come to claim her, had coated her in a death sweat. She fought the still night and her ragged breath cut through the air. The glassy night sea and coal black sky carried the echoes of her breathing to the far off places. I traced the lines on her forehead and I read the stories in each line. I read the life that had been lived and was coming to an end.

I wanted to know all that I did not know of her, to fall into the days that were hers, but they were already lived and gone.

'You have been a mother to me,' I said softly.

I pressed my lips to the whispers of hair on her forehead.

She tried to moisten parched lips with the tip of her dry tongue. I licked my own finger and ran it across them. I heard her words form in my ears, though those lips did not move to form them. These words came out of her heart and into mine.

'You have been a daughter. I am swimming in the death sea, Sive, it is warm and calm because I am glad to be in it.'

They were the last I was to hear from her.

We sat a long while, the mist pouring in through the open window. The room was bitter cold, but Myrna's fever was high. Though I did not know why, I began to hum low. The humming cooled and soothed her. She was frightened to go on. I spoke to her, through the tips of fingers on a palm, as Myrna had taught me to speak.

The spirit outgrew the body. It was as strong a spirit as I have ever felt, as strong as her bones were weak. Then I saw my grandmother and she took the Myrna that rose out of Myrna by the hand and I cried for being left behind. Her voice in me now. It spoke from a far off place that was closer to me than my own skin, 'The cards are yours and all that I ever owned is yours.'

The humming began again in the room of its own accord, for a time.

Then all was silence.

I put my heart to the bony chest and found it faint but beating, I put my lips to hers and breathed into her the love and regard I had for her. When I went back into the living room it was already morning, Eddie and Carmel were at the table.

'Is she gone?'

'Not gone entirely,' I answered. 'But she will never be back.'

I spoke without tears. Carmel wept and I went to her and put my arms around her.

'We will sit with her until she goes,' I said. 'I will sit with her for a while. Then I have to go. There is something Myrna wants.'

★ ★ ★

I slept over the body of Myrna and woke when the morning was still not fully underway. I ran to the gates of St Manis. Sister Mauritius had posted the caretaker and gardener to turn me away. I went across the field and tried to enter by the gap in the hedgerow. They had crossed the lawn and waited for me there too.

'Sorry, Mary Sive. We have the orders.'

As I walked away the wind lifted a little and the humming that had filled the room where Myrna lay now filled the whole sky. All was movement as the wind grazed trees and hedgerows and grasses and threw the sea up to reach the sky. The sun shone on the bare land of winter and the bare land stirred and the gentle humming passed over all and brought with it the message that the growing time was upon us and the bare time of winter was at an end. The humming brought life and death. Death to those who had served their time; life and purpose to those whose time was beginning.

The green shoots of the first flowers pushed through the earth to answer that call. The trees reached deep beyond the cold hard ground into the moist earth below and drank deep from it to push out the new buds of the new year.

All ending and all beginning in this moment.

Growth in the new year is a slow thing, so slow it is almost still.

To the knowing heart it was spring.

36

Death the Visitor

The card of white light in black surroundings. Death has come to visit.

★   ★   ★

Thomas awoke in the afternoon as lunch was cleared away. The men were preparing themselves. This was to be a different day, a day when one of them was going into the ground.

Joe and Margaret were running around, supervised by Sister Mauritius.

'This man needs a black tie, give him one.'

'This man has no white shirt. Give him Black's one.'

'We dressed Black in it, Sister,' Joe murmured.

'Well, go to the cupboard and get one.'

Thomas watched the men come and go, their startled looks at the change in routine.

He rose and took out his own black suit, his tie and white shirt. His black shoes, saved for special occasions, had a film of dust. He laid out all his garb and he gathered his shaving brush, razor and soap stick. Mauritius met him as he crossed the ward.

'Where do you think you are going?'

'To wash up.'

'For what reason?'

'Tony Black's funeral.'

'You are going no place.'

'You cannot stop me.'

'I can have you restrained.'

Thomas unbent himself, all stiffness gone. The giant returned.

'Do not speak to me like I am a child.'

'Well,' Mauritius was flustered. 'You have behaved like no child would.'

'I have that. I have behaved like a man wants to with a woman. I believe if you had behaved as a woman wants to with a man, life would be significantly easier around here.'

Sister Mauritius had no words except, 'Consider yourself homeless after today.'

'It will be my pleasure.'

Thomas walked on to the washroom. Later, dressed, he leaned over to wipe the dust off his patent shoes, which had not grown any less dull underneath. The two blurred halves of his own face stared back at him, the drawn limpness on the left, the firm set of sorrow on the right. He could not see his eyes. He looked for them a long while before rising on the first stroke of the chapel bell.

A dozen broken men attended the funeral service of Anthony Black.

The curate from Scarna said the Mass and he was stuck for words when it came to the sermon, because he knew nothing about the man except that he had been a sailor. He talked about death being a harbour from the high seas of life and he heard the hollow nature of his words as he looked at the sea of faces that showed that death was no harbour but the high sea itself and each of these men would put into it soon.

He broke off, then asked if anyone who knew Anthony Black would care to say a few words.

A very tall man in a well-cut black suit stood slowly, leaning on his stick. The curate watched nervously as Sister Mauritius turned from the front row and asked the tall man to sit down again. The man did not falter or sit. Silent Thomas spoke for his friend

'Tony Black did not lead an exemplary life. He was true to his own character. It is the best way to be and it was the best way for him. He died well. I was with him and he was not afraid. I think he would like to have been buried at sea, but I'm sure he truly does not care where he ends up,' there was a throat clear, 'once the place has malt, women and tobacco.'

The broken men laughed and Sister Mauritius and the curate shifted in the hope that that would be the end. Thomas had more to say.

'Tony Black taught me a shared death is easier. We should celebrate his going because it was a release for him. We should celebrate because his life was worth celebrating. But we will not. Because this is a place where people are expected to live and die without celebration. It is to St Manis that we come to die in the company of strangers. No one chooses that and that is not how it has to be. Black was a stranger to me, who became a friend. God bless Black and all here.'

He sat and the curate finished the Mass quickly and the congregation was dispersed.

310

The coffin was wheeled out to the ambulance to be taken for burial. Thomas followed it.

Sister Mauritius followed him and asked where he thought he was going.

'That is the second time today you have asked me,' Thomas looked down at her as he spoke.

'The residents don't attend the burial.' Mauritius felt unsure under his gaze. He seemed to grow taller by the hour.

'I am no longer a resident.'

Thomas Cave walked down the long driveway and out of the tall gates that had held him in for almost two years and he knew they would not hold him again.

★　★　★

At the graveyard the curate, who had travelled in the ambulance, mumbled prayers and threw soil as the coffin was lowered. He had already begun the walk back into the town by the time Thomas arrived.

Thomas spoke some words to the grave-diggers who were covering the coffin.

They agreed to give him five minutes and he stood, intending to pray and finding he could not. Instead he looked at the state of the large plot, there were no weeds but no care had gone into it. A plain headstone with no words but the names of those who lay there.

Thomas shed tears. He knew Black's was not the worst of deaths, but it was the most indifferent, buried with a single bystander.

Thomas knew now his dearest wish was to die

311

as he had not lived — to die in the company of loved ones who had been given all that he could give them. The sun was of afternoon and yet all around Thomas there were shadows as if the light was that of evening. He saw them when he looked up from the fresh grave into which he had poured his realization and from which he had taken resolve.

He studied the shadows. They shifted endlessly, so that they seemed to occupy the space between them and him. The closer the shadows came the more Thomas Cave realized that he knew not only them, but the light and darkness that formed them. He had created them.

They were images he had taken as photographs, their shadows the negative images that consumed him with all the feeling his existence had denied. Mine and my mother's eyes among them.

We covered his face and form in shadows, whispered and shrieked from everywhere.

We made music out of high notes of laughter mixed with low wails of despair, and all sounds in between. Thomas left Black's grave and the shadows danced before him and followed after him and ran through him as if he had not a body at all to protect his being. Mine and my mother's eyes led the way.

He knew only to follow us and soon he was walking down the wide market street of a grey town with thin sticks of people coming in and out of doorways and not staying long in the biting cold the day was fenced in by. They stopped and stared at him — a man so tall, clad in black with hair as brilliant white as the shirt he wore and walking with the aid of a stick — he must have looked like death himself come to carry off all those that came near him.

The shadows led the way and the shadow music was the only sound he heard.

We took him out of the town on the route that Carmel and I and Myrna had once walked in dead of night. Now it was early evening.

He was afraid that the shadows might lead him astray for his having betrayed their live flesh selves but he knew that his heart would have found the way, even if the shadows had not chosen to appear.

When he walked along the thin stretch of coast road the shadows grew impatient with him, soon they had run on ahead and he could barely see them at all. A car stopped and a man got out to see if he was all right and Thomas stood and thanked him and said he was fine, just a dizzy spell.

Perhaps, said the man, you have walked too far, would a lift be in order? No, said Thomas briskly and did not look back at the man who shrugged and drove on his way.

Ahead, the shadows had come across another car, parked across a laneway. We raced on to surround and wake the all-eyes-and-bones man who sat inside staring at the house at the top of the laneway without flinching. This man looked so hard at the house he could not see us.

We put needles and pins into him and hunger in his belly. And he shook his head and rubbed himself and felt it time to get a drink and something to eat. He had been there all night and day and already the little window cleaner had come down to him and advised him to move on or the police would be called.

So it was that the shadows dispensed with Jonah Cave and sent him in the opposite direction to the one in which Thomas Cave travelled.

Thomas Cave arrived at the bottom of the brambled laneway, the shadows had formed on either side of it, all but for mine and my mother's eyes, which led the way to him, back to ourselves.

And Eddie was the first to see the tall man with the white hair and shirt and dark suit and he, for he was one of the townspeople too, whispered, 'It's death. Come to get Myrna. Or a civil servant.'

Then he saw that it was Thomas Cave from the home. He called me from the back bedroom. Without a word I opened the door and he walked through it.

★ ★ ★

He looked at me a long while and I at him. Then I introduced him to my family.

'This is Carmel, my mother. You have met Eddie before. He cleans the windows at St Manis.'

'Used to clean the windows,' Eddie spat as he spoke.

What was in the air stopped Thomas from

314

making to shake the hands of Eddie and Carmel. I had fought with Eddie that morning, when he had learned of events at St Manis Home.

'That's a day's wages a month you've lost me. Now we don't even have you earning money. Where else do you think I'm going to get you a job? There's no one will take you if you've been let go from St Manis! Where else, do you mind telling me?'

'I suppose, Mr Cave, we might ask you to tell us why it happened that I have lost work and so has Sive?' Eddie spoke gruff and did not look the big man in the eye.

'You'll hear soon enough,' was all he could get from Thomas.

'Fair enough so,' Eddie said quietly. 'I'll just go to the bottom of the lane and see if the lunatic son of yours is still parked there and ask him please move on, seeing as how no one else is doing anything about it.'

'He is not there.'

'Well he'll be back soon enough I'm sure and I am sure I won't be told either whether him and you, Mr Cave, have anything to contribute to the running of this house with Sive not going to work any more.'

Eddie shook his head and got his coat, slamming the door violently. Carmel went after him. We heard them walking down the laneway, Eddie shouting and Carmel pleading with him to be quiet.

★   ★   ★

Thomas and I sat at the table, looking at each other. We had grown used to not touching each other in company. It was a while before he put his hand out across the table to me. I took it.

'It would never work if I came here,' Thomas said.

I nodded and said, 'You have come through my door. I have someone I want you to meet.'

We went into the back room, it was here the shadows had congregated having driven Jonah Cave away. Thomas saw the shrunken figure in the bed.

'Myrna,' I said to him. 'The woman whose image did not develop.'

Thomas looked at me in disbelief, then he looked at the shadows and knew I was not lying.

I took his hand and walked him to the bed. I put our hands on Myrna's breastbone and pushed the last of her breath out of her. She opened her eyes to witness us and gave it willingly.

The shadows took the last of her breath off. Noreen had taken all else. The townspeople and Eddie were right, Thomas had brought death with him.

I put my lips to Myrna's forehead and kissed what she had once been. Thomas watched.

I cried for her going and for our staying and the uncertainty before us.

Thomas put his hand on my shoulder and asked if we might go out into the day; that we might talk freely in a way we had never been able to.

Part of me wanted to stay with Myrna, but the

living in me wanted to go after life was with Thomas.

Together we walked out of the house and went down to the shoreline and silent Thomas was seized by talk as all he had held in came out and he took in fresh reaches of air and he began, 'I was not loved by my mother and father.'

'And I had no father and more than one mother,' I answered.

So he began at his beginning, and I began with mine. So he talked and all the life he had lived came out of him and I talked and all of my life went to him. We had waited for so long in the company of our separate secrets. Now they could be shared. As we walked and talked the coming into our own brought with it the heat we had so long denied ourselves. Our revealing to each other was more than words, it was a sense that grew between us.

The scent of my wanting was a low, dark, musk-scent that spoke of my years of nothing and no one. All that I had stored went to him. All that I had yearned for came back to me. Our two skins came alive.

And we had not yet touched each other.

All night the talk went on. Until we came to know all the corners and crevices that we had not shared. He talked most for he had a lifetime to talk of. I listened and I grew in the listening into a wider world beyond that in which I had lived. A world of ice and desert, of great rains and snowfall and burning sun and blinding blue skies.

I wandered where he had wandered and I saw

317

all he described. He followed me into a dark basement, a high attic flat, on to grey streets and into the house where I came to know myself.

In this way we came to know each other.

And in the morning we were ready.

37

The Meeting

There is the best to speak of, the talk of the loving time. The card of the sun facing the moon — the card of Meeting.

It began, as it had long promised to.

★　★　★

At the point of day when the rising sun faces the fading moon, it began on a wide open shore. The waves crashed into the silence between us and the silence between us remained. It began with the touching of our fingertips, my young firm life against his soft and loosened hold. So soft a touch I felt it to be only a whisper.

It was at the point in seasons when the winter meets spring and retires, but not before they have touched one another and lain together. Not until they have faced each other in their ending and in their beginning. Each naked in order to behold the other at its most truthful.

Then Thomas reached for my palms and opened them wide and watched the lines that had not yet been travelled and sought to put his life into them that I may not have to walk it alone.

He buried his head into my curved palms and

319

cried hot tears that ran into the lines of mine not yet lived and remained there until the years that I would live without him. And I would taste those tears in later times and I would grow strong from his weeping strength.

We had talked such a long while! Now all was silence and sleep tried to lure us, wrapping herself around us like fine silk. But we knew to close our eyes was to leave this chance for a time that might not come again. So we were naked and we walked to the water to clothe us. Two lost souls guided by the call of the sea.

The sea laughed and beckoned. With each returning wave came the sense that all things were to begin now and to continue on and to the end, all now contained in this moment.

The spring scent was mine and it was high in the air, luring winter into growth, the growing warmth between us hot summer and fiery autumn and we knew to reach warmth, coldness must be left far, far behind.

Thomas bent to kiss me and my lips were soft and shivering and cool as mountain streams on fresh days that do not know they will end. The spiced seawater took away all the need for sleep. Its fragrance was of all the loving and light of the newborn day that had begun without words and would not need them.

He held me to him. It was a long holding and I felt in him all that I had not felt and the wonder of it was that I knew it would be like this. He felt the still, closed places in himself open. He had been upright for so many years.

The sun opened its heart to us. A heron flew across its rising.

And he stood to mop the sodden hair and to stem my shivering, all the while growing blue with cold. I traced with one fingertip the vein map below his white skin and pressed hard in the places where they throbbed most prominently and felt the life course through him. Time would not wait for us and, as we dressed, the sun rose higher as it moved on to the whole world of moments, not just ours.

I saw his fear then and the grey of his skin not entirely gone. Thomas wanted to picture this moment and he could not picture and preserve it for he was truly in it as he had never been before. I was all soft and heart-heated now and when the feeling came back into his old bones, through me, it pained him with the life of it.

He had no example of love to go on, but he had experience and I had no experience but all example of love. I wished him everywhere. Inside, outside, beside, with, between, along, and all, all now.

But this was the beginning, the deepest touch was yet to come.

We walked up the steps cut out of the rock by unknown hands and crossed the stony fields that had been Joseph Moriarty's penance and beyond it the railway tracks.

We went into the woodland, my mother's familiar.

We walked through the tall trees and the light fell on us and the ravens called to one another to warn of our approach. A robin watched us quizzically, flying from branch to branch, his red breast strong against the bare breast of winter-not-yet-spring; against the greys and dull browns his heart spoke of all the colour in the world.

This was my mother's place. When Thomas stopped and held me against a tree I did not stop him. When he pulled my arms above my head and ran his hands down the pale inner arms and on down over the shoulders and on to my breasts and over my belly and into the deeper heart of me I did not stop him. His movements were rough as the tree bark I rubbed against and I welcomed the roughness and the taste of his heated lips on my salted skin.

But when he made to pull away the clothes and I made to help him I caught the robin's eye and the wind rustled in the trees and I knew it was not mine to know love here.

With each step we took we were bound together, with each stumble over knotted root we fell together. We did not stop for a long while, until the woods almost ended and the sound of a stream came to us, a stream that spoke excitedly of the hard night frost's melting and of our arrival.

We were all lips against hair and all breath in ears and all expectation and on we went, drifting out of the holding, moving onwards now.

The clearing we came to was alive with light, the frost had turned to sparkling dew and spiders had woven a silver web carpet to hold each dew jewel and we walked across it, leaving our marks on the now soft grass and in this place we lay together.

All clothing taken and all the earth's moisture became ours and the cleansing stream wove music from the birdsong. We traced the shape of our faces and our form and Thomas put aside his fears of capability and I put aside mine of sharing and we came to move together.

When he had known each part of me with lips and hands and I him, when we had tasted much and wanted more, I welcomed him.

Then it happened that he was brought down the road of darkness and the more he moved the more urgently he wished to move and the more he wished to cease moving for he could not bear it. I watched the flush of colour on his breastbone and in his cheeks. I watched, as the man who moved with me grew young again. The silver-white turned to dark chestnut hair that grew wild and thick and his lips and his form filled so that he was offered to me at the time of his life I would never know, when he was most beautiful.

I cried for my love then and for the young love that had never had the chance to grow old with me and the strong love that he emptied into me. When he was done I met him with my own doing. All done, the aged man was in my arms once more.

We stayed until the sun receded and the shadows were cast, turning them to a dullness that bore little reminder of what we had been.

We dressed and walked to Killeaden headland

and we sat to watch the rich sun set over the land and turn the sea to the reminding colour of red-gold. My lover, Thomas Cave, sheltered me from the high wind that had risen and he held me against him and when the last of the sunset had gone I felt desolate and he shared my desolation.

Until we looked at our palms and in each palm was a white snowdrop and a purple crocus of the heart. The day's events contained in them.

I have them. I carry them in the box the cards rest in. The flowers have dried but they bring memories as fresh as if they were picked only a moment ago. I lived all life in that day with him.

The light left us to walk the way home in darkness, sleep threatening to claim us before we even made it home. But we walked together and in that there was strength even sweet sleep could not conquer.

★ ★ ★

As the light of Solas came into view my lover left me to go his own way, but only for a while. He had to collect what possessions belonged to him from St Manis Home. He would knock on Peter's window and gain entry that way.

He would not leave me until we were at the bottom of the laneway.

'You are the only one I can talk to, the only one I can love,' he said. His voice was full of the future, talking and loving. Full of intent to use whatever time we had well.

I walked the last steps with the heat of the day in my heart and between my legs and I walked as a loved woman who loves. Never to be alone again.

38

Unspared

The shadows had taken and kept Jonah away.

He had gone to the Slip Inn on the harbour front at Scarna. He had been waiting for me a long while outside the house, without even a glimpse, and was glad to stretch out in the warmth and sip the neat whiskey that burned its way down his throat.

He drank until he was thrown out. Then he fell asleep in his car. When he woke with the next morning, he was tired from sleep and the pub doors were opening again. He went in for the cure. The cramps in his shoulders gnawed and nagged him into continuous shifting as he sat on his stool at the bar. The diehards surrounding him had grown accustomed to his face appearing at regular intervals and that did not mean they liked it any better.

So he was not asked to join in conversations that meant nothing to anyone. He was left alone to his thoughts and his thoughts were rough and ragged, snatching at him through the lack of sleep.

What he would do when he saw me, he did not know.

He wished me to know that I did not have to resort to the withered, listless pawing of an old man dreaming of younger days. I could have him and he would accept that I had allowed his father first to touch me. He imagined that once he had explained the situation to me about the money I would feel foolish and it would be the best way for me to feel.

Jonah Cave had it in mind to forgive and forget. He had it in mind to entice me with a small present or two and he left the Slip Inn, at dinner hour, to go up the main street and look into the jewellers.

The men watched him go and, one by one, they turned back to their drinks, one spat and the barman shouted for him to quit that.

'He's queer,' one said.

'A queer one indeed, with a skinful on him.'

'He'll drive the motor into a wall.'

'Or over the ditch.'

All these ends delivered slowly, with pint sips or whiskey nips in between. All these ends delivered with a certainty that they would be proved right.

'Who is he — do you know?'

'Not from around here.'

They dropped all talk of him then. It was not worth speculating on one they did not know. They would wait until he met his end behind the wheel and they would talk again of him and how he had sat with his back to them.

★　★　★

Jonah found a brooch with two pearls set into it. The lady behind the counter leaned back to

327

escape the fumes he breathed over her and the velvet-lined tray, clouding her pieces.

She rubbed a sleeve over them. The bundle of notes in the wallet he had produced was keeping her quiet.

He picked it up. She wrapped it silently. After a failed attempt or two at pleasantries in which lay the traps to determine who the man was and why he wanted a brooch at four on a Wednesday afternoon, the jeweller had given up.

She short-changed him and he walked away without counting. She laid her large bosom on the counter and sighed with satisfaction, imagining, as she did on most Wednesday afternoons, the likes of Rock Hudson unbuttoning her blouse. She undid one or two herself to remind her husband's brother when he came, as he always did on Wednesday afternoons, of what he had to do.

★ ★ ★

Jonah made to drive back to Solas and then thought it better to wait until he had a clearer head.

He would go to St Manis. If Thomas was still facing the curtain, Jonah would coax him to turn around. If Thomas was up he would tell him that everything could be sorted if only he would allow Jonah to handle things.

Jonah would give his father the money to be gone. To be gone back to where he came from before. In return for this money, Jonah had imagined, he would get information. On what

328

Sive liked and how he could give it to her.

The father would tell the son, as fathers should always tell sons, about the mysteries of women and how to control the vicious cat part of them that scratched at men and would not leave them be.

This, surely, would be the way to go about things. He was the forgiver and donator. They were the betrayers. They made a good fit, all these thoughts. Jonah's head was clearer than it had been for days.

It was not clear a few minutes later. He did not expect what he got from Sister Mauritius, so soon after his arrival. She was at the car before he even stepped out of it.

'Mr Cave, if you would just come this way.'

'I cannot,' he walked by her, 'just yet, Sister. I have to see my father on an important . . . '

'You will not find him, Mr Cave.'

Jonah stopped, turned.

'Where is he then?'

'If you will come to the office, Mr Cave, I will tell you.'

He was in a chair and the piece of paper was across the desk before he had much chance to think anything else.

Sister Mauritius snapped open a fountain pen.

'What are these?' Jonah asked.

'Release forms and settlement of account. Your father did not stop long enough to sign them. Since this home is no longer responsible for him we need to mark it officially.'

'Well, mark it with an empty bed then,' Jonah leaned back in his chair. 'I am not signing anything. And I am certainly not handing over any more money.'

'Routine. If you don't care to sign them then you don't care to collect what he has left behind.' Sister Mauritius's tone was clipped. 'If you don't care to settle the account then you don't care to know where he has gone.'

'What has he left behind?'

'Everything.'

Jonah took the pen and signed twice in the designated spots. He took the bill and looked at the amount in disbelief.

'He caused some damage before he left,' Mauritius smiled coldly, revealing yellowed, uncapped teeth. 'He also made the generous offer to pay for a friend's funeral.'

'My father has no money.'

'You, I'm sure,' she pointed a finger to the total underlined in red and then tapped the same finger at the place where his signature was required, 'can look after things. If you care to examine the figures they will tell you that we are owed for his last month's board and for some clothing we had to buy . . . '

'My father had all his own clothes!'

'Then there is the small matter of the member of my staff you assaulted yesterday.'

Jonah ignored this. 'You said you could tell me where he is.'

'I can, when we are finished here.'

Jonah passed over what notes he had remaining in his wallet.

'That is all you are getting and be glad you get that.'

Sister Mauritius opened a desk drawer, put the money in and locked it.

'He left yesterday afternoon. I have been told he was spotted in the town and then spotted with our former employee, on the beach. I think you will thank me that I have not brought the police into this matter.'

Jonah looked at her. Mauritius was a woman of many faults but she was not afraid of much. She feared what she saw in him.

'This has been a deeply disturbing encounter for all my staff and for myself. You will see to it that your father does not set foot here again. You will take his belongings with you I hope.'

'I will see he does not set foot here again. I will take his belongings.'

Jonah left the office and he took the boxes and suitcase of his father's that had been packed and left on the bed. They filled his car and the evening had already closed in by the time he was ready to drive away.

He felt the pressure of something between his seat belt and his breast pocket. He pulled the car in and opened the small package that held the brooch.

He turned over his wrist and stuck the pin into one of the blue lines running beneath the milk-white surface and watched as the red drops, thin at first, then thick, poured down.

'I am bled dry from all of this,' he whispered.

He would leave none of us unspared that, he decided.

★ ★ ★

331

When Thomas left me he decided not to set out on the road, but to walk through the woodland.

He wanted the blanket of darkness around him, no prying eyes. It was past dusk now and the night wind had picked up. It bit through the thin suit fabric. He tried to move more quickly to get to the shelter of the trees, but the events of the day and night had left him with little energy.

It was not the leaden tiredness of before. His heart was light and purpose was his.

Thomas felt himself to be a new man, a man restored. His only concern now to protect me from Jonah.

This was why he wanted to go to St Manis, to collect his belongings so that he and I might leave together. I had told him I would go with him once Myrna was in the ground. He would remain with me in Solas until then.

The steepness of the walk caught at his calves in vicious bites, he knew that if he stopped it would be a long time before he started again. In the end his legs demanded it, his bad arm was also stiffened with the cold, rest was needed.

So he took up a spot under a tree, which offered kind shelter and he listened to the growth of the night sounds and the steady beat of his own heart and his eyes closed.

When he woke it was with a start and there was no way of telling how much of the night had passed. He did not go on to St Manis, he cursed himself for having tried and having left me alone half the night. He turned and moved back down the hill with all the energy that had been lacking on the long walk up it.

Jonah Cave had been in the house for hours. There was no car; there was only a pile of Thomas's photographs burning along with his clothes and books. It would have made for quite a blaze, a clearly visible blaze with which the son was calling the father. But the father had been caught up in acts of love.

So the bonfire had grown down and almost out by the time I approached, nothing left but a few charred rags and shoes and leather binders. There were no images of Thomas's creation left. All was lost to him.

And to me. I walked into the kitchen. Eddie and Carmel in a twisted, still and bloody embrace on the floor. Jonah seated in a chair by the table, nursing a burned hand and bloodied head wrapped in a sheet he had pulled from over Myrna's death.

He smiled terribly when the door opened. He said, 'We are so glad to have you home. We were worried, you were away so long.'

★ ★ ★

Jonah had gone to his house and collected the things he knew he would need, he had gone to the garage for the petrol and come back to Solas. No longer watching, that was his intention. Doing from here on in.

He drove the car up the laneway and opened the boot and took out the things that represented his father's life and piled them high.

333

Carmel, seated with Myrna in the back bedroom, saying prayers of her own kind over her, smelt the burning and came to the window. When she saw the fire-maker she grew afraid and stayed hidden behind the curtain.

Eddie would be home for his dinner soon.

Eddie smelt the burning before he saw the great pile of flame. He feared it was Carmel's fire, the one she talked about in dreams. He heard the dogs barking frantically and dropped his ladder into the ditch and he cycled on without it and at the end of the lane he ran, pushing his bike up along, shouting, 'Carmel! Carmel!' He found only Jonah Cave, shivering, his arms wrapped around himself, his eyes on the fire. The dogs stood on the opposite side, snarling, afraid of what was around this man. The scent of Eddie carried to them over the burning only when he was right upon the house. The dogs scurried to him, tripping him up. Eddie kicked out at one and yelled at them to let him be.

'What in Christ's name are you doing?'

Eddie dropped his bike and ran at the tall man and the tall man looked up and cocked his head as if he had heard a phone ring and said, 'I have no idea.'

'If you've done anything to them I'll tear you apart. Get out of here, get out of here before I call the guards.'

Jonah's coat was long. It covered him entirely and it was only when he moved that Eddie saw the flash of steel. Carmel's pale face appeared at the window. Eddie made sure

Jonah's eyes stayed on him.

'Where is everybody?' Jonah asked. 'I knocked at the door and got no answer. What sort of a house is this where nobody's home and nobody answers the door?'

'The kind of house that has the measure of people,' Eddie backed away. 'What do you want with us? What are you burning, what right have you to burn on this property?'

'What I burn is none of your business. My father?'

'What about your father?'

'He came to see Sive, I know.'

'Well, you know they're not here,' Eddie insisted. 'They're gone since last night. Run out on us all.'

'They will be back. I have some things to say to both of them. Then I'll be on my way.' Jonah smiled a reasonable smile.

'You'll be on your way now. There'll be plenty of time to sort things out later,' Eddie suggested.

Jonah walked towards Eddie.

'You don't seem to understand. I am the one who rectifies all of this and decides.'

'I know that you have a quarrel with your father,' Eddie tried reason. 'But it is not with us. Why bring your trouble here?'

'Because it is here that it started.'

'Well, at least let me move myself and my wife away and off. We have brought you no trouble. We will bring you no trouble.'

'I am not allowing anyone anywhere,' Jonah's voice was heated now. 'You must go inside and wait. I'll be along presently.'

335

Eddie walked by him; he saw again the glint of metal inside the great coat.

'Where is your car?' Eddie asked.

'I dropped these things off and drove it somewhere,' Jonah smiled, 'discreet.'

Eddie went into the house. Carmel put her arms around him.

Jonah Cave watched his father's life-work and personal effects burn. He did not see the spirits of his father's creations rise and curl up in the black smoke and reach for the heavens. He did not hear their sighs of release in having their images set free. He saw his act as the destruction of only one life and one purpose.

★   ★   ★

'We have to find a way of warning Sive,' Carmel whispered.

'We cannot do that,' Eddie insisted. 'He is armed. Why did you not leave the house when he drove up?'

'I did not even know he was here. I smelled the burning. The burning came to me first, Eddie. The burning tells me he will kill her,' Carmel's voice was louder now.

Eddie clamped his hand over her mouth and pointed a finger between her eyes.

'No hysterics now, woman. This is not the time for them.'

Eddie watched from the window. The dogs had followed him inside and stayed close to Carmel. Jonah, arms folded, did not look at the house. Jonah, arms folded, studied his fire.

Carmel whispered again.

'Gomez.'

'We don't need to hear your ranting, Carmel,' Eddie spoke sharply. 'We need to know what to do. We have to figure out what to do. This is some house, Sacred Heart of God. If we get out of this, Carmel, we are moving back into the town. Just you and me. Away from all of this.'

'We have to make him stop,' Carmel breathed.

'What do you want me to do, Carmel? Go at him with my bare hands? Would you rather he killed me? We could go out the back way.'

'I won't leave until Sive comes!'

'We would have a better chance if one of us stays here, I suppose,' Eddie agreed. 'You go, Carmel. I'll make sure he doesn't follow.'

She looked at him.

'I won't go without you.'

She drew her nails along the tabletop. He could not leave her now. He could not take her with him.

They left it for a few minutes, because neither could be the one to go or stay, because they could not be apart and because they were afraid of running now.

Jonah was knocking at the door.

'If you had let me get the phone in here when I asked you — ' Eddie said as he lifted the latch.

'Don't let him in,' Carmel pleaded.

'Would you like him to blow the lock off? Get in the back room. Lock the door.'

'Easy now,' he said to Jonah as the tall length of him stooped to come in. 'You'd have had the door off its hinges in another minute. Easy now.'

Jonah smiled at him.

'I'm easy. I'm right as rain. A cup of tea please.'

Eddie went to stoke up the fire and hook the kettle over it.

'Have you no cooker?' Jonah asked politely, seating himself at the table, stretching his long legs out towards the fire. Eddie could feel the toe of his long boot only inches away from where he was stooped.

'Sure, you know from the last time we have a cooker. But it's nice to have tea from over the fire. It tastes better.'

Eddie had not gone into the scullery to put on the cooker kettle. He did not want to leave Jonah alone.

'Where is your wife?' Jonah enquired, again all politeness.

'She's in the back room. We had a death here only last night. She's praying.'

'Who died? The old woman?'

Eddie nodded. Jonah smiled and said, 'My sympathies. Could you call your wife in here please?'

'I told you, she's praying.'

'I'd like to see her please.'

'She's not gone anywhere,' Eddie urged. 'I'll call out to her. Carmel!'

A yes came from the back bedroom. Carmel removed the sheet that was over Myrna's face, she picked up the cold and lifeless hand and pleaded, 'Help us, help us.'

It was enough for Jonah, hearing the voice from the room.

'We'll leave her where she is,' he granted. 'For the time being.'

The kettle whistled.

'I'll make that tea now,' Eddie said.

The pot was drunk and the night grew darker. Eddie tried to keep the calm in his voice and movements.

'We could do with whiskey,' Eddie said soothing. 'We could do with it now.'

'Have you any?' Jonah looked at him and looked through him.

'I have,' Eddie whispered. 'It's in the kitchen.'

'Get it,' Jonah said softly.

There was half a bottle. Eddie wondered whether to pour some of it off, down the sink, or whether to give it all to Jonah. He was still deliberating when the voice came.

'Now. Get back here now.'

Eddie went to the back door, called, 'Coming!' as he unbolted it.

It opened.

Eddie came back with two tumblers. Jonah waited as he filled them and watched and sipped.

The hour slipped by and Jonah did not stop until there was an empty bottle. Eddie had matched him for every second drink.

'Waiting,' Jonah said, 'is a boring business.'

Eddie nodded.

The drink had rubbed off the edges of Jonah's need. But the ache was still there and the ache grew into a pain in his head that pounded against his temples. His stomach was cramped and rough gas rose up to the back of his throat. He rubbed his hands at his temples and his

339

stomach heaved and he leaned forward and retched.

'Have you eaten all day?' said Eddie. 'I could get you a sandwich.'

'I couldn't eat. What man could eat when his own father and his own woman go off together? What man could eat with all that goes on against him?'

Eddie nodded.

'I will have words with her about that. She should not have done that.'

Jonah looked at him.

'You're not her father.'

'God, no.'

'Then you'll say nothing to her. She is my concern now.'

Eddie rubbed his damp hands along his thighs.

'When did you start going with her?'

Jonah did not answer. There was silence for a time. Then Jonah said, 'She is not worth this.'

Eddie was quick to agree. 'You'd be better off with someone else.'

'I chose her. You cannot help who you choose.' Then it happened. Jonah's stomach heaved and his head pounded and it seemed as if I would never come home and he roared suddenly, 'Get your wife out here! She's been hours in there.'

'Listen,' Eddie spoke with the care a cat walks a thin ledge. 'You have no row with her. Leave her out of it and we'll sort this out together — man to man.'

'Get her out I tell you.' Jonah drew out the

gun from his coat and then the long blade. 'Get her out here.'

Eddie called Carmel. Carmel let the hand of Myrna fall. Myrna did not rise to help them. Myrna did not turn to watch Carmel leave the room.

Carmel went to Eddie and Eddie took her hand.

'That's nice,' Jonah said. 'Tell me about your daughter.'

Carmel looked at Eddie, Jonah sprang from his chair and pulled her by the hair towards him.

'Tell. Me. About. Your. Daughter.'

Eddie reached for Jonah's other arm.

'Get off her, get off her now. You're making it worse for yourself.'

Jonah threw Carmel back in the chair.

'Did you warn her that I was here? Did she come back another way? What is taking them so long?'

Jonah began walking up and down. Then he stopped and turned to Carmel again, who was weeping softly and curled up on herself in the chair.

'What sort of woman allows her daughter to take up with an old man?'

He moved towards Carmel carrying the blade, which glinted in the firelight. Carmel reached for Eddie.

'Easy now,' Eddie whispered, trying to keep the fear from his own voice.

'I'll be easy when she talks. Talk woman, talk about your daughter.'

Carmel looked at Jonah.

'My daughter is Sive.'

Jonah smiled.

'And what else can you tell me?'

Carmel wiped her eyes and watched the fire reflected in the blade, and it was to that fire she spoke.

'You don't need my daughter. Have me. I know what to do. I've done it before, many times. I know what to do, I do what makes you happy.'

'I don't want you,' Jonah's lips curled around the words. 'I don't want what any man can have. Sive had you for an example. No wonder,' he licked his dry lips.

Eddie put his head in his hands.

'We could all do with another drink, Carmel,' he said softly.

The overhead light was uncovered, it cast harshness all about, and there were no welcoming shadows to shrink into.

'Get the other bottle of whiskey, Carmel,' Eddie repeated. 'In the kitchen. The one by the door.'

Both Jonah and Carmel looked at Eddie.

'The big bottle at the door. Go and get it, Carmel.'

Carmel rose and Jonah did not stop her.

In the kitchen she saw the open doorway. She walked towards it. No one knew the ground here as well as Carmel. She went out into the night and had begun running when the first shot rang out. It stopped her in her tracks. The second brought her running back to the house.

Eddie lay in a heavy-breathing pile of blood

and bared bone. He moaned and Jonah kicked him over on to his back.

'I had to do it. You let her run off.'

Jonah did not hear the sound of the returning Carmel, her feet too light for that. She reached for something to bring it to an end and she found the poker. She brought it down on his head and Jonah brought his hands up with a great roar. He kicked at her wildly.

His foot found the soft hollow of her belly and it took the wind out of her, she rolled on to her back, gasping. Her long hair fell into the open fire. The burning began. Eddie wrenched himself around and began to crawl towards her. Carmel's long hair was all vibrant red for one glorious moment. She brought out a lump of firing with her bare hands and ran at Jonah.

He brought his hand up to shield his face. The burning woman put her coal into his open palm. He reached for the blade.

And it was the blade with the fire reflected on it that went into Carmel's belly and it brought fire with it. The air was filled with smoke. Carmel fell to her knees and reached for the dying man who had been her only love.

They held each other and they lay there, under Jonah's feet, until the moans stilled and the bodies with them.

Jonah sat, trembling, his hand joined the roar-chorus in his head and it throbbed and ached and he went into the back room where the old woman was laid out and took the sheet covering her face and left her death open to the air.

343

'It was not meant to go this way,' he reasoned with the still form. 'No one tells the truth. No one but me. I have to make sure that I tell Sive the truth when she comes. I have to make sure she knows what must happen and what must not happen. This has all gone wrong because no one will do as they are told. I will tell her that.'

He felt the ice-blade against his neck. The ghost of Noreen Moriarty had returned from taking Myrna off to where she was going. The ghost of Noreen Moriarty bared her teeth at Jonah Cave and followed him when he ran from Myrna to the next room.

Jonah sat at the table with the ice-blade against his neck. I did not come home for another hour. It was already night again. He could not forgive now. It had all gone on too long.

★ ★ ★

I cried out and fell on my mother and my mother's love, Eddie. I wailed and Jonah came to me and pulled me off them and said, with his hands around my waist, my neck, with his lips against my ear, 'This is all because of you, because of you. It is up to you to put this right.'

39

All Redemption Gone

'We will go to the room, the furthest room,' Jonah said. 'We have a lot to talk about. We can go to the furthest room from this one where we can talk.'

I would not leave them. I clung to them screeching and he pulled me, by the hair, to the room, and he held the blade against my throat. I prayed for Myrna to return.

'Why leave,' I whispered as I moved and bent and turned as I had learned in the dark rooms of before. 'Why leave us now?'

He told me to lie down on the bed.

I saw nothing, felt nothing. I reached out with the eyes I had through nothing and found Noreen Moriarty waiting at the end of it. In her sunflower hat. She had a boy with her. A young boy with tanned skin and fair hair and his hand in hers. Noreen smiled at me and let go of the boy's hand and pushed him towards me. He came to me and he put his lips to my forehead and the wrenching, gasping thing above me that twisted itself into me and was cold and heaving was no more. The young boy with fair hair took me off by the hand and we walked into the greenest of places and lay down and slept.

And while the fair-haired boy had taken me

off, Jonah had been left with the spirits of his own calling which tore at him and filled him with the savage knowing that he was a creature lost to life as he wished to live it.

And that is when he lost his mind entirely. All of him went over to the place he wished only to leave behind. All redemption gone. Still he would not listen. Still he thought to make me into what he wished me to be.

He would not give up trying while he had breath in him, he would not give me up while I had breath.

Out of this night, out of the darkness, comes Jonah Cave. He has lived all his life in it. Now he visits it upon me.

Jonah Cave. You use your blade again.

And you tell me that it is for my own good. For a woman who would let a man such as your father lay a hand on her.

You torture that which you love. And all the while my spirit watches you from the far corner of the room. It stays and it watches, with Noreen who has come to comfort me. She holds me and brings to me the realization that I have the power to bring death to you.

All my spirit has to do is wish you dead and the death wish would be yours.

The truth was put in front of you then, Jonah Cave, as it is now.

I open your eyes to what I am, not what you had believed you had created with your knife and your talk. I show you the torn-apart breast and heart. I leave you with the stillness. In it you have no place to hide.

You whimper and gather the shorn hair. In the hair you had loved you wanted to find life. But shorn from me it cannot live but takes on a lifeless, drab and dull form. Its shining black now faded — no longer my kind and alive night, but your dead and dull one.

I show you that your night will not end. I show you that your creation is death. I show you that the hair and the ring binders you had gathered were mementoes of people who did not love you. All, now, are beyond your persecution, except him that you had almost persecuted to death and beyond.

You had thought to wait for him, to take him with you. But you realize, no, it would be better for your father to arrive and to see that the son has taken that which he most desired.

★ ★ ★

The thought made Jonah sigh. He took the gun and lifted my limp hand into his. And he pulled the trigger.

It took some minutes for him to die and in those moments he hoped that his mother would come for him. But she did not. His spirit went as his life had gone, alone. On ahead of him he saw Carmel and Eddie walk together with the tall old woman, three shadows into the new light.

But his own limbs felt like lead and he could not join them.

He was left with the room and what was in it. A woman with the badness cut out of her. A man

347

shares that badness and sacrifices his own living to have his blood run with hers. Their shared blood a sign to all that they shared life.

A suicide pact some would say. Jonah smiled at that and shivered, a long shudder went through him, and the ghost of a word came to his lips.

He was gone. His last word left unuttered.

My soul was lost. My emptiness all around and no way of leaving it. I called out and no sound came.

★　★　★

Carmel and Eddie's moments of going. I only see them now, the ones gathered tell me what I do not know of their own story. It is a comfort to me, to see Carmel and Eddie standing above what they once were and holding on to each other and who they are now.

This is how they left us. They went from what they no longer needed. They left all that had gone wrong between them and took the pure drop of their love in a look they shared over their stilled bodies. Their eyes were the same as the moment when a living breath was in them.

The years did not fall away from them, they were not returned to youth and the lines on each of them were the map of their loving. It was not a paradise that opened for them, but the unlocked door to Solas.

★　★　★

'I cannot walk through it,' Carmel shook her head. 'I must wait and watch for Sive. He will do harm to her.'

'None that cannot be undone,' Noreen's voice between them, and her shadow cast itself clear on them, complete with hat. 'Life has its work to do with her, away with you.' Then the shadow walked out the door before them and off among the trees at the bottom of the field.

'We leave now or we stay in a place where we will intrude, Carmel,' Eddie took her hand.

They went through the open doorway and down the field into woods that had held all their loving. They walked hand in hand through the woods of goodbye to the far off place and they passed a just-roused Thomas who would soon set out from having slept in the woods. It was not for them to stop, Eddie said. But Carmel could not be prevented.

'Hurry on, Thomas,' she gave a whisper that came to him in the form of a breeze that gave more of a chill to him on an already cold almost-morning.

Noreen walked ahead of Carmel and Eddie not only because she knew the way, but because these were moments they must have to themselves. They would not walk this wood again — and it had been all and enough for them while living. The trees wept leaf tears and the woodland creatures hung their heads to their breasts in sorrow at such a going, for Carmel was their own kind and Eddie the one she loved.

They came to a place where I cannot follow even with my story. Carmel asked where Myrna was and Noreen kissed them both on their foreheads and they felt the cool surprise of it. The dead feel as the living do, for they live too, but in another place.

'Myrna has gone on ahead,' Noreen smiled and they saw the shape of her through the shadow. 'Time for us to follow.'

40

Thomas Comes

Thomas reached the end of the brambled laneway as light was breaking. No sign of Jonah's car. He breathed a sigh of relief. If Thomas had known that being left homeless and penniless and old and broken could have brought this much happiness he would have become so a long time ago.

'We will wander together,' he breathed. 'We will know the whole world.'

He did not linger in the yard of the house, before the smouldering pile of his belongings. The dogs did not even bark, did not emerge from their hidden places to challenge him. He went in through the open door to the kitchen and stooped over the bodies of Eddie and Carmel and on into the back room where Myrna's uncovered body lay.

Then up the stairs, two at a time, and into all the rooms until he found the one that held what remained of me.

And he saw, first, the end of Jonah had come and it was a bloody one. He moved towards the body and it was only then that he saw what remained of me — obscured by Jonah.

Thomas let out a great cry, which shook all the world. He gathered my opened skin and my

351

near lifeless bones into him.

He put his lips to the place where the hair had once been and then grasped the hands that had held him and he cried out that I had not deserved this. I had only loved. Why could it not have been him to suffer and die?

He did not glance again at the body of his son. But talked to him.

'It is a terrible thing,' Thomas wept. 'It is a terrible thing we have done, Jonah, you and I, to this young girl and her family. We have taken them with us, Jonah. May God forgive us.'

And he cried and in crying he gathered what he could not recognize to be me. He took shorn hair and pressed it against my head to make me whole and his, and it was impossible.

Then he felt the faint breath and he did not know whether to leave me to get help or spend the last moments with me. He fought going or staying and did not feel a hefty woman in a sunflower hat reach under his arms and pull him away from me and to his feet. Before he left he covered me with a blanket. He could not bear for me to be cold and dying.

He went to the town and his long stride took him to the door of the doctor. The doctor, sitting over his breakfast, was given no time to finish. His wife had tried to keep the tall man who might be death at the door but he had gone through the house until he found who he needed to find.

'Get your bag,' said Thomas Cave. 'And you,' he spoke to the wife, 'call an ambulance and the police. Send them to the place where Sive and

352

Carmel Moriarty and Eddie the window cleaner live.'

'Where is that?' The wife wanted to know, though she knew it well.

'The Hoar Rock.' The doctor grabbed his coat and stood.

★ ★ ★

They took me by ambulance to a white room and I lived there by a thread for a long time. And I longed for death.

Thomas sat by me. I was always cold and I did not wake or see Thomas.

Then one day I opened my eyes because I felt warmth rise through me from my feet upwards.

I found the white-haired man rubbing life into them.

'I brought socks,' he said to me. 'To keep out the cold.'

In that moment life won back Sive Moriarty.

★ ★ ★

There were long and terrible days. There were police and newspapers and all manner of inquisitions. They took what they needed to take from my grieving heart to know that Jonah was the one who had killed and torn asunder.

Many of them said, 'Sorry for your trouble.'

They let me home from the hospital. I travelled in a car with Thomas to Solas and I screeched on seeing it. But they did not hear.

I was beyond kindness and care. I roamed

long nights when I would not stay in Solas for all that had happened here. Thomas walked after me and I wept for my departed ones and for the alone future I faced with this stranger of a man who I had given up all for.

It went on for many weeks and it went for many days and nights and it would have gone on forever if the cold letter had not come to say the bodies were now free to be buried. The examinations of them were complete and satisfactory.

I did not feel complete or satisfactory. I wished for Myrna and Carmel and Eddie to live and for Thomas and me to die.

He bowed his head each time I said so, each time I would not eat what he made to eat or drink, each time he said a word I told him he did not deserve to speak. He bowed his head and he took the anger as he took the tears and the night walks and the raving and the emptying of all I had to make way for all that was to come.

Then the cold letter came to say that the bodies were now free to be buried.

And we had to bury them.

I could not bear to.

But then they said they would put them in cold, anonymous graves if we did not claim them. Thomas said he would make the arrangements. His money was returned to him on Jonah's death.

I left it to him to see to it.

At night I slept alone, as far away from Thomas as I could be. Though my body cried out for comfort. He slept in the room Myrna had

354

once had, with the dogs, who had taken to being not far behind him.

Thomas was not a housekeeper, the place was lost to neglect. I would have been the same if Thomas had not finally dragged me to the bathroom and forced me to pour water on my skin. And then I could not be prevented from going to that bathroom and spending many hours a day in it. Scrubbing what could not be seen with the slow deliberate rhythm that made my skin cry out and bleed.

Thomas had to force food into me then. And what he forced was brought up in angry spurts and he would clean it and begin again.

Then, one night, when all that was left of me was skin and bone and eyes, the door opened and the fair-haired child of before came and he put his hand in mine. I closed my eyes.

The sleep that came to take me was the kindest I have ever known.

★　★　★

When I woke a day was already half lived.

I rose and came down the stairs to find Thomas sitting at the table. He was thin and drawn. His face had set hard and hopeless again. I was a wild-eyed skeleton, my hair knotted and covering my half nakedness like a dark cloud.

'They will be buried here,' I said. 'They can be buried in the part of the wood that is ours. They were happiest in the woods.'

'Well,' Thomas sighed. 'What of consecrated ground?'

355

'There is no ground better than this.'

'Will you have something to eat?' Thomas asked.

'Something,' I said.

We ate in silence and each plateful that was put in front of me I cleared until I had eaten my way back into the living and breathing world. When I had finished I looked at Thomas.

'There is a lot to be done.'

He shook his head.

'No. I have done most of it. The bodies will be brought straight to the church. There will be a Mass and then they will be brought here. I will speak to the curate. He is a good man. It can all happen tomorrow if you wish, we are waiting for you to say when.'

He did not tell me that he had imagined this would never happen and that he had planned to bury the three without me. He did not tell me the humiliation he had suffered in walking into the town and being greeted only with silence and open stares.

The funeral home had charged him double what they would anyone else. The town had talked of nothing else but this house where all the murders had happened and the funeral home had to think of its good name and future custom.

Two men were hired to dig the plot. It cost a lot of money, Thomas had been advised by the men. He paid what was asked because he could not dig it himself.

After eating we walked down on to the beach so that I might gather what I needed.

356

He helped me with the driftwood. We bound them together into crosses of a fashion. He helped me to clear the house and to open all its windows so that the sadness could be taken by the air waiting to come in and begin the new life.

All this work we did in one day without a word between us. I did not ask him for anything, he was there with it before I had to ask.

That night I went to the room in which he slept, in which Myrna had slept. That night I slept in his arms. He held me and kept watch.

★　★　★

It was a fine day, the day that those three lives came to their final end. It was full of the promise of spring and the flowers that we put on the fresh earth were the first daffodils although they were not grown on our land. Thomas had bought them. They looked false to me, they looked severed and not in keeping with the wildness of the spot. But Thomas had done enough and I had not spoken to him to indicate otherwise.

The curate went back to the town in a taxi.

It was only midday when it was all done.

41

The Wanderer Reborn

I did not speak for a time. The silence was not disagreeable, it was a truthful silence, for there was nothing between Thomas and me in those days that grew into months, as the child grew in me.

Its first kick brought me back further into the land of the living, and it was only then that I realized how far, still, I was removed from it.

But this child was not one to lie in wait. This child wanted to walk into the middle of the world and let his presence be felt. He raced to this world with all the enthusiasm I had run away from it.

He grew big, so big, so quickly.

And with that child grew the love that had died. Then Jonah came in a dream and said: 'It could be mine.'

I was afraid. I had been taken in the best of ways and the worst of ways in the one day. I woke and would not sleep again. The cards called to me to let me know what way it was to be. I had not touched them since the day I had found blood and fire and hair flowing. I knew their truth would not be hidden and I wished to hide. But the child within had no wish to hide. He wished to be known and he shifted endlessly, urging me on and, finally, I could only do as he wanted or he would not let me rest.

I picked them up and took the chair by the fire that Myrna had always used. I meant to throw them on the fire if they brought more sorrow and pain to me.

But they did not.

I asked, 'Who's is the child? Who is the father?'

And they showed me only the card of New Beginnings and a voice said, 'It is the child who chooses this.'

'Who does the child choose?' I asked, and I turned the card and it was not the card of the One Who Watches, but of the Wanderer and I knew in my heart that all that was to happen from now on I should be thankful for.

'Will the child love me?' I asked.

The cards did not speak and I remembered, then, Myrna's words.

'Mine is the only fate they will not determine.'

And, since they were now mine, I knew it was the same for me.

I am glad for this. What I have known and felt and had these past twenty years was all experienced with the joy of not knowing it would come to me. I grew into my life. It was one of my own choosing.

In time I have come to realize that I am not one. I am a sum of many parts, all assembled in this room, this night. I have the strength of all of you in me. It has been a strength I have needed. It is a strength I am reminded of now, as this night is ending and this story is almost at an end.

It is coming, the alone time when you will depart and leave me.

More to tell. I am glad to tell it. Let me tell of clearing the way for the new life.

★   ★   ★

We put in a bathroom upstairs and we made a room into a nursery. I cleared the clothes of my loved ones. But I left all their possessions as they were about the place. It was still their home. I took Myrna's few dresses and objects and put them into her suitcase. In her grey coat I felt lumps and pulled at one. I pulled out a diamond necklace. By the time I had unpicked the lining there was a lot more jewellery besides. What we did not need to sell, I kept to wear and think of her, Jonah had spent most of his father's carefully earned money.

★   ★   ★

He came in autumn, my mother's season. He was born on the first day of the new moon and was as curious to grow as Carmel. We called him Simon and we laid him in the crib that was made for the child Eddie and Carmel did not have. Simon was a name all his own. We wanted, above all, that he would have a life apart from us.

We had been walking all day, collecting wood for the coming winter. Thomas had made a cart with wheels for the job. His health was fully restored to him, the limbs were stiff only in the morning and when that stiffness eased he was

360

thankful for each new day in which he could work on the place and make it ready for the new-born.

He had found some of his cameras in the pearl-blue Jaguar. But he had not taken one picture since the time when he had first been found by the postman of the year. He did not wish to photograph. He wished to live and he put his back into it. He took life on and it gave him a great force with which to complete each day.

He did all that had to be done in the town. I would not go there. I stayed with my growing belly and my shoreline and woods, as my mother had done before me. What need had I for strange looks on faces that bore no sign of friendship?

Thomas grew to talk to the townspeople, the formal talk that he had used all his life and many understand that. To him, now, as with me always, it had no meaning. But he could speak and was liked well enough for his courteous manner by the women and for his lack of curiosity on matters personal by the men.

He spent some hours there each day making purchases that would give this house its chance to welcome the new life. The townspeople did not forget how he had come to live among them, but did not choose to remember each time they came across him.

He made no friends and he made no enemies.

In Solas our love grew again, as all rooted things grow. It called out to the broken part of us and mended it.

The day the pains began the animals outside

361

shifted and called to each other and to me. I was carried with the waves of Simon's coming. I heard them call and travel with me and I did not feel alone.

Though Thomas was kind and loved by me when the pains began, I did not tell him, because I knew he would go to the town and bring a car and take me away from all I wanted to be near.

When I could no longer hide it, between the pains Thomas walked with me when I would not sit still and helped me into the fireside when I could walk no more. He had laid out blankets and sheets and it went on into the long night.

The new moon was at its height.

I bore down, my arms around the neck of my lover and I did not cry out, and the animals cried for me, their cries reached a great crescendo, and all the way through, movement and noise and rushing and fierce agony. When I could bear it no longer it bore me and my son's head came and his shoulders turned inside me and he was then whole in the world. In the place where he had been inside me was born the greatest love I have ever known.

It was for Thomas to cut the tie that bound us and he did so without taking the child from me. And he bathed and held us both and the animals rested easy and we two lost souls who had formed this new one between us, knew that we had found the way into a new life for all of us.

That was Simon's first gift to us. There were many more.

We slept by the fire all of us, that night. In the morning I woke and found the first magic of my

362

child was waiting for me. Thomas woke soon after and shifted and looked at us looking at each other.

'His eyes — they're open.'

Our son wanted to know all of life, all at once. His hair was fair, his skin was dark, though fairer than mine. It would welcome the sun on it. I held the fair-haired child of my dreams in my arms. And in all my dreams he had said the same thing without words: 'You are the one who will give me life. So you must live.'

42

Mothering Years

What can I tell you of my years as mother? None will match them.

Simon would not stop each day until each new thing set in front of him was learned. He loved me as the warm place he came to when it was cold and he loved me for the comfort I offered and the kind words. He grew sure under them.

He loved his father for the man in him and it was his father he reached to when the weaning was done and the walking was mastered. He watched the unbent nature of his father and he wanted to reach tall like him, he watched his father about the place, always doing, and he would want to be beside him, doing.

I loved my two men well.

From the first day of Simon's life, Thomas took out a camera and began to picture it. The pictures had a beauty, as all his life's work, now destroyed, had had. But these were different. They were filled with a feeling that even now is visible.

These carried the heart of the taker into them, showed the love and the days of rearing that went into our child to be the happiest of both our lives. We were complete in our world and it was a small one. It saw nothing of the outside until the boy Simon wished for beyond us and I was, at first, afraid to give it to him, because I did not know a world beyond that did not harm. But his father was the one to put my hand in his big hand and he said, 'We must get used to this. We will have the pictures to remind us.'

So I learned about the held breath of a mother. I learned about keeping hands by my side that longed to hold him and push cruel words and world away from him. He grew so fast; I could not catch my breath or hold on to a day.

When he held up a shell for me, when he traced the lines of my palm with his fat fingers, he looked with the eyes I had only grown into on Myrna's teaching. A child sees wonder in all things. When he tasted a new food he would look for me, surprised, and smile. A child tastes joy in all things.

When he heard the cock crow and the bitch's high whine he would laugh delightedly as if all life was contained in those sounds. When the thunder came he did not shrink from it, he shrieked and came to be held by me and he watched the lightning flashes with wonder. A child hears all the sounds of the world as the world's voice and adds their own sound to it.

When he picked flowers for me he would bury his nose into them and close his eyes and be lost in the scent. When he picked an unscented flower he would look at me with sad eyes as if something had been stolen.

He would stroke the ears of the dogs and cats for hours, and trace the shape of a leaf with his fingertips and rub the pebbles from the beach along his cheek and his palms along his father's unshaved chin in the mornings when he joined us in our bed.

With his clothes off on summer days he would roll around in the grass as the dogs did to scratch their backs and he would scratch and groan like the dogs did and sigh with pleasure. Touch was how he came to learn and love the world and to trust it. Touch was how I came to learn to love the world and to trust it. When he fed from me at night I stroked his forehead and his eyes closed and he would find sleep in that way.

Simon was the one who brought me back into the world.

It was for him and because of him that I went into the town for the first time, five years after the deaths.

I went, him leading me by the hand, him talking to me about the colourful people to be found there. Simon saw colour where we would see grey, he had a manner that brought out the colour in people. He had easiness about him, a ready smile and energy.

Thomas had woken me and said he was not in his health and I would have to be the one to deliver our son to the outside world. Simon came into our room and asked when it would be time to go. It was many hours before the time. The sun had not even come up. We begged for more sleep from our little child and he did not give into our pleas. He had his own purpose on that day.

By the time we were ready to leave, after we

had fed the animals, and ourselves, Simon had lost all patience and pulled on my hand all the way along the coast road into the town. Thomas watching us walk down the laneway.

And our son caught the fresh wind that had taken up on this early autumn day and chattered to it more than to me because I was lost in the world of my own fear.

In town there were lines of mothers with lines of children tugging at them, all walking in the same direction. We took our place among them and this was the first time I walked the ways of others.

I recalled the days when Noreen had dragged me towards school.

At the moment when we reached the gates Simon's hand left mine. This was the day he had been waiting for and he grasped it.

I was the one left behind then, as I am today. I caught other eyes on me, travelling the length of the woman they knew only by stories. I looked at them and they looked away.

The women moved off and in one or two of their remarks, which my ears caught on the same fresh wind that had travelled with Simon this morning, I heard revelations of my past, as told by strangers.

' . . . All murdered . . . '
' . . . Mother went with black men . . . '
' . . . Haunted . . . '
' . . . old enough to be her grandfather . . . '
' . . . poor child . . . '

Some of it was wrong and more of it was right and soon I was the one left by the gates with the mother of the last girl to enter the school gates this morning.

'You can't stay here all day,' she said softly.

I looked at her.

'What do I do now?'

'You go home, wait until three, and come back for him. You have a good cry for yourself. That's what I'm going to do. I've only got the one, too.'

I walked.

When I came into the house Thomas was waiting, with hot tea for us.

'I am not used to the world, Thomas,' I said. 'I will have to learn more about it.'

'Plenty of time,' he smiled.

'What can I do to see all of it?'

He knew then I was not to be kept waiting, which is the one difference our ages brought to us.

'Would you like to come with me?' he asked.

That is how it happened. We walked all over the town and he took pictures and when he had one taken he would hand me the camera and say, 'Look, what do you see?'

I saw that all life could be captured on a camera. This was Thomas Cave's way of holding time dear and he gave it to me on that day that I lost the first part of my son to the world.

Later he would give me books to read. I learned of places through my reading, places Thomas had been and which he could tell me more of. I learned that women wore clothes to please themselves and others. It was to please myself that I went into the town and bought cloth and it was with a book and the mother who

368

had stood at the school gate with me that I learned to sew, brought the world to me with my colour and movement and fabric song. I made the green velvet in those days. I made it to wear the green earth about me.

All the while I learned, my son Simon learned in the school and all the while I grew and my son Simon grew in the world. We did not notice that Thomas was growing down as we made our way into ourselves.

He had done what he had set out to do, give the child and the mother a start and feet in the world. He was ready to go on his last wandering. The preparation for that journey was to take many years. But he did not wait for it with longing, as he had done in St Manis Home. He waited for it with a prayer that he be given longer, since the world had taken on so much meaning for him. He prayed that he be spared until his son showed the first signs of being a man.

He was granted his wish.

43

All That Have Died Are Contained in Me

The death of Thomas Cave came when he had taught his son all he knew about being a man.

Simon was fourteen years old.

Thomas had woken early on this summer morning. He turned to me and I was sleeping. He left me to walk Killeadan headland for the last sunrise of his life. He had taken to spending his time here, in the last of the summer. But he found the warmth did not reach him and the beauty pained him. There was something overwrought about the late butterflies and last flowers, something so nostalgic and painful. Beauty is best remembered, than witnessed in its departure.

Thomas felt the chill of his going in the air. The darting swallow knew what Thomas knew. The time had come for movements to quicken and flee. The swallow would elect to leave until it no longer had strength. Thomas had the strength to elect to stay. It was almost spent.

I had opened my eyes as soon as he left the room and in each of my opened eyes the unshed tears swam and shimmered. I felt his going as much as he did. He had grown into a silence that was not restful.

I recalled Myrna's words: 'The old have the greatest of adventures.'

I knew my Beloved to be unafraid. I knew his only regret to be leaving us. But he had provided well for us, through the town solicitor. In these late days he had asked me not only to take photographs with him, but also to come with him to the darkroom and watch images emerge.

'It is for you to do this now, with Simon,' he advised as the forms of his intention swam into being. 'You must learn all this too, so that you can bring it alive for him.'

And I learned it and it was more fascinating to me to develop than to capture the moments. The camera tells no lies, it tells more truth than most dare see.

Thomas knew it and he taught it to me.

'Watch the lips, watch the curve of the mouth, the holding of one shoulder higher than the other, the turn of a neck and the placing of a hand. These say what the person will not say,' Thomas said. 'It will help our son to watch this. It will help him to make his way in the world, alone, if he can know the true nature of those he meets.'

Even Simon sensed the going, though he did not know it. He had taken to spending all his waking hours in his father's shadow, refusing school and friends who came to call and talking only to Thomas. Thomas and he would often go off for days.

★ ★ ★

371

The last sunrise rewarded Thomas Cave with a vibrancy, which celebrated his going. It brought him warmth that had escaped him in recent days. He had felt cold like he had never felt, even in the world's frozen reaches. He wished to sit by the fire and he wished even to climb into it. His only relief was at night when I lay close to him and put all my heat into him.

We would spend long hours looking at each other, no words or touching, just the look that spoke all and said enough for us.

Thomas had been troubled by a dream, in which a woman with a large and overbearing sunflower hat came and put her finger to his lips. It was a movement that stopped his breath. He would wake, gasping in the air she took from him. He would reach for my warmth and find it willing.

I knew in those moments before daylight that he felt great loss.

When he returned from walking the day in, Thomas Cave still had a warmth about him, which had been missing for a while. I put my hand on him and I knew the death heat, it had flowed through Myrna in her last moments.

I served him a breakfast and he ate it gladly. The appetite, which had been missing, had also returned.

'What does the day hold for you?' I asked him.

'I would like to spend it with Simon,' he answered.

I knew if the day was our son's, the night would be for us. He would give the day to the fair-haired child of dreams and the night to the dark woman on the edge of life.

I saw, then, his agitated look at the clock and I knew he felt the remaining hours to be short and too much to do in them. So I went to Simon's room and found him, not sleeping, but looking from his bed out at the sea as if it would contain some answers.

But it was calm as a mirror, and like a mirror, would only allow Simon's blue-green eyes to glide over its surface.

I kissed the top of his head and he looked at me and did not smile.

'Your father wants you,' I said.

This, on any other day, would have seen Simon spring up. But on this day he followed me and stood behind me when we came into the kitchen. One smile from Thomas took away his fear. Simon saw no change in the man he loved.

'Will we go out?' he asked with all the eagerness we had come to expect from him.

'We will not,' Thomas said. 'We will wash and shave first.'

Simon had grown soft and downy hair on his chin that did not need shaving. But Thomas wished to do this with him. In the bathroom, he lathered soap and put it on Simon's skin and he said softly, 'The first shave makes you a man.'

And the old man brought the blade along the young man's chin and took the soft hair of youth away from him and the first sting of air on freshly scraped skin brought a gasp from Simon, 'I don't want to be a man!'

But, when he was done, Thomas put his hands on the young shoulders, so thin then, so broad

373

now and said, 'You know, in other lands, you would have been a man long before now. But in this land, today is the time for you. It is a good thing to be, Simon, do not be afraid of it.'

And Simon knew that his father knew the way and had pointed it out for him.

His breath was deep and his courage came with it. He brought a laugh out of himself, 'My voice,' he said. 'It's gone down into my toes. But sometimes I still squeak like a mouse. It's embarrassing.'

'Don't be embarrassed,' Thomas said as he scraped at his own chin, closely, finely. 'Your mouse did well enough for fourteen years, it has to give way to the lion and that is not easy.'

Simon asked, 'Are all men lions?'

Thomas shook his head.

'Very few.'

★ ★ ★

When they were washed and dressed, Thomas and Simon went out to the work that had to be done.

Though Simon knew it all and had done it before, he did not mention this to his father. He watched and nodded and tried what he was told to try. He saw the correct way to cut the wood on the block, the way to hold a screw in place before drilling, the way a paint brush should be left after use, washed out and ready for the next job, not discarded and left to harden.

'Waste nothing and you will have everything you want,' Thomas said.

374

Simon stopped his father from showing him how the animals must be fed.

'I know this, I do it more than you!'

They laughed and Thomas went quiet then, they sat on the ground and watched the trace paths of the darting birds and then Thomas spoke once more.

'You don't have to do everything well around the place, you just do your best. It will be good enough for your mother. In fact she does not notice the need for repairs. Her mind is on other things and places, we must give her that time, always.'

They walked off then, the pair of them. The son thin, but filling, in the middle of the growth spurt that would leave him a tall and broad man in two more years. A tall and broad man his father would not see. But Thomas could see the shape of him breaking through and it was that shape he spoke to, the Simon of the future, in this long day where they walked to all the places they knew together and loved to be together in.

When they came back it was just before the sunset and it was a sunset we all watched from the yard and when it went behind the hills we three were gripped by a sudden fear that it would happen then, in the creeping darkness. But none of us said it and it was not time yet.

We went in and ate the meal I had spent the day preparing and we had good food and the best of what had been a good summer inside us. We rose from the table only when it was night. And night brought a mist with it over the hills behind which the sun had disappeared. A mist took the shape of the land and swallowed it.

All was soon darkness and the darkness took away all words. We went into the fire that had been lit only to give brightness, so warm was the night. Simon sat with us until its last glow went. He went to his father then and sat by his knees. Thomas pulled his head on to his lap and stroked the strong fair hair that grew so wild if he did not visit the town barber each fortnight to have it sheared. His father took him and they both laughed at my few tears each time Simon came back from one of those visits. I hated his hair shorn.

The man and the boy sat now, opposite me. Each known to each other, each sure of each other. Simon felt his newly shaved chin and smiled up at his father. Thomas then felt the chin and nodded his approval.

'A man now,' he whispered.

The words took the stillness out of the air and put movement into Simon. He reached out to his father and his father to him and they clasped each other. I left them that way, tied.

In the bedroom I pulled back the spread and pushed open the window to let the summer air take hold. I told the night that Thomas's death was not a death I would stand in the way of. I had learned too much from the times before.

I undressed. The door opened then and it brought in no light. Thomas had turned them all out and he and Simon had held each other long in the dark.

'One day I will go,' he whispered into the thick hair. 'This is what it will be like when I am gone.

I will hold you like this, be with you like this, in the dark moments. You are a boy I have loved and you will be a man I am proud of.'

Simon spoke then.

'How will we get on without you? How will it be for us?' Fear in his voice.

'As it has always been,' Thomas answered. 'I am always here. I will always be here. I am not going far away.'

It was enough for the son to take his father's words to his heart and they remained there and gave sustenance for the time ahead. That is how Simon came to be strong beyond his own years and reckoning. It was a strength that did not make him old. It was not a burden. If anything he grew a new zest for life on top of the old. The man-strength said it was time to let his father go to his mother and to let them have each other for the last moments.

★   ★   ★

My Beloved sits across from me now and in his eyes all the love he had ever had for me. I long for your hand now, Thomas. I long for your hands on me, as they were that night. Hands that spoke of all that you wished to put into me before you left. No need of words, no words could match them.

It was not love-making, it was life-making. A life given, a life received. I took the life from Thomas because it was offered as his parting gift to me. I took it through his loving and he lay beside me, after, in the halfway place between life and death and the soft wind beckoned him and the night called after the soft wind: 'Bring him to us and he will have the whole night.'

And all he wanted was the night in my eyes, so life clung on as death advanced.

But it was not a warring time. It was a peaceful going, the only noise that of our breathing. Even the wind was no more than a whisper.

I did not want to sleep, but sleep took me all the same. I would wake with a start to find him, still breathing, still watching. I was filled with the heaviness of life, he was light now, as death wished him to be.

Sleep was death's way of parting us. If I had not slept I would not have had the power of letting him go on to where I could not go.

His hand had held mine all the while, and the grip loosened and the hands parted.

All that have died are contained in me. Thomas the same.

★ ★ ★

When I woke it was the new day and my Beloved was not part of it.

He lay in the last sleep and it was not one I would have deprived him of, I knew, for it sat well on him. He was cold to the touch and that cold went into me and did not leave for a long while.

I cried ice tears and then the whispers took up and said my Beloved was not present, my Beloved was not cold. He was in a warm place

378

and this cold body was a shell on the strand, no longer used, ready to wear down and join the earth once more.

The body of Thomas was hollow and filled with the echoes a shell carries of the great rushing past it has shared with the sea. His heart was gone and so it was not Thomas but his memory the wretch in me clung to. I could not let it go until the young hand pulsing with life prised me away from the old and cold and dead thing my Beloved had become. I clasped and it was Simon's life I clasped and his need to go on and his urging me to go on with him.

My son and I held each other over the left body of Thomas Cave and wept our loss through the open window and the world about was filled with the full cries of our grief and the world went strangely silent on hearing them. All animals, all wind, all sea, all trees and grasses, still and silent and listening.

'They all go,' I cried to my son and to the still world. 'They all leave me in the end.'

'I am not gone,' Simon's voice soothed liked fresh mint. 'I am here.'

And I remembered I was a mother.

I did not speak aloud that one day he would be gone too. I did not tell him it was life's way and that already I had begun to prepare for it. I knew he believed he would stay with me always. I did not want him to feel the guilt of going along with grieving for his father. I wanted him to reach beyond this sadness and go on with his young time, which should be filled only with possibilities.

★ ★ ★

Simon would have nothing else but that he dig his father's grave. I watched the muscles in his back twitch and shine with the exertion. But he would not have me help him. This was his way of making a place for his father.

'I am a man now,' he told me, and he shovelled the soil to the side. 'I am to do a man's work.'

It was his way of goodbye. Mine was to prepare the body with the love I gave it in living.

The curate came from the town when Simon called for him. He was soon to leave the priesthood and so did not object when I told him that there would be no church visit. Thomas was a man of the open air. There would be no leaving our Thomas to rest for a single night in a cold and cavernous place not of his own choosing. He was to be kept close to us and this was to continue even after burial. He would lie beside Carmel and Eddie and Myrna in their clearing and I will lie beside you all when my time comes.

I placed Thomas in the ground under the now ex-curate's spoken words and silent ones of my own. I thought of Jonah Cave with my arm around my son whose shoulders sloped with the weight of weeping.

I thought of the anonymous place in which those who took him away from this house had put Jonah Cave. I felt pity.

Thomas had spoken to me of what he wished to be done for his burial and his wishes had been followed. He died in a place where he belonged, he had not gone the way of his son, Jonah.

He had often asked to be buried in the same manner as Carmel and Eddie, in the same place. He could not, he said, imagine a better heaven than the dappled sunlight of spring and summer falling through the trees on to his grave.

'And do not tend it,' he had asked me one day when we had spoken of these things. 'I want the brambles and dock leaves to grow over me — I want nature's covering and no other. I want no flowers but those that grow around me.

'Nothing but the simplest of crosses for me. Driftwood, like Carmel and Myrna and Eddie. And no name but Thomas. The name of Cave dies with me and I do not wish to carry it on to my grave. Simon must have your name, Moriarty, and all the possibility that you can offer him. He cannot be part of the miserable family I made. Let him be part of you and this.'

It was his last wish and I carried it out as best I could. But I did not take away the name Cave, because I knew to do that would be to make Thomas and Jonah and Patricia Cave as if they never existed. And they had existed, if only in the most painful of ways.

I let our son keep his father's name and he was glad to have it.

With Simon Cave I put Thomas Cave into the ground with no box around him, under the tree in the clearing that offered the best view of the sea and I knew it was the tree that suited the man's nature best. It was a tall elm, which grew apart from the others as if to observe them better and also to contain its secrets more easily. It was a tree that held itself upright and its branches did not reach out to touch others, but it shielded a younger ash from the harsh salt winds which blew in frequently from the sea.

This cover helped the young ash to grow tall beside its companion.

My son covered the coffin and stamped the soil down, again, alone, because he wanted alone.

The night Thomas went into the ground the cards called to me for the first time since I had read the birth of the fair-haired child of dreams from them.

I knew, then, that they had been waiting. It had not just been me leaving them, they had left me while I had made my family and lived it. Widowhood brought a coldness with it that would not be relieved. The warmth of Thomas's body had brought a surety to mine, now gone.

The days bound themselves tightly around me and with each day that passed I moved less and grew colder. Soon I could do nothing but sit and turn the cards, endlessly, reaching for the stories of each one. But the stories were no more than faint whispers in my ears. Whispers I could not hear and the more I strained the further away they sounded, so lost was I in my own misery.

I did not want the truth and so it could not make itself known to me. Each time I came to the card of a single figure walking through white emptiness I saw it as myself, the widow, walking alone again through the world. Then the figure turned and it bore Simon's face.

I turned my face away from the cards and

towards a young man, slope shouldered, head down, sitting close to me. When I called him, he raised his head and it was my son, Simon, and his face was cut to pieces.

'What happened to you?'

'The razor,' his voice had grown rougher with the weeks that had passed.

Though he spoke softly there was the grain and knot of pain in it.

'I cannot use the razor. He did not show me how to use it properly. I can't make it follow the shape of my face, I can't do that without him showing me again what to do.'

The claws of grief cut into him to take the joy he had been born with and had carried even before birth. My son had come to me in a time of grief and saved me. It was for me to do the same. I took the mother's promise to put the child's pain and joy before my own and it is a promise I have kept.

I held my arms out to Simon and he came into them and we cried joined tears for the one we had lost and when we could cry no more, we laughed for the times he had given us. When we could laugh no more we slept a sleep his spirit brought to us and it was one without the dreams of his loss.

And when we woke we were ready to live without him.

44

The Years Go By

The card of the Leave Takers falls again.

You will go and I am left with the last of the night in which a new moon rose and heard a story and watched us all through a thin, narrow slit, a cautious eye that said all stories must come to an end. The years in which Simon grew went too quickly. I want to linger on them and make your time with me last but I know that you are fading, all of you, fading for me and from me. The years go by, Simon grown as tall as the man he chose to father him, tall and away from me.

My fire grows weak and the daylight stretches her long grey fingers and curls them round my throat and stems the talk that I would use to keep all that I love in this room and keep night with us always and day forgotten.

I could begin the story again. And I would tell it in the company of no one.

My loved ones prepare to leave. Carmel and Eddie shift on the couch that was theirs, Thomas stirs in the chair, my baby in his crib wails, Myrna stands.

★   ★   ★

The story is at an end. My throat dry from the telling. The moon has gone and may well have grown from new to full in one night. All lifetimes told. Day cannot be prevented.

How will you leave me? One by one.

I cannot watch it. I study the card of the Leave Takers and close my eyes, feel your going, each one a whisper down my spine. I am left only with Thomas. When I open my eyes, he is still here.

He takes my hand. The touch, all its warmth and the warmth of our time brought back to me. The opening of arms and I go into them. Then the words he once said to Simon: 'I am not far away.'

I leave the room of telling, the cards in my hands, and step out into the early morning. I watch the grey stir of a heron across the sky.

Myrna's words come to me through the thin film between life and death, 'Each beginning means an end, each end a beginning. All the dead and gone are contained in you.'

The lost souls have left the way they arrived. From my heart they came and into it they travel again. I have no need to pass through doors to visit with them. Their company is to be had. I will have the cards in my hands and eyes. Old friends for new times.

New times are upon us, and my heart, though sore, listens. The cards are my constant. I learned not to be afraid of them and always to respect their truth.

I learned truth in these years and will learn more from those that follow.

The years go by, people pass with them. The

crib rocks, empty and ready to be filled again — we are all that is left of the lost souls who have come this way and gone. Life has all the answers and death takes them away.

End and Beginning

X The leave Takers

ACKNOWLEDGEMENTS

There is something to be said in thanking everyone and mentioning no names. If I do leave one out you know who you are and that I am grateful to you.

Chubb, Michael, Johnston did everything in his power to help me and so the book is dedicated to him. My sister Amanda read it and helped me to produce a manuscript in presentable form.

My friend and ally Tony Baines was the first to set eyes on the book and did his utmost to encourage me. Marian Keyes, who happens to be married to him, is one lucky woman and also a constant source of support.

Ailish Connelly also read it as it was being written and gave me her valuable thoughts. Gai Griffin kept me going with her words and criticisms and insight. Morag Prunty — fabulous woman, fabulous friend — took it upon herself to believe in the book. Biba Hartigan had her own words for me and they made me get over the hump of sending it out into the world of publishing.

Julie Duane, Moira Reilly, Pauline O'Hare, San Orme, Susan Byrne, Sorcha Schlindwein, Birna Helgadottir, Frankie Smith, Clem and Jula Cairns — all of them have offered encouragement.

Marianne Gunn O'Connor is phenomenal — she stayed with *Lost Souls* and myself and proved that there was a point in trying to get published and not just hiding things under sofas.

At Picador — Peter Straus saw something and for that I will always be grateful. Becky Senior and Maria Rejt both worked with me to get to what I was trying to say. Becky in particular — thank you for all the work you put in.

Sue Townsend hid things under sofas for years and was kind enough not to let me do the same.

Julie Lombard hides things in teapots unashamedly and pours excellent kindness and inspiration.

Claudia Nielsen — a Brazilian with a wardrobe the size of Rio and a heart to match helped me more than she will ever know.

My mother and father — Jimmy and Marina — housed me in hard times while my brother Alan and his wife Siobhan gave me their daughter Emma to play with and take my mind off things like trying to find endings — since Emma is such a wonderful beginning.

Alberic reintroduced me to my life force.

Catherine reintroduced me to myself.

Then there was Albie. Now there are Rory and Finn.

Other titles in the
Charnwood Library Series:

EATERS OF THE DEAD

Michael Crichton

In A.D. 922 Ibn Fadlan, the representative of the ruler of Bagdad, City of Peace, crosses the Caspian Sea and journeys up the valley of the Volga on a mission to the King of Saqaliba. Before he arrives, he meets with Buliwyf, a powerful Viking chieftain who is summoned by his besieged relatives to the North. Buliwyf must return to Scandinavia and save his countrymen and family from the monsters of the mist . . .